SCORPIO RISING

R. G. Vliet was born in Chicago, the son of a naval medical officer. He lived in American Samoa (as a child), in the Southwest, New England, and Mexico. He was educated in Texas and did graduate work at Yale. Vliet three times won the Texas Institute of Letters Award, twice for collections of poems and once for his novel *Solitudes*, which Penguin will reissue in 1987. A Rockefeller Foundation Fellow in Fiction and Poetry, and a Dobie-Paisano Fellow in Fiction, Vliet was the author of three collections of poetry, *Events and Celebrations*, *The Man with the Black Mouth*, and *Water and Stone*. His two earlier novels, *Rockspring* and *Solitudes* were, like *Scorpio Rising*, set in Texas. Vliet died in May of 1984, in North Adams, Massachusetts, just days after completing *Scorpio Rising*.

R. G. VLIET

SCORPIO RISING

PENGUIN BOOKS

a mi Vida

PENGUIN BOOKS
Viking Penguin Inc., 40 West 23rd Street,
New York, New York 10010, U.S.A.
Penguin Books Ltd, Harmondsworth, Middlesex, England
Penguin Books Australia Ltd, Ringwood, Victoria, Australia
Penguin Books Canada Limited, 2801 John Street,
Markham, Ontario, Canada L3R 1B4
Penguin Books (N.Z.) Ltd, 182–190 Wairau Road,
Auckland 10, New Zealand

First published in the United States of America by Random House, Inc.
and simultaneously in Canada by Random House of
Canada Limited, Toronto, 1985
Published in Penguin Books 1986

Copyright © Vida Ann Vliet, 1985
Introduction copyright © Viking Penguin Inc., 1986

The author is grateful to the University of Texas at Austin
and The Texas Institute of Letters
for a Dobie-Paisano Fellowship
during which part of this novel was written.
Chapters of this novel appeared in *Agni Review*,
Pawn Review and *A Texas Christmas*.

LIBRARY OF CONGRESS CATALOGING IN PUBLICATION DATA
Vliet, R. G., 1929–1984
Scorpio rising.
Originally published: New York: Random House,
1985. With new introd.
I. Title.
[PS3543.L5S4 1986]   813'.54   85-19242
ISBN 0 14 00.8513 0

Printed in the United States of America by
R. R. Donnelley & Sons Company, Harrisonburg, Virginia
Set in Fairfield

Except in the United States of America, this book is sold subject to
the condition that it shall not, by way of trade or otherwise, be lent,
re-sold, hired out, or otherwise circulated without the publisher's
prior consent in any form of binding or cover other than that in
which it is published and without a similar condition including this
condition being imposed on the subsequent purchaser

INTRODUCTION

In the case of Death versus Russell Gordon Vliet, the gods badly let us down. Preoccupied as they are with divine governance and each other, Jupiter and Juno maybe couldn't be expected to tender their mercy to a merely mortal wordsinger. But Minerva, she of art and culture, must have had a Walkperson in her ears the day the prose of R. G. Vliet arrived vibrant on the wind. Listen. *"Over near the curb, perched on a candy wrapper, a monarch butterfly rocked back and forth, its orange-and-black wings, veined like a church window, slowly opening and closing, opening and closing like breathing. In the fall those things migrate clear to Mexico."* And again: *". . . The sermon was snubbed down, cinched, saddled and rid. Feet scraped, babies waked, coughs played over the gathering like chips and scraps of thunder. Fans were tucked into the racks on the backs of pews. Everyone stood. The Doxology was forced up through the roof and the benediction laid out over grateful heads."* One last dab: *"Thunder ain't rain."* No clemency, even for one so devout unto his particular literary calling? Especially not for one so devout, say They. On May 11, 1984, eight days after Vliet finished the manuscript of this novel, the careless deities let cancer take him. It all makes a person want to shout out across the cosmic prairie on his behalf, "Dammit, Minnie, Jupe, Junebug—what does a guy got to do, whistle *Eleanor Rigby* upside down and back-wards?"

He just very nearly did, you know. This *Scorpio Rising* is a performance that turns time around blithely and rearranges the sad balladry of solitude. The troubling everybody-reaps-the-whirlwind ending of this novel is amended by its first section, for we would not have the memorably appealing narrator Rudy except for the Castleberry family tragedy of those last pages. What catharsis there is in this fate-bound tale occurs in its *middle*, in the astounding 1907 visit into the mind and circumstance of Velma Castleberry. Next, you can set yourself for not one but two plots. A contorted young man of only yesterday—1976—"whose spine had slithered like a snake in two directions" yearns for a self-centered young woman whose black hair flows to her waist. Another contorted young man, "hunched-up, toad-looking," of yesterday's yesterday—1904—yearns for a willful young woman whose black hair would flow to her waist "if I let it." Aha, twin tracks of narrative, we say in I-spy style—just as they diverge to utterly different and inexorably sure destinations. All this in a distinct lyrical style. One of Vliet's editors tells me that whenever she reads the opening page of his 1977 novel, *Solitudes*, she can just feel him wanting to sculpt that prose into poetry. Amid *Scorpio Rising*, he goes ahead and does it:

> When Victoria Ann was thirteen ever'body thought she was sixteen. She thought so too. But I knew better
> > dinner table. Serafina reaches over Victoria Ann's
> > shoulder to put some food on the table. She screams
> > and drops the dish: pet green lizard hanging from
> > Victoria Ann's ear
> squeeze its jaw, its mouth'll open, you can catch it to your ear
> lobe

Literature "presupposes the unexpected," Vliet once said, "the unexpected in style, structure, character perception, vision." His last and best book, here, does all those kinds of surprising and then some.

Born in Chicago in November 1929—like his protagonist Rudy Castleberry he was a Scorpio although evidently an impious one (". . . Write Your Own Horoscope, *one of those how-to books like* Raise Your Own Heliotrope *or* Build Your Own Fluoroscope, *and about as useful . . .*")—Vliet grew up on military bases, an environment that if it don't squish your soul like a pissant under a parade will sharpen your ear for vigorous lingo. He went to college at Southwest Texas State in San Marcos, coincidentally the alma mater of another artisan of the Texas vernacular, Lyndon B. Johnson. A year of small-town school teaching, then onward and northward to Yale to study playwriting. Plays, poems, fellowships ensued. The constants were his literary striving and the support, financial, moral, and whatever other kinds there are, of his professor wife, Ann.

In 1972 cancer came.

Vliet's harrowing survival struggle across the next dozen years (chemotherapy, remission, then even more virulent recurrence in 1981) makes all the more remarkable the vigor he managed to put forth in his prose. He wrote with sharp No. 2 pencils and as Steinbeck's needlefine Mongol 2 ⅜ Fs did for *East of Eden*, they led his hand and mind to old remembered country. Ann Vliet sites *Scorpio Rising*'s fictional Balcones County as "about a hundred miles straight up from the Rio Grande and 150 northwest of San Antonio." Hot, sparse and yet compelling land where, R. G. Vliet tells us, "*if it's late February or March, an agarita bush puts out its yellow show, on blood-red stems. In June, quail eat the berries. Sometimes you can hear the quail from the highway, CHUCK-too, CHUCK-too, CHUCK-too.*" On my map of life, Texas is written in with *Here be barracks, B52s, and blue northers*, but if my own military base stint there was much briefer than Vliet's Texas time, I nonetheless hear familiarity in his voice. More Western than Southern, his twangy slang sounds right as rain. "*It was a starve-out proposition.*" "*I got to git.*" "*Shame*

*enough to fill all four corners and then some." "I ain't about to."
"Well, if God was to listen to the prayers of crows, there'd be dead
horses lying right and left."*

A regional fellow, then, this R. G. Vliet, of little renown be-
yond his adopted Southwest? No more so than Faulkner writing
so many of his books about his postage stamp county in Mississippi. Writers of caliber can ground their work in specific land
and lingo and yet be writing of that larger country, life, as well.
"Fiction lives by the energy of its prose," says Thomas Flanagan,
who knows. We have had noble proof of this in two of the most
alive and little-read masterworks of recent fiction: *The Book of
Ebenezer Le Page* by the late G. B. Edwards, a bewitching
narrative ramble of life on the English Channel isle of Guernsey,
and *Riddley Walker*, Russell Hoban's reJoycing creation of
tribal life after a nuclear holocaust. Tiny geographies, galaxies of
imaginative expression. R. G. Vliet was exploring those territories,
too: *"Scorpio, rising, its red star spitting and twitching just above
the edge of the Plateau."*

So Scorpio rises, destinies fall. Do you truly want to spend eye
time on a dying writer's fatalistic book? Betcha. You're going to
miss wonders if you don't. For me the loveliest portrayal here, and
the most deft, is the affection between Rudy and the little
daughter of his blacktressed sproutbrained friend Lita. *"I put my
mouth to Pearl's ear and said, 'What'd you have for supper?' She
put her mouth to my ear and said, 'Busghetti.' I put my mouth to
her ear and said, 'I did too.' Pearl has blue eyes the color of a
clear, Texas sky in October. She's a towhead and, like all four-
year-olds, has the rounded bulging forehead of a genius."* The
same wordsmith who gives us that portrait of innocence also
creates Victoria Ann Castleberry, who rules the last half of the
book like the sexually awakening princess of the prairies. *"Oh,
Mama that I never knew, make me beautiful! Let me be like you.
The main thing is to be pretty. Everything depends on that. Let
me wear your face, let these be your hands and arms. Bring me
love."* And always, always, there is that unmarked grave near the

Castleberry family plot. *"The body was buried eight feet deep. A little closer to Hell than all the rest."*

All of which is not to say this is a perfect book, for a work of such striving and tricky angles of grasp never is. Either astrology is more mystifying than I already thought, or it and the novel's title don't have all that much to do with the actual story. The characters whom Vliet does bring to more-than-life—Rudy, Velma, Victoria Ann—are so richly drawn they tend to dim out the rest of the population of the book; truly a conundrum of success. But we put up with more serious woes in almost everything we read or, alas, write.

Best to let the writer say it himself finally. "I'm so conscious lately of what must, apparently, be the *strangeness* of my novels to others," Vliet near the end of his crafting of this book and his life wrote to his editor. "But my vision seems to me so *clear* and true, the compulsive passion behind it so powerful, and my demands upon the language so necessary to me that I don't believe I can write any other way."

The gods maybe thought they could bray along in their lordly way and ignore this lone little-heard lyrist. But thunder ain't rain. Death did get what was mortal of R. G. Vliet, but we have here and hereafter the lasting part, his unforgettable words.

—*Ivan Doig*

BEATRICE JOANNA:
Beneath the stars, upon yon meteor
Ever hung my fate 'mongst things corruptible.
—T. Middleton, *The Changeling*

Antares, the red first magnitude star in Scorpio,
rises to the southeast about May 10. . . . Viewed
through opera glasses, the star shows a rare,
rich, ruby light, and in telescopes of moderate
power, a tiny emerald companion may be found
so close beside Antares that it appears actually
wrapped in the red light of the larger.
—W. B. White, *Seeing Stars*

♏

By nature, inclination and temperament you are
an extremist. Whatever you attempt, it is
usually done with the full force of all your
being. Your will is so strong you stick to a
fight to the bloody end, regardless of the out-
come. . . . You like very much to operate behind the
scenes. You hate and love with a white-hot fire,
yet you are able to keep things to yourself
until some plan of action is mapped out. Scorpio
is exceptionally resourceful and self-reliant,
and frequently malicious. . . . The undeveloped type
is capable of almost any outrage.
—J. F. Goodavage, *Write Your Own
Horoscope*

I

1976

1

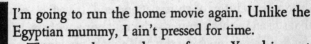I'm going to run the home movie again. Unlike the Egyptian mummy, I ain't pressed for time.

There are three roads out of town. You drive out the one headed east. Or you can walk it if you want, it's not all that far—Highway 43, one of those Balcones County roads through scrub brush and cleared-off sections of goat range that looks like it's headed straight to nowhere, just smack into the hithering sun if it's morning or up against the evening star at dusk. A state highway, not a farm-to-market road, though it looks like the Texas Highway Department has about decided it *is* one. It does have a picnic area alongside, with a cement table and a green-painted trash barrel, about five miles out from town.

I think I'll walk. I love the smell of browned grass and oily, heat-pressed cedar needles. I like the prickle of sudden sweat, the thickness of the hot, still air that feels like it's holding time in a cube of packed stillness. The sky is bleached white as a shirt on a bush. Anyway, to get out of an air-conditioned car will like to kill you.

Heat lifts from the pebbled asphalt. I walk by the baked schoolground with its big stone schoolhouse the size and shape of a dirigible hangar (grade school and high school combined: I'm in its dark halls, varnished walls and scuffed, wooded floors, the noise before the bell, the green door opening onto my place in a row of scarred, initialed desks)—the same building, built up of blocks of pale limestone that look like they were quarried from somewhere along the Nile, that's been here eighty years. ALTO SPRINGS, each letter as big as a pickup truck, is painted on its tin roof, with an arrow pointing north towards God or something.

Past the gymnasium (1940), stucco fronted by a couple of junipers, the brown football field with its wooden scoreboard, a few white clapboard-or-asbestos-sided frame houses, the Mexican school. At least it *was* the Mexican school until recently: now it's all piled full of old school desks and worn-out Ag equipment. Around the curve and past the trailer court on one side, its tiny stone office building set amongst brush and vacant cement slabs, and on the other side the rodeo ground, an oval of fenced-in dust with a cluster of chutes at one end. If you've seen the energy that's been in those chutes—the quivering withers, laid-back ears, the flank strap pinching the bull's dick, the kidney belt and tight britches, the spurred shoulder, fingers grabbing the surcingle— then the weathered posts and rails fencing in blank space look like the sticks and drift of the morning after death.

A few coneflowers if it's June, mesquite, cedar brush, burnt grass at the edge of the caliche shoulder, a wire fence and then a rock fence, and we turn in at the stone-arched gate.

This is where the exiles stay, the "put away," the ones who one way or another got so flat unsociable they couldn't talk or walk or even breathe. Some got knocked from a runaway horse or pitched through a car window, some got cramp colic and took a dose of Black Draught, some, crawling through a bobbed-wire fence with a deer rifle, settled for a bullet and some settled for one anyway, several tried to cross the Nueces or West Nueces in flood, dozens met up with a twister in 1881 (its ghost still hangs over the Plateau: every bush and tree keeps a low profile like it figured to be ripped up, and in town folks store their canned goods in storm cellars), some came down with typhoid, pneumonia, or the influenza of 1918, or membranous croup, milk fever . . . and some, amazing grace, just quit.

The white caliche road goes up to the top of a slight rise, where it'll make a brief circle back onto itself. The ground, littered with rocks and sparse pokings of Indian grass and curly mesquite grass, is the same caliche—a kind of clay—mixed with black, mealy, limestone dirt. Four acres of the cemetery are for the "Anglos" and one for the "Latin-Americans," a single-strand, bobbed-wire fence in between. The Mexican side is a crowd of wooden crosses, weathered or still white, with a cement Virgin here and there. The yellow mounds, still heaped up (the spring fogs don't wet the ground more than an inch deep or the winter rains more than two inches and at six feet under the climate's bone dry, nothing rots) are covered with bleached seashells, pieces of broken glass, their colors softened by the sun, pictures of Christ in medicine bottles. The place looks like a town dump. Some plastic flowers—all the violent colors of grief—are in their coffee cans, but most, and most of the faded red and pink and yellow crepe-paper flowers, scattered by the wind, are all over the place. There ain't any trees over there.

On this side it's the blue shade of cedars and the darker shade of live oaks, but even here most of the graves are out in the sun. Grasshoppers tick against the headstones. In March or April, yellow-cheeked warblers build their nests of torn cedar bark in the scrub cedars, and sometimes there are doves' nests on the ground. From the highest part of the cemetery you can see the town water tower and the tin-roofed courthouse, over to the west, and here and there way off yonder on the Divide a windmill sticking up. As far as you can see in any direction the gentle, stalled swells of the Plateau lift and fall, lift and fall like an ocean sea. Days the sun goes on overhead and nights the stars, which are so close they could wellnigh scrape the top of a dead man's grave.

Like I say, lots of headstones on the Anglo side, especially those bounded by rusty iron cribs amongst the mountain laurel and black persimmon bushes at the middle of the cemetery, are dated April 12, 1881, the day the sky turned to boiling stone and a black arm reached down and cut a swath a quarter-mile wide through the brush, taking half the town with it. The earliest grave, anyway the earliest with a marker still to it, has got a headstone that, if you can parse it out of the smudge of lichen and flaking letters reads:

RICHARD A DRIS

COE WAS BO

RN SEPT THE 26

1849 AND WAS KILL

ED BY THE INDIANS

JULY 19 1873.

Everybody in town knows everyone here: the schoolteachers who became ranchers' wives, the sheriffs, the doctor who learned his anatomy dissecting dead Indians, the dry-goods clerk who window-peeped, the woman who grew fifty-two kinds of rose bushes and shrubs and flower plants in her yard year after year, even through three or four bad drouths, the blacksmiths and freighters and grocers and a projector operator from the movie house, town drunk who lost his false teeth at least once a week tossing up in the early morning hours at the curb around the square, barbers, mechanics, beauty-parlor operators and one who, with the bases loaded and two away, in the last inning of the ninth knocked a home run in the game with Junction City in 1923 and was "never able to wear the same size hat again." I could go on and on. The citizens here outnumber those in Alto Springs three to one.

Most of the plots on this side are family plots, squares of concrete curbing, each with a slightly lower, poured-concrete threshold—like the houses Marybeth Crozier and I used to outline with pebbles and sticks in the bare dirt under a chinaberry tree in her backyard when we were four years old. The monuments are the furniture.

All day long, from the four or five live oaks, leaves tick onto the ground, and dark-blue cedar berries drop into the grass. Slightly to the southeast of the middle of the cemetery is the Castleberry plot. It's the largest plot here—big enough for three families—but there are only five monuments on it, including the small granite block for my brother, who died at age three and a half, before I was born. There's not a tree or bush on the plot: the four tall marble shafts and the little granite block are the only things that throw any kind of shade. The lot's set off by a curb topped by a cast-iron fence just like the one in front of the house in town. The fence gets a fresh coat of black paint every eight or ten years. There's an iron gate that opens onto the plot and latches shut when you close it behind you. The name

CASTLE

BERRY

is set in raised concrete letters on the threshold.

The four marble shafts are exactly alike—white marble base narrowing to a four-sided column, capital cut like a dormered roof, blunt, pyramidal peak. Set in a row facing east, over the heads of my great-grandpa and his two wives and my grandma, they're like the markers an ancient army might of left at the farthest point of a long, foreign-country march.

CATHERINE S. CASTLEBERRY
1866–1887

ALTON TRAVIS CASTLEBERRY
1850–1914

8   R. G. VLIET

VELMA SIMMONDS CASTLEBERRY
1862–1954

VICTORIA ANN CASTLEBERRY
1886–1907

"*Love Is Love Forevermore.*" "*Gone Home.*" "*Reunited in Heaven.*" "*All Shall See God, the Pure and the Impure.*" The stone over my brother's grave looks out of place next to the four tall, marble shafts, like it was the grave of a puppy or something. Its dates are AUG. 12, 1937 and MAY 9, 1941. The rest of the family's in town, doing whatever-all they generally do in the late morning heat. My mama's cooking dinner. My sisters are cooking for their own families or watching television. My daddy's fixing to walk home to eat, from his job at the wool-and-mohair warehouse.

Ringtails scream at night. Days the red ants crawl up and down their sand cones. Once in a while dust devils explode out of an open patch of ground to spin trash across the brush and of a sudden dissolve. In winter the northers throw the sleet in long horizontal lines, and in spring, for three or four days after a heavy rain, rain lilies whiten the ground. Sometimes hail scratches the headstones, but mostly sunlight scrubs them.

In a corner of the cemetery, no marker at head or foot, raked out flat and overrun with agarita and scrub cedar and mountain laurel alongside the rusty bobbed-wire fence, is another grave. It's been there seventy years or so. You can make it out: the outline still shows. The body was buried eight feet deep. A little closer to Hell than all the rest.

I don't live in Texas anymore.

2

The month before I was born my mother went out onto the gallery to watch a total eclipse of the moon. She was just curious. Last night the moon was full. I couldn't sleep. I have to lie on my back when I sleep, anyway, on a hard mattress, and the moonlight came in through the window like a sonofabitch. I put the pillow over my face and like to choked. Then I got a sock out of the drawer and put that across my eyes. But cars kept roaring back and forth down in the street: high school kids picking up their girls or drinking buddies to go up into the mountains around about town. I thought of them parked out up in the turnarounds or getting their fingers caught in their girlfriends' zippers while the moonlight beat on the hoods of their cars with both fists. So there I am, with my chest pitched up on top of my back and my hand sneaking down my belly toward my crotch. Hands are the sorry angels of a celibate life.

I didn't have back spasms, though. And towards morning I slept. But when I woke I felt like I was crawling out from under a root. I must of watched too much television last night.

Two glasses of orange juice laced with brewer's yeast set me to rights, plus some vitamin A and D capsules, two vitamin C's, iron and an all-natural-ingredients multivitamin out of a bottle with a pair of naked, radiant Adam and Eve types on the label running across a field, their genitals and other primary sex characteristics blurred by the speed at which they're running and the tall savannah grass. Also bee pollen. I'd take rhinoceros pollen if they sold it.

Hot shower. Did my morning exercises. Put the Band-Aids on my toes. I tucked a clean handkerchief, wallet, comb and breathmints in my britches pockets, a flock of ballpoint pens in one of the pockets of my blazer and slipped on my digital watch. Took a quick look in the mirror. I'll never get quit of the yellow on my teeth. It's systemic—that damned water I had to drink through four years as a business major back in State College, Pennsylvania. If you want to have your own teeth, keep away from central Pennsylvania. There're folks back there who've been wearing false teeth since they were sixteen. Anyway, as if I didn't have enough trouble: I've got a *third* set of teeth coming in right behind my second. That happens once in a hundred thousand. But if I'd stayed in Texas, where the water's fit to drink, leastways they wouldn't be yellow. When I smile it looks like I've got field corn in my gums.

Down the dark stairwell and on outside. The early morning sunlight on the empty sidewalk, closed shops and fence row of parking meters made it seem like Sunday. Some sparrows flew up from the gutter, and across the street pigeons scraped and cooed on the slate roof above Martha's Bakery. The stores don't open until nine.

I walked up to the end of the block, where the Union soldier, Springfield rifle in his fist, chipped nose and pigeon wash, stands on a pedestal inside a breastworks of barberry bushes at the head of Main Street, staring down the drag, probably appalled to see what he'd really died·for or got his balls shot off for or whatever. Four New England churches surround the rotary, one of granite, two of brick, one of white Congregational clapboard. The spires stick up like fingers from four fists. There are still a few elm trees on their lawns, plastic plugs in the trunks where the trees are being treated for Dutch elm disease. The buds of imagined leaves are just beginning to crack. In the sugar maples, branches drift through a yellow haze of tiny flowers. (Back in Texas the hard nubbins of plums are already on the plum trees. The okra's flowering. They're picking collard greens, watering the onions and the lettuce is past. —*Here*, just three days ago, we had four goddamned inches of snow. On the twenty-first of *April*, for Christsake. The Berkshires were white. In town the crocuses were poking up through the white stuff.)

Forty-four degrees, seven Celsius. The dots of light change on the board in front of the Muskapec Savings Bank: 8:28. Almost no one's on the street—everybody gets to work about five minutes to nine.

I sidestep some dog shit. A police car goes by. A little farther down Main Street I nod to Phan Son Xuan, who was sent from Vietnam by the Xtian god to sweep McDonald's hamburger wrappers, cigarette butts, candy wrappers, smashed ice-cream cones and aluminum sodawater cans from the streets of West Hesper. Right on schedule, he's in front of the movie house, pitching a shovelful of trash into the barrel on the little cart he pushes around all day, six days a week. Phan Son Xuan's one of your last examples of the American work ethic.

If we have any more snow I'll commit suicide. I think of yellow puffs of flowers on a branch of huisache, back in Texas. I walk through a stricter sunlight, heat so thick you can cut it with a knife. Oh, well.

The loudspeaker in the belfry of the Congregational church intones the half hour.

At Business Way Office Equipment and Supply I unlock the thick glass door, step in and turn off the burglar alarm. The next thing I do is water the *Rhoeo spathacea* that's flourishing in a tinfoil-wrapped flowerpot on my desk. I hate the damned thing.

Maybe you want to know what-all a good ol' Texas boy who's still got angora goat dung on his boots is doing way up here in nowhere, amongst the Massachusetts income tax and sugar maples, native Italians and Poles. I'll make it short.

In 1972, the year I graduated from Alto Springs High School, the town set up a scholarship, which I won. The hitch was, you

had to go to an out-of-state college. Buddy Gilpin, who had graduated from A. S. H. S. years before and had got up to working
on a doctorate in anthropology at the University of New Mexico,
then one in American Culture at Bowling Green, then one in
philosophy at some place in New York state—straight *A*'s and
never finished a one—was a forty-year-old graduate assistant in
English at Penn State University in State College, Pa., and he
got me in there: it was a way of life, like changing stock from
Herefords to sheep to goats on a ranch. (The year after he got
me into Penn State, he transferred to Temple University, in
Philadelphia, to concentrate on speech and drama. Every four
years or so he'd go back to Alto Springs for a rest before com-
mencing on a new dissertation. He'd sit for three or four days on
the gallery of his folks' house at the edge of town, drinking Lone
Star beer and swatting flies, and stare at the heave and fall of
the Plateau, the miles of brush. Told me once it was the "moral
equivalent of getting comfort from the stars." Then he'd change
his major and apply to another university.) Anyway, my roommate at Penn State, Frank Bertolini, was from Massachusetts. His
dad owns Business Way Office Equipment and Supply in Worchester, with five branch stores, one in West Hesper. Frank's
dad gave me this job. Chief cook and bottle washer.

That was about as short as the new bride's pie crust.

Art supplies, adding-machine tapes, pads, envelopes, desk
lamps, typewriters, calculators, office furniture—that's the desert
I roam through forty hours a week, one of your contemporary
saints. Every once in a while I have a cold beer or a glass of milk
from the refrigerator in the stockroom, like a lizard snapping
flies off a prickly pear.

The first thing I do is itemize the accounts and take the cash
to the bank before the store opens. When I get back I do the
bookkeeping on charge accounts for the previous day. Then I
start putting up shipments for phone and mail orders, to be sent
out each day by delivery service.

Folks come in.

"Hi, Rudy. Do you have typing paper?"

"Hullo, Rudy. I'm looking for some small rubber bands, but wide."

About three times a week some guy or other'll come in off the street. I know right off what's up. They look like what you'd see kicking fenders in a used-car lot. They'll walk back and forth in front of the typewriters, their hands crammed into their britches pockets. They ask me about this machine or that one, peck a few keys, tilt the damned thing up to look underneath. I don't know what-all they're looking for—transmission, crank case, whatever-all it is they're checking out. I answer all their questions. After about fifteen minutes they'll say, "Now, what can you do for me on this?" or "What kinda deal can you give me on it?" They must think I'm selling pineapples in a Mexican market.

"That's the price."

I get this sly look, like they've really got me by the balls. That kind never buy.

I was setting up a display of Pres-A-Ply get-acquainted badges when Lita came in. "Hi, Rudy." She stood over by the El Marko Color Center rack, her head cocked, squinting at me like she was sizing me up. "Where've you been hiding yourself?"

"Under a rock."

"Long time no see."

"I only come out at night."

Lita smiled. I wish I had teeth like that.

"Pearl's been asking for you." Pearl's her little girl. She'll be four in three more months. "She keeps pestering me about you all the time."

"Tell her I think of her a lot."

Lita went over to my desk. She had on her back-to-the-land commune outfit: white flowerprint pioneer dress with scalloped hem, pullover sweater, work boots, floppy black felt hat. Her long black hair streamed down to her waist. She bent over the *Rhoeo spathacea*, pulling at the big leaves like they were rab-

bits' ears. "It's really growing! *Look*, it's got a *flower!*" She knelt
to smell the flower. It's got no odor at all. A homeless bee wouldn't
be interested in it.

Joe, Lita's live-in boyfriend, gave her the plant to make up
with her after a quarrel. But Lita's thumb is about as green as
Vietnam defoliant. All the plants in her apartment have a dead
look. She's always forgetting to water them, and when she does,
half of them drown. Right now Lita's in love with Joe and I'm
the one who has to feed and water the plant. She wants to put
it on the apartment table as a big, fat, thrifty centerpiece on their
"anniversary" when it comes up in a couple of months. I wish
she'd take the stupid tinfoil off the pot.

Lita poked at the flower. "Will it get any bigger?"

"I hope not."

Lita laughed and stood up. She turned to me. "The guys don't
have a gig tonight." Joe plays trumpet in a local band, The
Applegate Outfit. "We're having a party up at the apartment.
Why don't you come up?"

"I don't know."

"Come on, dammit. I haven't seen you in *weeks*. And when
are we going to take another trip?"

Lita and I like to drive to the towns around about West Hesper to look at the buildings. We drive around in Lita's beat-up
green Volkswagen, mostly on Sundays, trying to find old houses
and business buildings—anything built before 1910. We're both
Victorian gingerbread freaks. We'll spread a picnic lunch out on
our laps on the sidewalk across from some building or other and
spend all afternoon checking it out. What we like best are buildings that are such a mess of architectural styles it looks like
they're about to explode. Then we try to figure out what, not
counting mortar and nails, is holding the whole damned thing
together. It's a sport.

In Wylie, the next town over, there's a building we go back
to see two or three times a year: the old Muskapec County National Bank Building. It's been empty since the early 1950s, when
the bank moved its moneybags to a new location. Of all things,

it's never been vandalized. On the ground floor, just inside the fly-specked, flaking gold-leafed window, there's still an old roll-top desk. The sun-yellowed shades with their bleached tassels still hang half-pulled in the windows. Two corner plinths each support a marble column topped by an abacus and echinus that can only be called East Coast Midwestern. A narrow, polished, red granite shaft with quilted, almost Egyptian Revival base and Corinthian capital, seems to be the only thing holding up the center of the building. The second story is divided from the first by a marble stringcourse, with MUSKAPEC COUNTY NATIONAL BANK carved into it. Above this is an arcade of three windows, each separated by projected columns, also with Corinthian capitals. At the top of the building is its crowning glory: the moldings, carvings, corbels, rosettes, cornices, arched amortizement and finials of draped globe-and-vase like John D. Rockefeller the First flinging silver dollars into the air. The date on the building is 1875. For all the hassle of shafts, columns, projections, moldings, entablatures and bas-relief the whole thing pulls itself together, expresses itself upward, the stone and glass and wood vibrant, almost lifting itself off the ground: amongst buildings, a kind of half-assed, ascending angel.

"Well, are you coming to the party?"

"Tonight's Thursday night."

"What's that got to do with the price of eggs in China?"

"Thursday's the night I reserve for cuddling up to my teddy bear."

"Aren't you a smart bundle of mouth? We ought to put you on some talk show."

"The commercials'd give me acid indigestion."

"*I'll* give you acid indigestion if you don't show up. Us westerners have got to stick together." Lita's from California and I'm from Texas. We're the only two sunbelters in West Hesper.

"I ain't said yes and I ain't said no."

"Why do you always say 'ain't'?"

"Pure orneriness. I don't say it to customers, though."

"Just us lower classes."

"It reminds me where I'm from."

Lita jerked a pencil from a rack. She came over to me and said, "I'll break this damned pencil on your head if you don't quit your fooling. You come to that party tonight, you hear?"

"All right."

Lita laughed. She stuck the pencil into my blazer pocket, straightened my lapels, dusted them, leaned forward and gave me a peck on the forehead. "You've made my day," she said. Next thing I knew, she was out the door. At the curb, just in front of the store, she turned and waved, then started across the street.

Lita's tall. Her arms are long and smooth: they look so cool. She always walks with her head slightly back, her hair hanging down so straight it hardly touches her back, just the tips of it lightly brushing the top of her butt. I'd recognize her a mile off.

I've seen her barefoot. There's a little web of skin between each of her big and second toes. It troubles her. It means she was born imperfect.

What I need is a glass of milk.

In the stockroom, surrounded by cases of Ezy-Rase, Eaton's Corrasable, looseleaf-notebook fillers and other mementos of the intellectual life of the nation, I opened the refrigerator, reached over the boxes of wax crayons and such, and got a fresh, unopened carton of milk. I drank two glasses. The buzzer sounded: Somebody'd just come in the store. They wanted a package of file folders, some legal pads, a roll of adding-machine tape and a box of Dennison's seals. I added up the sale, wrote out a receipt and bagged the purchases.

At one P. M. Herbie came in. Herbie's a senior at the high school. They let him out three afternoons a week to get work experience, and he works for me. I went up the street to the Towne Restaurante to have dinner. When I got back, the weekly restock shipment had come. We spent the afternoon checking the invoices, getting the stuff into the stockroom and some of it on the shelves. Customers came and went all afternoon. At five-thirty I closed out the cash register and locked up the cash.

Herbie emptied the trash baskets. He swept the floors and ran
an oil mop over them. After he'd gone home I sat at my desk to
write up the day's receipts. At five minutes past six I picked out
a pack of blue index cards and a box of wax crayons for Pearl.
Then I turned on the burglar alarm and locked the glass door.
The street was already almost empty.

Bought some Twinkies in the pizza shop and walked up
Main Street towards my place. A few teenagers were huddled
around one of the benches that line Main Street, planning the
night's vandalism. To the west the sun, not yet propped up by
daylight saving, was touching the top of the Taconic Range,
over in New York state. It threw long shadows on the cold sidewalks and long sheets of late sunlight up the slopes of the Muskapec Mountains to the east. Fifty-one degrees by the Muskapec
Savings Bank, and I can feel the wind from Canada, the chill
of melting ice off the Great Lakes. They've got a saying here in
West Hesper: *I missed spring this year, I was on the toilet when
it came.* Christ. I'd give my eyeteeth, all four of them, for the
hot shade under the mesquite tree.

I cook my own suppers. I usually eat canned spaghetti, but I
can make a pretty good meat loaf, with baked potatoes. Tonight
I had spaghetti. A salad of lettuce and spring onions for my green-
food. Coffee. A couple vitamins. Vanilla ice cream and a
Twinkie.

What I hate is washing dishes. I left them in the sink, changed
into a Levi jacket and faded jeans and hit the street, headed for
Lita's place. The wind had picked up. Candy wrappers and
paper cups skittered along the sidewalks. Above the fluorescent
streetlights the stars, if you could see them, were rotating on
their crystal axles amongst the rest of the litter of space.

Lita's apartment is above Early's Department Store, on the
third floor. The building, part of the Blotner block, was built in
1928. It's one of the nicest buildings in town, especially on the
inside. From the landing on the third floor you can look two
stories up. The whole enclosure is topped by a skylit roof. Apart-

ment windows face the landing. Lots of the windows are open, and potted plants sit on the sills. The wainscoting, molding, window facings and doors, all varnished oak, are the color of dark, golden honey. Even in winter the place is warm and sunny. You could grow a stand of banana trees in here.

There are eight apartments in the building. Each has a fireplace in the living room and one in a bedroom directly above. The rent costs a mint, but Lita's dad takes care of that, just like he took care of her college expenses and forked out for her wedding and her share in the commune in Colorado and her bail when she was arrested during a nuclear protest in New Hampshire and her back-to-the-land farmstead with its sick cow, imported seaweed fertilizer, kerosene lamps and sauna bath in Vermont just before she and her old man split. Lita's apartment is furnished with Le Creuset cookware and Cuisinart blender, Goodwill rugs, chairs, floorlamps and an expensive sofa. There's always a sleeping bag somewhere on the floor.

A stick of incense was burning in a saucer on the meter box by the door. Below it, on the floor, was a dish of catfood and a box of Kitty Litter. Lita feeds all the cats that manage to get into the building, but Joe won't let them in the apartment.

Pearl opened the door.

"*Wudy!*"

I wanted to scoop her up, but my back can't take it. I told her to close the door.

Her eyebrows twisted into a frown. "What *for?*"

"*Close* it."

She closed the door slowly, opened it partway again, squinted up at me, commenced laughing and slammed it shut quick. I got down on my hands and knees, worked up a mean face and got ready to grab her. The door opened again and I was staring at somebody's knees. It was Joe, Lita's boyfriend.

"For Christsake, what're you doing? Get out of that catfood." Pearl was standing right behind him, jumping up and down, screaming and laughing.

"I'm classifying cockroaches."

"Shit. Get up off your knees." He turned back into the room and walked away, leaving the door open.

I went into the apartment. "Get away from me," I said to Pearl. I sat on the sofa and Pearl climbed onto my lap and I gave her the blue index cards and the box of wax crayons.

The noise from the stereo was enough to make you deaf— The Kinks or The Grateful Dead or a socko combination of shot-down World War Two kamikaze pilot, Eighth Avenue subway and chain saw, I couldn't make out which. I'm a country-music boy, my ownself.

Everybody was passing around joints. Already all the mice and cockroaches were high. Ralph Staples and Steve Newcombe, who are with The Applegate Outfit, were popping pills. Trish Meyerson was pressing up against Dom Trisorio, the local Walt Whitman poet, over by the fireplace, and Dom was holding a bottle of Scotch against her spine. There were books on the guru's craft and mayonnaise jars full of paintbrushes, their stiff bristles clogged with acrylics, on the mantel and astral charts and occult and science-fiction posters all over the walls.

I put my mouth to Pearl's ear and said, "What'd you have for supper?" She put her mouth to my ear and said, "Busghetti." I put my mouth to her ear and said, "I did too." Pearl has blue eyes the color of a clear, Texas sky in October. She's a towhead and, like all four-year-olds, has the rounded, bulging forehead of a genius. She was in her pajamas, ready for bed.

Hollis Waltermire was back from Boston. Avery Linscott and Julie Alcombright were in from the farm. A girl named Janice Something-or-other came in from the kitchen. She was braless. Her breasts bounced with every step. In fact, every ounce of her bounced, a kind of muscular Morse code. She yelled "Hi, Tex" at me and commenced to pass around the marijuana brownies. I don't even know her. I wouldn't mind knowing her, though. Pearl opened the box of crayons and the package of index cards and started making squiggles on the cards.

Of a sudden, after a final volley like the sun coming up, the record quit and in the early-morning hush I could hear the clear

noise of birds in the bushes. The only problem was it wasn't
morning.

"The Bo Diddley beat."

"In sync."

"Megastud."

"Shit. Megaturd, you mean."

"Cosmic consciousness."

"Feedback effect."

"Run a riff on the electric bass."

Somebody put on a John Coltrane. Lita came in from the
kitchen carrying a bowl of miso dip in one hand and a dish of
carrot sticks in the other. She was wearing a blue Indian sari
edged with white and her hair was done up on top of her head.
Her face looked paler than usual. I could make out the faint
sprinkle of freckles on her nose. She hadn't any makeup on. She
looked like some goddess come out of the ocean or a law of
nature fetched down from a mountain somewheres, simple to
understand as a tree in fruit bloom or a burning bush. "Hi,
Rudy," she said. She put the carrots and dip on the coffee table
in front of me. "Haven't you got anything to drink?" She looked
around the room. Joe was over in a corner with Dave Howcroft,
sharing a joint. (Joe's last name is Cwiertniewicz. Can you say
it? I'll spell it again: C w i e r t n i e w i c z. He's from New Jersey.) "Hey, Joe," Lita called to him, "didn't you get Rudy anything to drink?" Joe didn't even look at her. In fact, he didn't
talk to her all evening. I saw it. If she was in one part of the
room, he'd go to another. She followed him all over the place,
all evening. He'd just turn away. Lita would talk to whoever
was at hand. She kept laughing louder and louder. Once she
bumped into Joe as if by accident. He gave her a look that would
of drove a tapeworm back up a dog's ass. Joe is tall and dark, with
thick, black hairs on the backs of his wrists. Black, brushy eyebrows. Scars all over his neck and face from ingrown boils. His
eyes are as black as a pair of Mexican persimmons or the stare
of a ringtail from a cedar bush. Some women are mighty queer
feeders.

Lita went into the kitchen to fetch me a Guinness. "There's more where that came from," she said. It was foamy and cold. She said to Pearl, "Come on. It's time you got to bed." Pearl started to make a fuss. Of a sudden Lita grabbed her by the arm and jerked her off my lap. "Goddammit," Lita said, "you get up to bed." The crayons flew every which way. Pearl commenced crying. Lita sent her up the stairs with whacks on her fanny, following up after her. I didn't even get to tell Pearl goodnight.

I picked up the crayons and took a swig of the porter. It went down smooth, bubbly and thick. Frank Kimberly came over and sat down beside me. For the next half hour he carried on about the Maharaj Ji, little butterball guru who's going to save the world. My back was killing me. Finally I said, "Can you get me another bottle of stout?"

He stared at me a minute and said, "Sure."

I had two more Guinnesses and things were looking good. Words fluttered past my ears like moths. The bulb in the lamp on the table next me was a protective angel, hovering and bright in the circle of the shade. Janice came over and talked to me a spell. Who *is* she? At one point I got up and wandered to a window overlooking the street. The street was still there. Then I made my way back to the sofa, plopped down and stayed there the rest of the evening. After the fifth Guinness I just leaned back and smiled. My back felt great. Once in a while I'd lift my hand, examining the wonder of it, or turn my head. If somebody offered to fetch me another Guinness, fine, but I wasn't about to get up and go after it my ownself.

Sometime during the evening Avery Linscott gave me a lecture on organic gardening and manure composting. I just smiled. At about a quarter to twelve my coach began to turn into a pumpkin. I figured I'd better get home while I could still walk.

I went to the john first. Man, did I piss. It was the most interesting piss I've ever experienced. I mean, it was endless. Then for about twenty minutes I stared at the picture on the wall above the toilet. It's a photograph of Lita's grandma and great-grandparents in a gilded frame. The family is in a studio. There's a backdrop of painted vases and flowers and curtains behind. A Turkish carpet is under their feet. The mother, dressed in black silk and a white lace collar, is sitting in a chair, her arm around the child, Lita's grandma, about five years old, who's wearing a huge black ribbon on the top of her head. She has on a waistless sailor dress and button-up shoes. The father stands directly behind them, in black suit and celluloid collar. They all look so serious, like they hadn't yet ate dinner. It's interesting to see what Lita's grandma and great-grandma-and-pa were like. Lita picked out the picture from a box of them at Goodwill's.

The moon was directly overhead as I walked home. I took my time. Back in Texas the moonlight is likely pouring down onto the Plateau. Under cedar bushes the ground is as black as pitch. Deer browse near the fencelines. At the edge of the Plateau, along the breaks of the Balcones Fault, the canyons drop down into darkness and the Nueces River and the West Nueces and the Agua Frio, bright ribbons in moonlight, rush over the rocks.

It's godawful lonesome here in West Hesper. As lonesome as the Valleys of the Moon.

3

 I could go to the house with its long gallery, its cast-iron fence, live oak tree and fig trees and pyracanth bushes, but I'm going to stay here on the square. The courthouse is behind me. I know its hulk, the tall, narrow windows, the pale blocks of squared, unmortared limestone. I can feel its dark shadow begin to inch away, grass stem by dead grass stem, from the base. The courthouse lawn is brown beneath my feet. The sun in a fit of triumph's just on past overhead. There ain't a sound of a bug or a bird. The shade under the wooden awnings of the stores around the square is so dark it's like parceled-out chunks of night, and pickup trucks in front of the Bluebonnet Café shimmer in the heat. Everybody with any sense has got his head under a roof somewhere, his knees under a table and a glass of beer or ice tea in his fist. But I like the heat. I've got my own shade, such as it is, here on the courthouse lawn next the whitewashed trunk of a pecan tree.

All the stores have wooden awnings. All the sidewalks are still stirrup-high. The business buildings are mostly stone. They're might'near all single story. Some are quilted with white-washed tin. Some are built of rough, undressed stone stuccoed-over and scribed with lines to look like the joints of good cut-stone work. But mostly they're just plain stone. Hoesstresser's Dry Goods Store has a false second-story front of wood, behind

it nothing but wind. Price's Drug Store, right across from me on
the southwest corner of the square, does have two stories, the
tallest building on the square excepting the courthouse and
the hotel. Downstairs, in the drugstore, Mrs. Price is putting the
latest *Redbook* and *Look* on the magazine rack and Cleota
Twelves, who's been working at the soda fountain since her
husband, Nate Twelves, fell from a windmill twenty-three years
ago, is serving Cokes and chicken-salad sandwiches to the three
or four women—mainly ranchwives with a second house in town
so the kids can get to school—sitting at one of the two glass-
topped, wire-legged tables in a corner of the store. Upstairs is the
Masonic Temple, which used to be the Woodmen of the World
Hall, which used, before the twister came along and knocked
additional religion into the survivors' heads, to be the dance hall.
They rebuilt a lot of church buildings after that twister. But one
time I saw, on my way home from a horrible first day in the first
grade in school, a devil cutting across the square: he was dressed
in new black, was dark and good-looking as all get-out, and had
roosters' feet.

> *"My nose itches.*
> *I smell peaches.*
> *Here comes Rudy*
> *with a hole in his britches"*

the girls used to yell at me on my way home from school. Cram
their jump rope.

Next to the drugstore, if you head north along that side of the
square, is the Balcones Power and Light office, then Gus's Barbershop and the hardware and the *Alto Springs Staple & Star*,
the local weekly newspaper (staple being the long, curly mohair
of the angora goat—the "diamond fiber"—in its clip), and an
alleyway and then the movie house, the Gem City Theatre.
Dorr Beecroft owns the movie house. He runs the projector and
his wife works the popcorn machine and sells tickets. They show
two shows a week and on Sunday nights a Mexican movie. If
you're late, and you're the last one in, Dorr will start the movie

over: at the exact same place you came in the film stops, the lights come up and it's time to go home.

Past the movie house is the American Goat Breeders' Association office and then Van Zandt's variety store and the post office —narrow corridor with tinned ceiling and dark, varnished walls, ranked postal boxes and postmistress' window behind which Miss Fern Quarternight, bent and tiny as a dwarf, has kept hold to her job through the administrations of nine presidents—and then the white-painted locker plant on the northwest corner, where hunters in season have their deer weighed and tagged and sometimes hung in cold storage. That's on the west side of the square.

Across the street from the locker plant is the Ranchman Hotel. The doctor has his office there (the dentist's office is in the courthouse). Across the street from *it*, in a triangular building on the corner, is the Humble gas station. Along that side of the square, I know it all by heart, is a vacant lot and Hoesstresser's Dry Goods and a vacant lot and then the city hall—two small rooms, the only building on the square built after 1920.

On the east side of the square, not counting a lot of empty lots, are the Gem City Grocery, Harvey's Cleaners, Valdez' Grocery and Market and the Gulf-gas-station-and-Chevrolet dealer. (The wool-and-mohair warehouse, where my daddy works, takes up almost all of the southeast block, off the square, and has for eighty-seven years.)

The Stockman's City Bank is on the south side, along with the Bluebonnet Café and The Western Wear Shop and then a wide-open spread of cockleburs and sandlove grass with concrete pillars and girders still sticking up—the start of Alto Springs' finest building, a department store, that commenced going up in September 1929, quit the same year and never recommenced. The pillars and girders, weathered by the sun and wind and tufted with bull-nettles, are like the guardians of some ancient archaeological site. Next to this is Roy's Garage and Pool Hall, catty-corner from the drugstore.

Three blocks in any direction and you're in the brush. The

schoolhouse is two blocks over to the east, the town water tower
a block or so to the south. The sky up above is a pale blue—a
color of blue that in the summer won't change for weeks.

But towards evening the west turns plum-colored. In the
windows in town and out on the ranches, curtains stir: the
breeze that comes up out of the southeast every night. Night
after night it comes back, crisp with odors of dry grass and
cedar brush and with a hint of the saltiness of the Gulf. A small
red light starts blinking on top of the water tower. The motor
comes on in the shed under the tower and runs for an hour or
so, hauling water out of a deep underground river. The stars
come out, bright as Xmas: you can see by their light. Tree frogs
trill in the live oaks, and nighthawks *peent* overhead.

At night, in bed, you'll have to pull a blanket up over your
shoulders.

Even if you try to separate your fate from your people, will
your heart let you do it?

4

Every morning I straighten out my toes. Both feet. I tape a Band-Aid to the big toe, run it under the second toe and on top the next, then another Band-Aid from that on under the next and end the whole kit and caboodle atop the little toe. You think that's funny? If I don't, my toes are like pretzels. They climb on top of each other like drowning swimmers onto a buddy's back. It gets so I can hardly walk. The Band-Aids fix up my toes.

Last night was another bad night. Came near to having muscle spasms in my back. It scared hell out of me. I think I was about to have heart palpitations too. I took some Dantrium. It loosened me up in the nick of time. I lay on my back. My mind climbed out of my skull and hovered in the dark above me like a moth. I was so relaxed I could hardly move. I didn't sleep. It's like when you've just died and you know your legs are stretched out straight and your hands are on your chest loose and useless but with the notion of warmth in them, the remembrance of motion. You know there's light around you, and people in the room. You can't hear them. You can't see them. You just *know*. And you don't even *want* to move. There's just your brain, shining like a grub in dirt. It can't contract a muscle or lift a breath out of your gullet anymore. It can only wait. The thing is, it's got everything in it you ever knew, and even the bad is good.

That's how I got through the night. This morning I was really dragging my hub. Felt like I was about to croak. I got up early and stood in a hot shower for an hour. My fingers were so wrinkled afterwards I could hardly button my shirt. Drank a quart of orange juice, laced with plenty of brewer's yeast. Took my vitamins and my bee pollen and a handful of aspirins. Then I went to work. I was sick to my stomach all morning. But I'm going to live if it kills me.

Outside the store, on the other side of the plate glass, it was a bright, sunny morning. I could wellnigh *taste* the spring air. Folks walked back and forth in it without hats or jackets or coats and every blessed one, it looked like, in good health, with perfect bodies. When they came into the store, it was like they were stepping in from Acapulco—they were lighthearted as foam hitting a Mexican beach. You could smell the springtime air and sunlight coming off them. Even the old ones were in perfect health. It made me want to run out onto the back parking lot, fling myself down onto the hot asphalt and let the sunlight bore down into my back, changing all the atoms until I could crawl out of myself like a raw, smooth snake out of a new-shucked skin.

I had to settle for another couple aspirins.

At about a quarter to eleven Lita called. She said, "What time are you eating lunch?"

"One. Herbie's coming in then."

"Come up to my place. I'll fix up something nice for the both of us."

"I'd intended to take luncheon at the Waldorf-Astoria."

"Rudy, *stop* it, *please*. You're going to drive me crazy one of these days."

Something was wrong. I said, "What's the matter?"

Lita didn't say anything for a minute. Then she said, "I need somebody to talk to." It sounded like she was about to cry.

I said, "Jesus, Lita. I'd come up right now, but I can't leave the store."

"That's all right. I'll be all right. Do you like shrimp? I've got a package of frozen shrimp here." It sounded like she was brightening up some. "I'll make a salad."

"That sounds great. Should I bring some wine?"

"There's a bottle of Chablis in the fridge. Just bring yourself. And *don't* bring any more of those damned Twinkies. The last time, Pearl got sick on them. You know she's not supposed to eat stuff with sugar in it."

"You won't let her eat sweets. You don't let her drink Cokes. Life is hell for her."

"Don't bring any Twinkies." The line was silent again for a moment. When Lita did speak, her voice was way down in a lower, softer register. She said, "I'm sorry I pulled Pearl off your lap like that the other night. I just wasn't myself."

"It's O.K." I could live for a week without any nourishment but just listening to the changes in Lita's voice. At night, when I'm alone and Lita's probably already asleep or being made love to, in my mind I can fetch up every tone of her voice. Or sometimes I've been half awake, about to stumble into sleep, and of a sudden I'm in a room, sunlight crowding in from somewhere, and I hear Lita's voice as close to my ear as the pillow, as pure as that sunlight.

Lita said, "Pearl didn't get to see much of you."

"I'll see her when I come up."

"Rudy, I mean it. Don't bring any Twinkies."

"Christ, the whole country's going organic. It's a Communist plot."

"See you at one. *Ciao.*"

"Chow."

That was four days after the party.

When I walked into Lita's apartment the place was a mess. Pearl's toys were all over the floor. Clothes were on the floor, Pearl's and Lita's both. Magazines. Crumpled tissues. A plate with dried spaghetti sauce was on the end table, and cups with floating cigarette butts in dregs of cold black coffee were everywhere—on the arms of the sofa, on the floor, on the windowsills.

There was a canopy of blue haze in the room. Lita won't eat anything but natural foods, but she smokes like a fiend. She called from the kitchen, "I'm going to clean that mess up in a while. Not that I give a damn." I bent down into fresher air, tossed a blanket out of the way to the end of the sofa, brushed off the granola crumbs and sat. My back was feeling a mite better. Pearl, happy as a lark, climbed onto my lap. She was still in her pajamas. She said, "I wanna see your munny."

"What money?"

"The big one." She poked a hand into one of my blazer pockets.

I took a silver dollar out of my vest pocket. It's an 1884 silver dollar, minted in Philadelphia. The eagle's breast feathers are gone and Liberty's cheek is worn smooth, but the thing is as solid as if it was new. You can pitch it at the floor and it'll bounce a mile, it's got that much silver in it. It rings like crystal. It's the first silver dollar my great-grandpa, A. T. Castleberry, took in in trade when he opened his general merchandise store in Alto Springs in 1889. It's been handed down through the men in my family for years. My daddy gave it to me when I left Alto Springs. He was almost crying when I left. The silver dollar would of gone to my brother Leroy if he hadn't died. I keep it on me all the time. Like the saying goes, *Money in your pocket when you see the new moon is money all month.*

Pearl grabbed for the silver dollar. She said, "I want it."

I curved the coin through the air and plopped it in Pearl's hand. *"Keep it out of your mouth."* Pearl pressed it against her cheek, her eyes scrunched shut in concentration. She said, "It feels *hot.*"

"I'm trying to get it to hatch."

"I wanna keep it."

"You give me that." I pretended to grab for the coin. Pearl held it away from me and laughed. I pushed her over onto the sofa and tickled her and tried to pry the silver dollar from her fist. Pearl was laughing like crazy.

Lita came out of the kitchen. She said, "What are you doing to my daughter?"

"She's got my silver dollar." Pearl was churning from side to side on the sofa and laughing like crazy.

Lita said, "Good God, you're both a couple of kids."

I held a finger against Pearl's chest and kept it there until she lay still. She had hiccups and tears were running from her eyes. I said, "All right, you can have it for now, but give it back when I leave, y'hear?" Pearl looked up at me with her big blue eyes and nodded. She hiccuped. As soon as I let go of her she jumped up, laughing and squealing, and ran to a corner of the room. She said, "No, you can't have it."

"Haw, haw," I said.

Lita was setting the dinner table, over by the window. She tossed a bean bag that Pearl had left on it into a corner, wiped the table with a wet dishrag and set out three plates. I said, "Where's Joe?"

"Off on a gig."

Maybe the room was a mess, but Lita wasn't. She was as spruce as if she'd just stepped out of springwater. She was wearing a blue work shirt tied in a knot over her belly button, and Levi's. She wore an apron. She said, "I'll have lunch on in a minute." She moved around the table with the cool motions of a priestess, setting out honest-to-God heirloom silver and dime-store wineglasses. Lita has the long, slender fingers of a pianist. I just wish she'd quit biting her fingernails. Look, Lita's one year older than me. She went to a fashionable, private high school in California where everyone had their own late-model car. She went to Stanford. She spent two years putting up geodesic domes at a commune in Colorado. She don't know *anything*. So why am I in awe of her? I'll tell you why. I could stare all afternoon at the seams on her Levi's. But it's not only that. I mean, there's *her*. Look, I don't want to think about it.

Right now she's sad. I can tell. A second ago I saw her of a sudden stand stock-still, her hand about to set down a fork, and stare into space. I can guess what's likely standing there in front of her: that sonofabitch Joe.

I studied the astral posters on the wall. Lita's a Cancer— ❀ —with Mercury in the ascendant, whatever-all that means. Lita believes that crap. But I've seen Cancer in the east, in Texas in December, way up in the dark over the dust and brush. It's got six stars. You've got to work hard to make it out from the crowd of other light. In February it stands up high. What I like best is the soft, small bunch of light in the center of the hard-shelled crab back. To me, that's Lita. I'm the bright star twitching and snapping to the left, in Leo.

If Lita was to ask me to kill for her, I'd likely do it. She won't ask me to. In fact, she'll never ask me to do anything real.

Pearl ran back over to me. She flung herself against my knees. She said, "Tell me a stowy." I'm a sucker for kids: I love their small, round faces. I said, "Give me back my dollar first."

"Aw wight."

I put the silver dollar in my vest pocket and Pearl climbed back up onto my lap. I said, "Once there was an old woman named Abbie Amelia Davis Dobbs. One day Abbie Amelia Davis Dobbs went out to her garden to dig potatoes. She dug and dug, and suddenly—*she dug up a silver toe.*"

Lita, who had started back to the kitchen, stopped in the kitchen doorway and said, "I don't want to hear that."

I said, "A golden arm?"

"No, dammit. It gives me the creeps. You're just going to scare the daylights out of Pearl."

Pearl said, "Tell me! Tell me!"

I said, "Pearl, I promise you. When you grow up I'll tell you ever' blessed story I know, about silver toes and golden arms and diamond noses and I don't know what-all. And we'll drink all the Cokes we want. Your mama won't be able to do a thing about it."

"*Huh!*" Lita said. She went back out to the kitchen.

Pearl said, "*Tell me the west.*"

But Lita's good to me. Once she gave me a birthday party: all

Pearl's friends came. I said, "I'll tell you a better one. Once there was an old woman that had two daughters. They were called 'Good Gal' and 'Bad Gal.' "

"Why?"

Lita came out of the kitchen with food and the bottle of Chablis. She said to Pearl, "I swear, you're nothing but a question box from morning to night. It's time to eat."

I said to Pearl, "I'll finish it later."

Pearl said, "Oh, foo." She slid off my lap and ran over to the table. She said, "What's that?"

"Shrimp salad."

"I don't like swimp salad."

"Well, you're going to eat it."

We sat to the table. There was a bowl of shrimp salad, fresh seven-grain bread that Lita had baked herself, mung sprouts with tofu, applesauce and the Chablis. Pearl had milk. Pearl ate three helpings of shrimp salad. Afterwards we had herb tea. It tasted just like boiled goat fodder. It was a real good meal. All it lacked of putting a bottom on a man's stomach was a couple of Twinkies.

During the meal Lita was quiet. She didn't eat much and she didn't talk much. Pearl did most of the talking. When we'd finished, Lita said to Pearl, "Go upstairs and straighten up your room, sugar."

Pearl said, "I don't want to."

Lita said, "Pearl Elizabeth."

I said, "Straighten up her *room*? She's only three years old."

Lita looked at me. She said, "You are cruising for a bruising. She's almost four. A four-year-old is big enough to take care of her own room." She said to Pearl, "And while you're up there, get dressed."

"Do I got to?"

Lita pushed back from the table. "Goddammit," she said.

Pearl slid from her chair. She said, "I *never* get to play. Do I have to take a nap?"

"No, you can come down and play afterwards."

"Will Wudy be here?"

"He won't be if you keep on wasting time. And if it'll make you any happier, *I'll* be cleaning up *this* mess."

I said, "I suppose you mean me."

Lita said, "Stop it, Rudy."

Pearl ran over to me and gave me a hug. She whispered in my ear, "*I got a jump wope.*"

I said, " 'Had a dog and his name was Rover. When he died, he died all over. Excepting his tail.' " Pearl laughed. She ran over to the stairs. She said, "Don't go back to work, Wudy."

"I'll be here. Just don't take all day."

Lita said, "And don't you dare pile all that stuff into the closet. Put everything right where it belongs." Pearl ran up the stairs.

Lita started to clear off the table. I said, "I'll do that."

She said, "How's your back?"

"It's fine."

"You're a darling. Just dump the dishes in the sink and set the leftovers on the drainboard. I'll put them up later."

While I was clearing off the table, Lita did a quick job of picking up in the living room. Not perfect, but quick. She said, "What I'd like to do is sprinkle a little kerosene and put a match to it."

When I got through, I poured myself another glass of Chablis and sat back down on the sofa. Sometimes I have to sit. Lita picked up one of Pearl's socks and pitched it up the stairs. She emptied the dregs from several coffee cups into a single cup and poured that into one of her potted plants, a suffering hydrangea. She stuffed the paper plate with dried spaghetti sauce into the fireplace along with some other trash. She said, "Rudy, I'm sorry I neglected you like I did the other night."

"What do you mean?"

"At the party." Lita dumped a heap of contorted cigarette butts from a saucer into the fireplace. She wiped the saucer with one of Pearl's socks and put it back on the end table. She pitched the sock up the stairs. She said, "I was in an awful funk. I hardly knew what I was doing. I should have spent more time with you."

"I didn't notice."

Lita sat on a chair near the sofa. She lit a cigarette and looked at me through the thread of blue smoke. It looked like I was about to get an utterance from the Delphic oracle. I drank some Chablis.

She said, "You think I take you for granted. You think all I want you around for is for you to come up and fix my broken toaster and leaky faucets or change the tires on the car"—I've done all of that—"or help me move in my furniture." She took one more puff on the cigarette and snubbed it out in the saucer on the end table. "You don't *mind* coming to see me, do you?"

"Don't make me laugh."

She bent forward and touched my wrist. The spot burned. She said, "Rudy, what's happening to us? We hardly see each other anymore. We haven't been house-hunting in weeks. I'm going to forget what the old Muskapec County Bank building looks like."

"I've been awful busy. We put in a whole new line at the store."

"It's like you've been avoiding me the last few weeks."

I laughed. That's how much it hurts. It hurts like a knife in my chest. Who wants to come back, to have the knife twisted? Shit, *I* do. But I've been fighting it hard. Like I say, I'm one of your contemporary saints, made pure by suffering, wandering in my white, invisible robes amongst the stones and scorpions, eating bugs and possum plums. I *try* not to feel anything. I read a lot and take long walks and cold showers and fetch work home from the "office"—everything virtuous. The only salvation I've been able to find is the manna of T. V. or the dew of a good drunk. And now here I am, back in the lion's den.

I am not in love. Believe you me, I ain't about to go through the "Penn State Caper" again. I ate at that trough once. Never

again. I know what I am. "Love," the lousy psychosis. What's
the word "love" *mean*, anyways? You lift up a rock. You've got
hold of its flatness or roundness and it is goddamned solid and
you can feel the heft of it in your back and guts. What's "rock"
got to do with it? Or hit your fist against a live oak tree: what's
"oak" or "tree" got to do with what-all's green and puts out
snaky branches, or the washboard roughness you're knocking
your knuckles against? I can think up a plenty better words for
"love"—like "terror" or "shame" or "Hell." I wouldn't touch that
word "love" with a ten-foot pole. And if I'm in the lion's den, I
ain't scared to be here.

I was in "love" once, and let me tell you it was nothing like
what you see in the movies. I metamorphosed into a goddamned
fool. That was back at Penn State, in my sophomore year, and
it like to ruined me. I like to flunked out. Her name was Alex-
andra Huffstickler, and she was pretty and gentle and sweet.
Excepting not to me. Not later, anyway. She was from Ephrata,
Pa., where Amish farmers in black coats and hats drive around
in black buggies. Sandra wasn't Amish, not anywhere near it:
her daddy owned a drugstore there. She had long blond hair,
dark at the roots but otherwise honey-colored, and brown eyes.
The first time I saw her, she was sitting on one of the cement
steps in front of the Forum Building, where the College of
Business Administration holds some of its overflow classes, with
a book on her lap. It was the start of the summer trimester. She
was reading the book and pulling abstractly with her fingers at
a long strand of honey-blond hair, sometimes looking at it, sep-
arating the strands and then reading again. It turned out we
had a class together.

The class was Marketing 122, under Dr. Pettigill, a professor
who took snuff in his office between classes. He bought it,
Garrett's Snuff, in little tins, and before class tucked a pinch
behind his lower lip, just like old Mrs. Tate back in Alto Springs.
During his lecture he'd turn aside ever so often and make a
small, soft noise into a handkerchief. Sandy sat three desks in

front of me. She spent a lot of time running her fingers through her hair.

After about the fifth class, Sandy came up to me in the hall. She said, "I can't hack it." I'd been doing pretty well my own-self, and I said I'd help her. I went over the assignment with her and worked out the statistics. After that we studied a lot to-gether. I even wrote a biology paper and an English paper for her. Several times we went to the movies together. It got to where I was thinking of her all the time. It got to where I was looking to be with her every minute I could. I thought she liked me. It turned out she was laughing at me the whole way.

Then once when I asked her to go to the picture show with me she said something real mean. She said the one thing I can't stand to hear. And she laughed. It like to killed me. The crazy thing was, I still couldn't keep away from her. I craved to be with her more than ever, even when I knew she didn't like me. She'd stung me, but still I tried to be wherever-all she was: to look at her, to watch her run her fingers through her hair or jerk her head back flinging the yellow strands from her face, to see her bent over a desk taking a test, her breasts nested in her blouse like ripe fruit, or watch her go down a stairwell, one foot dropping to the next step, the click of her clogs, her hip bones perfectly articulated and not just perfectly articulated, but with *her* perfect articulation. I made to meet her in the halls. I signed up to be in the same classes she had and tried to sit next her. I even changed my minor so as to get to be near her. Mornings, in rain or sun or snow, I stood in the parking lot across from her dormitory, hoping to see her come out. It didn't matter what-all she said to me, it didn't cut ice how mad at me she was, just so she said *something*. It got to be as changeable as the weather in Texas: one minute she'd turn her face to me and I'd be standing in the sun, next minute her words were hitting me like hail-stones. I knew she hated me. She would of liked to of had the hide off my back, tanned and cut to fit her for a pair of dancing pumps.

I followed her around like a dog that comes back for another swift kick, its belly scraping the ground. And if I couldn't be near her, if she'd ditched me some way or another and I couldn't smoke her out, I'd wellnigh have a mad fit. Like I say, I turned into a simple-minded idiot. Nights alone in my hellish bed I'd touch her hair, I'd kiss her shut eyelids and her blond eyebrows and her lips with the hardness of the teeth behind. I kissed her forehead, half-mad to know the thoughts behind the bone. I kissed the puckered points of her breasts. I ran my hand over the rollercoaster of her hip, down the slope of her back, across the smooth belly and crisp, kinky hairs as she lifted her pubic bone against the ache. I climbed through a rage of grief and tenderness to my own Golgotha, the forsaken emptiness, the cry to un-answering air.

It was a starve-out proposition. I ain't about to study it again. I *like* Lita, and that's that.

Lita got up and commenced walking back and forth. She said, "Oh Jesus, Rudy, don't desert me. I need you for a friend."

"I'm here, ain't I?" I took another swallow of the Chablis. It takes a lot to get drunk on that stuff.

"Put down that drink. I'm serious." Lita lit another cigarette. I'd had a good health-food dinner and now she was going to poison me with smoke.

I said, "Lita, you know damned well I didn't come here for the food. I'd eat scalloped cow plop if that's what you'd fixed."

"Well, why have you been avoiding me? You never drop by anymore. I just about had to drag you to that party."

"I told you. I'm busy at the store. I even have to fetch work home nights."

"Shit."

"Anyways, lately I've been so damned homesick I ain't felt like seeing nobody."

Lita snorted. "*Homesick?* I thought you were glad to wipe Texas off your boots."

"I go back sometimes."

Lita snubbed the barely smoked cigarette into the saucer and said, "If you like Texas so much why don't you stay there? Crap."

"I've got my reasons."

"Yes, and then I'd be the only damned fool left in West Hesper who knows what a kumquat looks like." Of a sudden she said, "I wish you *would* go back." She commenced to cry. "*I don't like anyone. I'm just about alone here myself anyhow.*" She plopped down onto a chair and bent forward, her face cupped in her hands, her shoulders heaving. "I wish I was dead!"

"Jesus, Lita." I jumped up and went over to her. I knelt beside her and touched one of her hands. I said, "Oh, sweetheart, don't cry like that."

After a spell she quit. She snuffed and snucked. She looked up. Her face was wet, and prettier than ever. She said, "No, I mean it. You can put Pearl in an orphanage or turn her over to the Jehovah's Witnesses."

I laughed.

"It's not funny."

"I know it's not."

"That sonofabitch Joe. I hate his guts. No, I don't." She let out a wail, stuck her face in her hands again and commenced rocking back and forth. I didn't know what the hell to do with my own hands. I put one on her shoulder and said, "Shhh. Shhh." It was pure afternoon soap opera.

I said, "Pearl'll hear you."

Lita looked up again. Her eyes were getting red around the edges. "Oh, Rudy, you don't know what it's like to be in love. It's awful. I'm going out of my mind."

"What's so terrible?"

"Joe hasn't been here since the night of the party."

"He'll be back."

"If he does, I'll kill him."

"I thought he was out on a gig."

"Gig? Crap." Lita plucked one of the Goodwill doilies off the arm of the sofa and blew her nose into it. "I know where he is.

He's got my car, and he's in some off-season chalet up in Vermont or New Hampshire with that little shithead Denise Prevear."

"Well, Christ." Denise Prevear's a brittle, small-breasted, dark-eyed girl who works off and on in one of the clothes shops in town, The Alternative Twist. She's a friend of Lita's. Or was. She's a hard-rock freak who used to spend a lot of time in Lita's apartment, passing joints and listening to Lita and Joe's tape collection. She wears lots of jewelry, beads in her hair and a turquoise in her left nostril, and talks all the time about being "laid-back." But under the calm surface of a Percodan trip you felt her lurking like an alligator. I could see her whipping her tail back and forth in that off-season chalet right now. Sometimes I used to notice her in The Alternative Twist when I went past, looking out from amongst the hippie clothes and recycled Levi's on hangers and racks with the innocent face and dark, smoldering eyes of a wild animal.

"He's been sleeping with her the past two months. The way I found out, he was doing a gig in upstate Vermont and spent the night at the Fox Hollow Motel, and they mailed some of her underthings back here. Christ, you'd think we were married."

"I figured something was wrong."

"That shithead Denise. Coming over here and smiling at me and helping me cook. So when I shook those little things in front of his face he said he was in love with her and loved me too and wanted her to move in with us. No goddamned way! He wanted to have her to the party the other night and I said, 'Piss off. If that little fart comes in this apartment again I'll take her ass and pin it up behind her ears. What's more,' I said, 'it's either her or me.' He didn't talk to me the whole evening. Then, when the party was over, we had a terrible fight. That's how come the toilet bowl got cracked."

"The what?"

"I'm not going to go into it. The thing is, he took my car and his sleeping bag and his trumpet and took off. I've been out of my mind the last three days."

"Maybe he's not with Denise."

"*Huh.* Try calling her place. Her roommate says she's visiting her mother."

I gave Lita my handkerchief and she dried her face with it. She said, "I must look like a mess."

"It'd help if your nose was shorter."

"My nose is perfectly all right. It doesn't stick out like a ski slope, like yours does. Why do you keep teasing me? I *hurt.*"

I took hold of Lita's hands and looked into her eyes—her eyes that were filled with hurt intelligence. I said, "What's the use of me telling you how pretty you are? It gives you the big head. You *are* pretty."

"It's worse than when Mercer and I were splitting up." Mercer's her former old man. He's back in California selling real estate now so as to pay Lita's alimony. "At least I never *liked* that asshole."

"But you loved him?"

"Oh, I loved him. I just never liked him. But I *like* Joe."

"And you love him?"

"Shit, Rudy. I wouldn't live with a man if I didn't. But it helps if I like him."

I laughed. She laughed too. Then tears rushed to her eyes again. She put my handkerchief to her face. "Christ, nobody believes in anybody anymore. It's dog eat dog. Fall in love and you know you're gonna get kicked in the ass. Everybody finally splits. God. I hope I never see that sonofabitch again. I can't take it. It makes me want to crawl in a hole. And *nobody* likes me. All Joe's friends—everytime I open my mouth they say I'm uptight. And they're probably right. My goddamned *parents.* I'm just going to turn out to be a shriveled old bitch." Her shoulders shook.

I waited until she quieted. Then I said, "Are you all right?" She snucked and nodded. I said, "*Look* at me." She looked up. I said, "Lita, there's *scads* of men that'd swim the Atlantic *Ocean* for you."

She perked right up. "There are?"

"Yes, and pitch the rest of their natural lives into the bargain." But I was feeling sick. I stood up. Pearl was at the top of the stairs, watching. I said, "We've got a visitor."

Pearl said, "why you cwyin', Mommy?"

Lita blew her nose in my handkerchief, then dabbed at her eyes with it. Without turning to Pearl she said, "Did you finish your room?"

"It's all done."

"Then I'm coming up to look at it." Lita stood.

"No, don't!" Pearl darted back up the stairs. Lita blew her nose in my handkerchief again. She looked at it. "Well, I've certainly made a wet sponge out of *this* thing. I'm such an idiot."

"Anybody who falls in love is bound to eat some backwater."

"You're about as romantic as a bucket of mud."

"It's just I've got real clear vision."

Lita laughed. She said, "Rudy, you're sweet and you're good and I couldn't have got through another day without you." Of a sudden she took my head in both her hands and gave me a kiss on the forehead.

I said, "He'll be back. Denise Prevear can't hold a candle to you."

Lita said, "Christ, I love you. Just keep on telling me those things." She walked over to a window. She said, "I feel a hundred percent better. And I'm *not* going to put up with it. People can be as faithful in this kind of relationship as in a marriage, dammit."

Pearl, at the top of the stairs, said, "Mommy, you can come up now."

Lita said, "Come on down, sweetheart. I'll look at it later. Would you like some cocoa?"

"Cawob or choc'lit?"

"Jesus Christ. *Carob.*"

"Oh, aw wight." Pearl came down the stairs. Lita said, "Someday I'm going to let you have all the chocolate you want until you get good and sick. Then you'll never look at chocolate again." She went out into the kitchen.

Pearl said, "Tell me the 'Good Gal.'" She sat on my lap.

I told her about how the good gal went down to the magic spring, and the wild horses let her pass and the two mean bulls let her pass and the gate let her through and when she got to the spring she was taking a bath and up came a little thing and said, "Wash me and comb me and lay me down softly." She washed it and combed it and laid it down softly. Up came another little thing and said, "Wash me and comb me and lay me down softly." And she washed it and combed it and laid it down softly and it said, "Pretty you are and ten times prettier you'll be and every time you comb you'll comb out gold and silver." And the first little thing said, "Every time you spit you'll spit diamonds," and she went home combing out gold and silver and spitting diamonds and got prettier all the time. But the bad gal, when she saw all that, went to the spring, and she said to the horses, "Get out of my way." They kicked her something terrible. She said in a rough voice to the bulls, "Let me past," and they nearly killed her. At the gate she kicked it open and when she was going through it slammed to and like to tore off her heel. At the spring she plopped into the water and up came a little thing and said, "Wash me and comb me and lay me down softly" and whack! she slapped off its head. Up came another little thing and she killed that one too. Then a voice said, "Ugly you are and ten times uglier you'll be. Every time you comb you'll comb out nits and lice. Every time you spit you'll spit a toad." And she went home, combing bugs out of her hair and spitting toads and getting uglier by the minute.

After the story, Pearl looked mighty sober. She drank her cocoa without saying a word. Lita gave me another cup of goat-browse tea, without sugar, and after I'd drunk as much of it as I could I said, "It's past four. I got to git."

Lita and Pearl went with me to the door. I gave Pearl a good-bye kiss. Lita said, "You're awfully good to Pearl."

"I like her."

Lita said, "We're still friends, aren't we?"

"Sure. Why not?"

"Let's go out driving when I get my car back."

"O. K."

Lita took my hand. She said, "Rudy, you know what I think? I think you're one of the kindest, sweetest persons I've ever known." I felt her handbones in my hand. I could even feel the blood pulsing. Christ, life's so *physical*.

Joe's jogging shoes were by the door. I said, "If you want Joe back, all you've got to do is get the foot of a rabbit killed by a cross-eyed black at midnight in the full moon in a graveyard by the grave of a young girl that—"

Lita laughed. She squeezed my hand. We looked at each other and she said, "Thanks, Rudy." She gave me a kiss and I left.

When I got back to the store, Herbie was already mopping the floors. I let him go home early. I wrote up the day's receipts and locked up.

I walked down Main Street. It was summery and warm. There wasn't a cloud in the sky and the sun, on daylight saving now, still hadn't touched down onto the hemlocks and closed-down ski slopes on the mountains to the west. Folks were hurrying home from work, the men in shirtsleeves, the women in summer dresses. The high school kids hanging around the pizza shop were mostly wearing T-shirts. The girls didn't have on bras. I kept my mind on my own business, which is to be goddamned alone. I might as well be exiled to Siberia.

> *All the lonely people,*
> *Where do they all come from?*

Maybe I'll pick at my guitar tonight. I don't do it good. Even on the chords I get like cataleptic fingers. But it soothes the Hank Williams in me.

5:15 by the Muskapec Savings Bank. 71 degrees. *Doctor Zhivago*, a long thing about three-horse sleighs, ice and a stalled train (I don't mean that's what the book's about), was billed for a rerun at the movie house. Over near the curb, perched on a candy wrapper, a monarch butterfly rocked back and forth, its orange-and-black wings, veined like a church window, slowly opening and closing, opening and closing like breathing. In the fall those things migrate clear to Mexico.

5

 Lon Chaney swings from saint to gargoyle, his hump strapped to his back. He thumbs his nose at the Xtian mob below, stalks crabwise across cathedral floors, scuttles with Esmeralda on his shoulder up stone passageways to the bell tower. She is saved—Esmeralda of the Cupid's-bow lips, new, clean gypsy rags, washed and combed filthy beggar tresses, probably all bone now in some Hollywood cemetery, stained ribbon, a hank of brown hair. She touches him tenderly, the movement of her fingers frame by frame. Lon climbs a bell rope and the great bells boom silently above. He scrambles amongst the timbers. He rides a giant bell in ecstasy.

I do *not* have a ski nose. Maybe it's long and slanted to one side, but it's good-looking and puts a roof over my new mustache. My left cheek's a smidgen sunken. When I was born, that side of my face was smaller than the other, so they say. It went away by the time I was three. Even I can't hardly make it out.

Heavy chin. Brown, soulful eyes: my gaze sinks deep into them until the mirror fogs. A big knowledge bump on my forehead. Heavy eyebrows. Straight, dark hair with a reddish show to it, trimmed singles-bar style. Full lips under a soft mustache.

I ain't about to open my *mouth*.

I was born way late. It was a pure surprise to my folks, since my mama'd already gone through her changes. The moon didn't call to her anymore, she'd thought. And there I was, hairy, wrinkled thing annunciating on the breast of a forty-nine-year-old madonna. I had black hair on my *face* even, for a spell. It went away. When I finally looked to be normal my folks were crazy with joy. They'd had girls three times running. They'd settled they weren't going to get another boy. They named me Rudy Earl, after my dead brother Earl Leroy. That's my daddy's name too—Earl Leroy.

I had a dimple in the small of my back. It's still there.

I remember the light and the shade, dark leaves, the frenzy in the pyracanth bushes, the scream. I was five. After a snack of cornbread and cold milk, I'd run back out to play. My sisters were all at school: I could hear the sound of recess four blocks over. Mama was in the kitchen starting dinner. It was a hot spring day. The sun was so bright it hurt even to look at the dust, but it was shady under the pyracanth bushes foamy with flowers. That's where I always played when I was by myself. Under the bushes were roads patted out of dirt, winding amongst roots, and pebble gates and stick cattleguards and houses of chalky limestone that water sometime somewhere had made doors and windows through. The tiny red cast-iron play-toy car was there that used to belong to my daddy when *he* was little.

The family got into the car. There was the daddy, a prominent rancher, the mama, known all over the world as a great country-music singer, greater than Kitty Wells even, and the three brothers. The three brothers had had famous adventures in Africa and South America and Junction City and the North Pole. They'd driven the red car up mountains and across deserts. They'd captured doodle bugs and fought in many wars. The bravest brother was exactly my age. He was younger than the other two and had saved their lives over and over. The governor of Texas had heard about it and become the brothers' best friend. In fact, they'd gotten the governor out of several fixes his own-self. Now the whole family was making to drive to the state capitol, which I'd seen pictures of in the *San Antonio Light*, to

see the governor and have pimento cheese sandwiches and ice
tea with him. Probably there was Indians along the way.

The car roared along, its engine humming in my nose. Then
I heard myself scream. I heard it almost before I felt the pain. I
fell down on my face in the dirt. It was like I'd been hit in the
back by a sledgehammer. The pain shot through my ribs and
out along my arms to my fingertips. It went down my legs to the
soles of my feet. I thought my back was broke. It was like some
paralyzing light had struck down through me and turned to
flint rock in my bones. I couldn't hardly move my ribs to breathe.
But my mama had heard the scream and was out there to me.
"*Rudy*, what on *earth*?" I couldn't talk. "*Oh, God!* What *is* it?"
she said. She got me turned over. All I could do was stare, and
I remember everything was light and bright edges like I was
looking up into some fierce stone of solid air. Mrs. Stephenbalm
ran over from next door and they got me into the house. In
twenty minutes Doctor Stovall was looking me over. He couldn't
figure it out. I tried to whisper, "*HURTS!*" He prescribed aspirin. I hurt for nine days and all I got was aspirin. I wanted to
die. Then the pain went away.

That was the start. Slowly I grew into another world I hadn't
asked for, or even dreamed of before. There wasn't any more
pain, but in eight months it was over. In eight months my spine
had slithered like a snake in two directions. Congenital something or other. My folks watched it happen with horror, like
they thought it was some kind of fate. Maybe if they'd had a
doctor who knew what he was doing things would have been
different. But by the time they took me to Krugerville a year
later, and then to San Antonio, it was too late. The boy in the
bed next to mine in the hospital in San Antonio went into the
operating room and came back with a severed spine—never walk
again. My pa fetched me straight home . . .

I give the cheery guy in the mirror a wink, slip off my bath-
robe, fit the pink plastic bath cap onto my head and step into the
shower.

It feels queer without my elevated shoe.

I adjust the hot and cold. The water stings my face, massages my forehead, peppers my chest and back and butt and streams down my legs. I work up a lather on my chest, wash my face and neck and shoulders. Then I imagine myself again, frame it all over, run my hands over the slick, soaped skin, the strong, broad shoulders, one lower than the other, the short, thick trunk with no waist, the slight indentation on my left side, the not too noticeable roll of bunched muscle on my back. What the light did to me under the pyracanth bushes was make me six inches shorter than I ought by rights to be.

Gladly the cross I'd bear.

Gladly, the cross-eyed cow.

That thing on Lon Chaney's back is nothing but a fake. I saw that movie in a class at Penn State. There wasn't one bone right. There wasn't a lick of it, watching him, I could feel in my own-self. I don't like Hollywood movies anyway, even old ones.

I eat when I'm hungry, I drink when I'm dry.
If a tree don't fall on me I'll live till I die.

They kept me back from starting grade school until I was seven. Marybeth Crozier went on to school. She didn't come play with me anymore. I didn't play under the pyracanth bushes anymore, either. I killed that whole family off in my head, in a clearing in Africa surrounded by Ubangis with bones through their noses and parrot feathers in their hair. *I* was one of those Ubangis and I put a spear through the mama and papa my own-self. I danced with the others around the bodies of two of the brothers. The youngest brother got away, to live on bugs and poison plants in the lion-infested jungle.

When I did start school, a year late, everybody stared at me even though they knew all about me already. The first day in the first grade was hell. The *room* was Hell, with its green walls and big windows and blackboards and pinned-up alphabet, and Miss Hendricks up front. Even she stared at me, when she thought I wouldn't know it. Maybe I didn't cry like some of the others. But I died a few times.

I hated grade school. If we played "Drop the Handkerchief" at recess, nobody ever dropped the handkerchief to me. But when we played *Frog in the Middle* I was usually the frog. Somebody'd come and turn me three times around and push me down into a squat. Then the circle would sing

> *"Frog in the middle*
> *can't get out.*
> *Take a stick 'n'*
> *stir him about,"*

but they didn't just run in and touch me. They *slapped*. Even the girls.

Once at recess, under a live oak by the swings, a girl kissed me. She did it on a dare. Her friends popped up from behind the schoolhouse steps, laughing and screaming, and she ran from me quick as a jackrabbit.

There is *no* King's X.

I skipped as many grades as I could—second and fifth.

I'm going to tell you something. You know how come I won that scholarship that got me up to Penn State? Maybe I had the highest grade-point average of anybody in the senior class, but that ain't why. When I gave the valedictorian address folks looked at me like they were seeing a ghost. They stared like I was something that had stepped up out of the ground. The town set up that scholarship for *me*. It was a good year for mohair, and the ranchers had plenty of money. The main thing was, whoever won it had to go to an out-of-state school.

You want to know why?

Go to the grave in the corner of the cemetery, the one with no stone to it that's all weeds and brush but you can still make it out, over by the bobbed-wire fence.

Like a song you can't get out of your head, not only for its tune but on account of what it says cuts right to the bone, the shock waves of an old violence in a Texas town don't go away until the story's been told over and over. And maybe not even then.

6

Sometimes in spring beads of fog hang from the bobbed-wire fence. Winters the wires, strung from cedar post to cedar post, can be the cores of ice ropes. Or a blue norther lifts: the rusty wires hum, a broken strand clicks against a lower strand. The grave, raked out flat, still shows. On days so hot birds don't fly—they can hardly *breathe*—ants thread across the grave or go in and out of their holes. Scrub cedars drop blue berries and dead needles to the shade below. Laurel leaves flash in a wind, the pods rattle, later they split and spill red beads onto the grave. Or the air is still. Or a dust devil hisses across, tearing off leaves. Sand slides down an ant lion's funnel. It's quiet under the ground, though. On top the grave, if it's late February or March, an agarita bush puts out its yellow show, on blood-red stems. In June, quail eat the berries. Sometimes you can hear the quail from the highway, CHUCK-*too*, CHUCK-*too*, CHUCK-*too*.

In the center of the cemetery the graves are all crowded together—the ones dug for the twister of '81. I remember the graves of three girls, fifteen or sixteen years old or thereabouts, from different families but their graves right next to one another, each with the same kind of plain slab with a hand carved on it, a finger pointing up, and all the same date: April 12, 1881. Killed when the twister took away the roof of the schoolhouse.

They probably onetime ran to show each other a new dress and wrote in each other's school autograph albums and traded valentines.

Over and over, the sun and the moon.

A black-painted, cast-iron fence of arrowhead pickets sets off the Castleberry plot. Once a year, in the spring on my brother's birthday, my mama and my daddy and my three sisters weed the plot. They rake off the trash and pick the shreds of blown crepe-paper flowers from the pickets. They pick wildflowers—phlox and verbena and black-eyed Susans and Indian blankets—and put them in a jar against my brother's stone. The other four monuments don't need that support.

The four pillars—freckled with mold and leathery liver spots of lichen and each alike excepting for their inscriptions and the stone carvings just under the eaves of the pyramidal capitals—point up at the naked sky. On my great-grandmother's column the carving is of a marble fist holding lilies; on my great-grandfather's, two hands clasp; on that of his second wife, my "Aunt Grammie," who died when she was eighty-nine, a dove flies with a rose in its beak. An angel with a scroll is on my grandmother's column. The marble shafts are cemented with lead to their broad granite bases. They rise out of the ground as if from roots of bone.

Sometimes, mornings mostly, the sky above the marble shafts is red, flecked with clabber. Other times it's heavy as lead. Or blue, heaped up with bundles of white clouds. But mainly it's pale bright. Nights it's black or there's a moon up or millions of stars. The four tombstones look like they could wellnigh scrape the stars, they're so close—the stars in Betelgeuse or Arcturus or Vega or the Seven Sisters, the big and little stars in Andromeda or Scorpio, depending on the time of year.

That grave by the bobbed-wire fence is my grandfather's. I know it.

7

 I was born in November, a Scorpio, which—according to the beat-up paperback *Write Your Own Horoscope*, one of those how-to books like *Raise Your Own Heliotrope* or *Build Your Own Fluoroscope*, and about as useful, that I found bleaching in the sunlight on the dashboard of Lita's Volkswagen and got to poking through while I was waiting for her and Pearl to come down from the apartment to go for a drive one day—is the sign of "change, growth and decay, creation and destruction." Right now I'm in my decay phase. I see a lot of Lita. She got her car back, and she piled Joe's stuff out in the hall. I got rid of the *Rhoeo spathacea*. Sometimes Lita and I drive around looking at houses. Sometimes I take Pearl for a walk. Since Lita and Joe split, all Lita's friends have been extra-special protective of her. She had more friends than she thought. It's been one damned party after another. But I feel like warmed-over Hell. I wake up of a morning and I can't seem to get going at all. At Business Way Office Equipment and Supply, right in the middle of whatever-all I'm up to, I forget what I'm doing. Or I'll come home from work and I'll sit all evening staring at the wall. I can feel my blood knocking in my wrist, against the arm of the chair, and I don't even care. I don't even fix myself supper. Terrible things go through my mind: I forget 'em as soon as they crop up. I'm like to be pulled seven ways for Xmas. One minute I'm about to put a fist through the bathroom wall, next minute I'm prissing around delicate as a see-through tea cup. The world is perfect butter, wrapped in a dog's skin.

The one time I perked up was when Lita and Pearl and I went out on a Friday in the middle of June to a big blowout and picnic at Avery Linscott and Julie Alcombright's place, an old, tilting barn, half-rebuilt farmhouse and outdoor privy in a clearing on a mountain top about fifteen miles outside of town. We went in Lita's car. Hollis Waltermire was with us. Hollis is studying mime in Boston. He wants to go to Paris next year to study under Marcel Marceau. He's about a year older than me. He's got long arms and long hand bones, a caved-in chest, and he wears a hearing aid. His hair is long and mouse-colored: he ties it back with a rubber band. Blond eyebrows. Swedish-blue eyes. He's always joking and teasing. What I can't figure out is how come his skin is so *creamy* looking and damp. It makes me think of those white salamanders they say are in the caves of underground rivers in Texas. But Hollis is smart. He ran his dad's electronics business, in one of the old mills in West Hesper, for two years. Then he decided he wanted to be a mime. His dad had a fit.

Hollis had to do a mime show that evening—part of a benefit performance in the American Legion Hall in West Hesper, sponsored by the local Arts Council—so he came out to the picnic for an hour or so, borrowing Lita's Volkswagen to drive back to town to do his act and then on back out to pick us up. He'd come from Boston by bus. On Saturday afternoon he had to be in Worchester to do another show, and then on back to Boston.

Hollis drove the car. I'm going on twenty-three years old and I *still* don't know how to drive. About twelve miles out of town we left the highway and started up a dirt road. It's called Klondike Road, on account of it's so steep and gets so cotton-picking cold up there in winter it'd freeze the balls off a brass monkey. There were enough stones on the road we'd of done better to of drove up the creek bed. That little Volkswagen was hopping all over the place. Pretty woods, though.

Lita said, "Sit down, Pearl."

We turned right at the mailbox at the top of the hill, drove through some woods and then out into an open space with a hayfield on one side and a blueberry field and a pond on the other. Two little boys were running across the blueberry field, and one of them fell. Pearl said, "Look!" There were some white ducks on the pond. Frank Kimberly and a girl I didn't know were standing by the pond, tossing chunks of bread to the ducks. They waved. Over at the edge of the field, under some trees, Avery Linscott and Dom Trisorio and a bunch of others were tending a fire. Blue smoke curled up. Here and there in the blueberry field were broken-down cars, like pop art. Also two tractors, some stoves and a bathtub, and a red, one-ton truck up on blocks under a sugar maple near the road, its hood up and the engine out. The engine hung in chains from a big branch of the maple.

The house and barn were in the middle of the clearing, and we drove into the yard, where there were already four or five parked cars, one of them with New York plates. Chickens scattered. A pony trotted off the porch and out under the apple trees to the east of the house. Pearl went crazy, seeing that pony. "No, you *can't* ride it," Lita said. "He's one mean son of a bitch." Six puppies ran up to us when we got out of the car. One of them licked Pearl's face.

Somewhere off in the woods a chainsaw snarled.

Julie Alcombright, Avery's woman, came out of the house carrying a bowl of green salad, fresh out of their own garden. She looked hot and sweaty. She was wearing sandals and jeans and an army fatigue undershirt that came clear down to her knees. Her breasts under the undershirt were as flat as a couple of pie plates. She smiled and said, "So you finally got here! Can you take this salad with you? Everybody's over on the other side of the pond." There ain't enough flesh on Julie to pad a crutch. Everytime I see her she looks skinnier. She's a Zen

macrobiotic. It's a kind of religion. At first, whenever macro-
biotics eat, they leave off red meat. Then after a spell they leave
off milk and cheese and fish. Then eggs. Then bread. Then
fruit. Then vegetables, until they're down to beans and brown
rice. Then they live off the beans. When they die, they're laid
out in their coffins on beds of cooked rice. I just wish Julie
would quit before she disappears into thin air.

Somehow or other I was the one who had to carry the bowl of
salad. Pearl and I started out across the blueberry field. Lita and
Hollis were still back at the house, chatting together. I turned to
look at her. So much cool, late-afternoon sunlight was coming
down I felt light-headed. Pearl grabbed hold of my pantsleg and
I helped her over a log. The ankle-high blueberry bushes all
around were filled with tiny white flowers. Over at the edge of
the field, under some trees, Avery and the others waved to us.
Everyone had a can of beer in his or her hand. When we got
there somebody popped open a can for me. "Hi, Tex," Avery
said. I said, "Who's using the chainsaw?" Avery said, "Dave
Howcroft. He and his girlfriend just broke up. He'll probably
spend the whole damned evening in the woods."

Avery introduced us to his friends, some of whom I didn't
know: a couple from New York City, both of them artists, who
were staying with Avery and Julie for a few weeks, and another
couple—the Allyns—who lived about two miles off, down on
the side of the mountain. Elaine Allyn's a potter. She makes
bowls and vases and fetches them around to craft shows to sell.
Elaine had an eight-week-old baby girl, cute as a thimble. It
poked its face out like a little monkey from under her shawl.
Frank was there, and a girl named Iris Petropulos or Petrapolis
or somesuch and the two Linscott/Alcombright boys, Justin and
Jason, and another little girl, named Mandy, that belonged to the
Allyns.

There was a roast beef turning above the fire and fresh-baked
bread and potato salad and a tub with iced-down beers in it as
well as bottles of grape juice and apple juice for the kids. I said,
"Man, that looks good."

Hollis and Lita came up. I put the green salad with the other stuff. Pearl said, "I wanna see the ducks."

Lita and Pearl and I and the two Linscott/Alcombright boys went over to the pond. Justin, the oldest boy, hunkered down at the edge of the pond and said, "C'mon, Squiffy. C'mon, Squiffy." He held out his hand and the biggest duck, one with a lot of red, warty-looking knobs around its bill and eyes, paddled over to him. It wouldn't let Justin touch it though, and when it saw it wasn't going to get anything to eat it paddled on back to its buddies. Pearl watched the whole thing with her eyes wide and her thumb stuck in her mouth. I think she fell in love with Justin right then.

Up at the house a dog barked. A breeze stirred the surface of the pond and rustled the leaves of the blueberry bushes around about. Swallows were circling and twittering overhead and one dropped down and flew right across in front of us, its breast almost touching the water. Lita said, "Oh, Rudy, life's so goddamned beautiful it's a crime."

It was getting up onto the shank end of evening, headed into one of those long New England twilights—not like the almost sudden way night falls back home. There was a thread of new moon down low over to the west, what in Texas we call a dry moon. Lita and Pearl and I and the two boys walked on back to the crowd around the fire. Trickles of fat dripped from the roast of beef, popped and sizzled on the coals. "I'm hungry as a hound with nine pups," I said. Everybody laughed. Trish Meyerson and Janice Rondeau (I'd found out her name was) came across the field from the house lugging a freezer of ice cream to be turned. Julie was with them. Somebody was pouring grape juice for the kids: for a minute I was back on the Plateau, wading through a stand of mountain laurel under a hot sun, the air heavy with the sick-sweet grape-Popsicle smell of the beanlike purple flowers. Avery said, "Let's EAT!" Julie and Elaine started serving the kids. Dave Howcroft came out of the woods, carrying the chainsaw and some chunks of wood. He dumped the wood by the fire.

Lita and Hollis and I sat together, under a sugar maple. Pearl was with the other kids. I thought for a minute I heard a mourning dove in the woods: they say that in the past few years they've been turning up more and more this far north. Of a sudden I had this feeling come on me, I don't know how to say it: it was like something with so much time and weight behind it, and at the same time so gentle, was about to light onto me. I just knew it was. It was about to put a hand or something onto me and whatever-all ever happened to me after that couldn't hurt me at all. I saw right off it'd been about to touch me like that all afternoon. Nothing *did* touch me. It's just how I felt. I didn't tell it to anyone. But it made me so damned happy I could of cried.

The food was good. Hollis put his away fast. Then he said, "I have to go. I've got to get my props set up." Lita said, "Here's the car keys."

The lightning bugs were starting to come out. Lita and I took a walk in the woods. It was getting on towards dark, so we didn't go far. We sat on a boulder with a cushion of moss on it two inches thick. Some of the birches around about were bowed clear to the ground, from ice or old snows. I said, "I bet in winter it gets cold as a well-digger's elbow up here."

"They were snowed in for three weeks last year."

"Don't the town plow the road?"

"No. Avery and Julie have to use a snowmobile."

"Think I'd just head on back to the city."

Lita laughed. "Listen, even in the *summer* sometimes I wish I was back on the West Coast." Then she told me about California, about how she and her mama and her sister used to go every day to the pool at the club and lay for hours baking in the sun. Evenings, when they got back home, they sat on the patio, their sunburnt noses iced with Noxema, and ate cantaloupe halves filled with vanilla ice cream and counted the stars. The air would be heavy with the smell of orange and lime blossoms and, from underneath the trees, dropped, rotting fruit.

They were calling us, back at the fire. When we got to the clearing, Pearl came running. "Ice kweem!" she shouted. Lita picked her up and carried her. Over by the fire Dom was spraying beer from a just-opened can all over the place. Everybody was laughing and yelling. Frank Kimberly's transistor radio was going full blast.

Lita and Pearl and I sat with the others and ate homemade, hand-cranked ice cream. It was damned good ice cream.

I heard, or maybe felt, a bat. I looked up. The moon was gone. There were zillions of stars. A shooting star scratched across.

The rest of the evening we drank beer and sang and goofed around. Elaine Allyn breast-fed her baby next the fire. It was so beautiful it made me sad. Over under a birch tree, in the dark, Dom was trying to make out with Trish Meyerson. Pearl fell asleep on my lap.

At about eleven-thirty Hollis got back with the Volkswagen and I carried Pearl to the car. "You want to drive?" Hollis said. Lita said, "No, I'm bushed." I sat in back with Pearl. She was still asleep, making sucking noises. She had a thumb in her mouth and her index finger in her ear. I kissed her on top of her head.

When we got back to West Hesper, Hollis dropped me off at my place, then took Lita and Pearl on home. I crawled into bed and slept like a log. I didn't even have to take aspirin.

In Texas right now they're driving in from the ranches in their pickup trucks. In Alto Springs and all the other ranchtowns on the Plateau, in another hour or so, the pickups'll be parked in front of the Methodist or Baptist or Church of Christ churches. The men in their ranch-cut suits, string ties and cowboy boots, with squint-wrinkled, weather-burnt faces dark as a Mexican's, a white half-moon across each brow from the shadows of their hats, the women in pink or off-white or robin's-egg blue suits or dresses and a conglomeration of hats and purses, the little girls in organdy and shiny patent-leather shoes and the older ones in their graduation or Easter outfits, the boys, big and little, in their own stifling suits, will crowd the church steps and sidewalks in front, sunlight bouncing back up from the hot cement against the undersides of their faces. Town latecomers will hurry from their homes through blinding, late-morning light and alternating shade under live oaks, the constantly falling live oak leaves crackling under their feet. It'll be so hot the snakes will stay under their rocks. Around the square the closed shops will look like houses of the dead. Even the drugstore will be closed by church time.

It was sunny here in West Hesper too, going on eleven in the morning the Sunday after the picnic—cool New England sunlight. Lita had put a basket of cheese and bean-sprout sandwiches, fruit and a thermos of herb tea in the back seat of the Volkswagen and she and I were about to hit out to Edgefield, forty or so miles from West Hesper, to scout out Victorian gingerbread. Lita had left Pearl with Mrs. Trombley, a little old widow woman with wasp's-nest-gray hair and eyes so light blue they're the color of skimmed turned-blinky milk. Mrs. Trombley can see as good as a twenty-year-old, though. She lives across the landing from Lita. She's gone through three husbands, and she's as brisk as a sparrow. Mrs. Trombley loves Pearl. In fact, when she opens her door to have Pearl in it's like Pearl was going into Heaven. The first thing Pearl gets is graham crackers and a cup of egg custard, then, if she wants, a glass of lemonade. When Pearl's in Mrs. Trombley's apartment she can play with anything she likes. It don't matter if it's a photograph in an oval frame or a brooch or earrings out of Mrs. Trombley's treasure box or her fox furs or a pair of shoes—Pearl can play with it all day if she's of a mind to. The only thing Pearl has to do is once in a while comb Mrs. Trombley's hair, which, when Pearl pulls out the gray hairpins, falls clear to Mrs. Trombley's waist. Pearl would like to comb it for hours. You can't fetch Pearl along with you if you want to drive around trying to smoke out Victorian architecture though. "I'm hungwy." "I gotta pee." She'll drive you bananas.

Anyway, Lita and I were just circling the rotary, about to head east. Lita looked flushed and excited. I said, "What's up?"

"I'm just happy."

Folks were going up the sidewalks into the churches, under a simmer of green leaves. The church lawns were littered with yellow suns of second-crop dandelions, like hundreds of small, frame-stopped explosions. We had to wait while a policeman, in clear violation of the separation of the powers of church and state, held up his hand to let the Xtians cross—all those pagans in their Sunday finery like Aztecs plastered with feathers about to dance around a rock. I got about as much faith in most folk's Xtianity as I have in a mule's. Inside, in the stained-glass light, they'll whip up a storm of magic, prayers and calls for a bigger collection than they got last week and hymns and the like, amongst a passel of criss-crossed sticks and carved idols and sips of wine and pieces of soda cracker, whilst the women show off their new hats and the Chamber of Commerce, Rotary Club businessman types eye the high school girls—"Love Lifteth Me." After a man's been dead as long as Jesus Christ he's bound to have a wonderful reputation. But there ain't no magic, no matter what way you cut it, going to change the bloody mess we were at scratch or the dirt we're headed into quick as a dog. There ain't nothing going to lift an inch of that dirt—you're going to be stuck there solid as a cockroach under a Gideon Bible. Nobody's come out of the grave yet that I know of excepting *maybe* Christ, and if he did it's a wonder it didn't make him sick.

Anyway, the last pagan and the last dog following a pagan from home went on across, and Lita and I drove around the rotary and over to the highway and out of town. Pretty soon we were driving past Dairy Queens and billboards and farms, headed up into the mountains. Lita had lit another damned cigarette, but the car windows were down and the fresh air, smelling of warm grass and cow manure and, farther up the mountain, the shade under birch trees and evergreens, rushed in. Near the top of the climb was an observation tower and a place that sells honey and maple candy and Indian moccasins. But pretty soon we were up over the pass, winding and twisting down the twenty-mile-long downgrade towards Edgefield, mountains on either side, and the Green Mountain River, whitewater tumbling over rocks to the left, sending up a wall of air as cold as if it'd just been let out of a refrigerator door.

Lita said, "Got a letter from my mother the other day."

"What's she say?"

"My sister's dropped out of Berkeley and gone to live with a guy that's a fire warden on top of some mountain in Washington state."

"Sounds like fun."

"Hell, my sister can't cook. She couldn't start a fire in a wood stove if you gave her kerosene to do it with. And she's never washed a dish in her life, not even in a dishwasher, let alone in a creek."

"Maybe *he* cooks."

"Yeah, and she goes out and pees on the forest fires. My mama's all depressed. Farley was her baby. Mama thought Farley was going to be a nuclear physicist. Just like she thought I was going to be the next Gloria Swanson. My mother's just turned fifty anyway, and she says the only consolation she's got is that they let the women tan naked at the club nowadays and she's got a nice brown bottom." Lita laughed.

We were driving through an open space, the river broader and slower now but still flinging up spray wherever it hit against the upstream sides of boulders.

On the other side of the road was a meadow with a roadside sugarhouse, a Howard Johnson restaurant, a bronze, Hartford-Insurance-Company-type elk with a set of antlers on it that looked like a rocking chair, and then a row of red-and-yellow-painted, concrete tepees—the Chief Something-or-other Motel. We drove across a bridge. Lita laughed again. I looked at her. She had a grin on her as big as all get-out.

"What on earth's got into *you* today?"

She said, "I'm in *love*."

"You're *what?*"

"I'm always so damned *happy* when I'm in love. Shit, Rudy, I'm not even *alive* when I'm not in love."

"Who *with?*"

"Hollis."

"Here we go again."

Lita laughed. But to tell you the truth, my heart was pounding like it was about to blow off the top of my head. I couldn't even see the road, my head hurt so much. I said, "I didn't even know he was—seeing you." My voice cracked when I said it. I watched Hollis get out of the car the other night, at Lita's place, after they'd dropped me off. There was a taste in my mouth like I was going to be sick.

Lita said, "Oh, he's been back a few times, since Joe left."

So he had.

"Rudy, I'm *scared*," Lita said. She pulled over to the side of the road and stopped the car.

"About what?"

She switched off the ignition. "When I'm in love it's like the ground's shaking under my feet. I'm always afraid I'm going to get hurt. You can't depend on a damned thing you were sure about before."

" 'Ever' feller to his own notion,' like the old woman said as she kissed the cow."

She laughed. "I don't care. I'm so damned happy I can't help myself. Christ, I sit in this car right now and look at the trees and rocks and stuff and the world's so goddamned beautiful I'm about to go nuts." She laughed again. I watched a bug crawl across the windshield. It stopped at the edge, tested the rubber molding with its feelers, then turned around and headed back across. Of a sudden I was so mad I wanted to cry. But I got hold of myself. I said, "It sounds just fine." I said, "I'm going back to Texas pretty soon, my ownself."

"You *are*? You don't mean for good?"

"No, I'll be back, dammit. I got a good job here. There ain't no work in Alto Springs. And I couldn't stay anyways."

"Why not?"

"There's reasons. I usually go for Christmas. But if I don't get away from here pretty quick I'm going to have a nervous breakdown."

Lita laughed. "I'll bet." Of a sudden she touched me. "Oh Rudy, I'm sorry. Do I bore you, carrying on like I do?"

"Hell, no."

"Look, if I can't talk to you who *can* I talk to? You're my best friend."

"It's just, I'm irritable. I think I need an R and R."

"What brought that on?"

"Cost overruns."

> *"Her eyes as bright as bright can be*
> *Like sun rays on a summer sea.*
>
> *Her hair is like a sunset crown*
> *O'er fields of wheat just turning brown,*
>
> *And in her lips the mantling blood*
> *Is like a pomegranate bud."*

I said, "I got to get out of the car a minute." I got out and went over and leaned against the gray, smooth-barked trunk of some damned northern tree and threw up. Lita ran over to me. She said, "My God, what's the matter?"

"I ain't felt well all morning. I didn't sleep too well last night, and when I got up this morning I felt like homemade shit. I shouldn't of never of come."

Lita touched my shoulder. "Poor darling. Why didn't you tell me?"

"I thought I could make it." I wiped my mouth and chin with my handkerchief and bent down and wiped the spatterings off my shoes with some leaves. I said, "I think we'd better head on back."

"You're angry with me."

"No. Hell, I just don't feel good. It's probably something I ate. I ate at that damned seafood place last night, and even then I thought the stuff had an off taste."

We got back into the car. Lita said, "Well, I'm upset."

"Jesus, Lita, can't a body be sick once in a while?"

"I don't like you to be sick. It makes me worry for you."

"Let's go home."

We drove back to West Hesper. Lita didn't say much most of the way and I didn't feel like talking. I turned on the radio and the first thing I got was a religious program. It was as bad as Oral Roberts. We listened to the goddamned thing the whole way home.

8

I didn't get to go back to Texas for five lousy weeks. Mr. Bertolini didn't want to let me go, but I told him there was a terrific crisis in my family back home, what with the death of my grandma and the serious condition of my brother Leroy and all, and anyway if I didn't get to go home for at least a short spell I was going to go nuts. They had a hell of a time finding somebody to take my place for just two weeks, but finally they got a guy to come out from Worchester. I stuffed some clothes and my vitamins and bee pollen into a suitcase, gave my replacement the keys to my apartment along with a gift bottle of Irish Mist, told him where the cooking gear was and the dishwashing detergent and the toilet paper and took off. It was eleven o'clock at night, July eighteenth. Moths were freaking out around the streetlights and bugs knocking against screens. Once in a while, in the time before I left, Lita and I saw each other. I went over to her place to have dinner a couple of times.

Once Lita and Pearl went to Boston for a week.

Hollis and Lita drove me over the mountains to Edgefield to catch the train. I went by train. I could of gone by bus, but the last time I did it like to broke my back: three days and two nights of pure torture, where, after the first day or so, no matter what way you sit your ass feels like it's crawling up your back and you can't stretch out your legs to save your life. And I'm scared to death of planes. The one time I went up in one, at takeoff my heart dropped down through my britches and through the seat and the fuselage of the plane and I looked out and could see it pulsing like a small red light way back down there on the runway.

Pearl slept most of the way to Edgefield, her head on my lap. It was a godawful time to have to catch a train—1:20 A. M.

Amtrak don't give a damn about their passengers anyway. No matter where you get on the train, at the beginning of the run or somewhere farther on down the line, you always have to catch it in the middle of the night.

It was a pitch-dark night, damp and cold. We drove through fog. Lita had her window down and I felt the wetness prickling against my face. When we drove into Edgefield it was onto one of the loneliest streets I ever saw. There wasn't even anyplace open to get coffee.

The depot was on the other side of town. The waiting room was about the size of a bathroom. It had a couple of benches in it, some schedules and posters tacked onto the walls, and an attendant hiding somewhere behind one of two closed doors. Four or five people were already there waiting for the train, their suitcases and backpacks and duffel bags stashed around them.

Pearl said, "Where's Wudy going, Mommy?"

"Home for a visit."

"Don't he live here? I mean, in Wesper?"

"He'll be back in a couple of weeks, sweetie."

Pearl tugged at my sleeve. She said, "I don't *want* you to go. You're gonna miss my birfday."

I said, "I'll fetch you back something real nice." We heard the foghorn snore of the Amtrak coming in. I gave Pearl a kiss. Everyone went out onto the platform. The yellow beam of the locomotive twitched and poked through the fog, the corrugated, wet, streamlined walls of the passenger cars slid by like stainless-steel canisters. The iron wheels squealed as the train came to a stop.

Lita touched my shoulder. I turned to her and she said, "I've hurt your feelings and I'm sorry." I said, "No, you didn't." She gave me a hug and a kiss. There were tears in her eyes. I kissed her too. Then I turned and shook Hollis's hand and said, "Thanks for everything."

"That's all right."

Pearl started to cry.

Folks were getting on the train. The conductor took my ticket. I said, "Where do I sit?"

"Anywhere you want."

I climbed up the steps, turned and waved goodbye. Then I slid open a heavy door and went into what I guess was the lounge car. The lights were on full glare. A bar was at the far end of the car and behind it a black man in a starched, white serving-jacket was selling soft drinks, coffee and sandwiches. He looked embarrassed. There was a hell of a crowd in the car —what looked to be mostly college-aged kids talking and yelling, singing and playing guitars, laughing and goofing around. Food and paper cups and sandwich wrappers were all over the floor.

I looked for a seat on the side of the car opposite the platform. A girl with brown, Asiatic-looking eyes and an Afro hairstyle was sitting in a seat next the aisle, her legs over the armrest and a Dixie cup of soda pop in her fist. " 'Scuse me," I said. I got past her with my suitcase and sat down. She looked at me, then got up and took another seat.

My seat was next the window. I saw my face in the glass. Of a sudden I hated my face. I couldn't stand to look at it. I turned away, trying to get used to the noise and light. But I couldn't take it. I'm going on twenty-three years old and I'm already a hundred years older than these kids. I turned back to the window again, pressed my nose against the glass like diving into dark water, and tried to look out, my hands cupping both sides of my face to keep out the light. All that was out there were five or six far-off, lonesome streetlights, made even smaller and more lonesome by the fog. The train jerked forward. I sat back in my seat. The train jerked again and I could feel it picking up speed. The coach began to rock from side to side. Across the aisle a bunch of kids were laughing and yelling over a game of cards. I couldn't hear myself think. I was dead tired and it looked like I wasn't going to get much sleep. In fact, I wasn't going to get a goddamned bit.

Some track signals flashed by the window.

Of a sudden it struck me I didn't *have* to stay here. I got up and hefted my suitcase to the aisle, trying to keep my balance in the motion of the coach, and up the aisle through hoots and jeers to the rear.

The sliding door slid shut behind me and I was in another world: shift and clang of metal, racket of couplings, clack of rails, cold, rushing air and night. Through another sliding door into a coach of shadowy dark and body heat, snores and a bee hum of soft, regular, in-and-out breaths—likely a carload of sleeping Canadians headed for New York. Every seat was taken so I went on through to the next coach and found a seat there. I fell in love with the quiet and the dark, the hiss of breaths, the rocking cradle of the coach. I dropped off to sleep like I'd been knocked on the head.

I was waked by somebody trying to get a suitcase past my knees—the fat, motherly woman who'd been sitting in the seat next to mine. After she'd gone, in the sway of the car bumping her suitcase or her hips against one or another of the seats along the aisle, I slid over onto the hen's warmth she'd left. It was gray out, with a thin, orange streak behind black houses, billboards, trees. In the empty suburban streets sodium streetlights hung on poles like trophies of past sunups. I was homesick for Lita and Pearl. I wanted Pearl on my lap, her hands poking around in the pockets of my blazer or vest. I wanted Lita beside me, or even across the aisle, where I could look at her face and hands, the sprinkle of freckles on her nose, the long fall of her black hair. *Oh, Jesus, I'm sick to death of beautiful women. I'm sick to death of the whole fucking world.* I didn't mean to think that. It came on me like a sickness, lit down onto me like a grief.

I closed my eyes. I felt the train rushing me through space to nowhere. It struck me of a sudden that most women, even the nicest ones, think ugly men, all on account of their ugliness, are pure eunuchs. Or ghosts. They don't *see* you. I just wanted to crawl under a rock.

The sky was pale. Apartment houses and cemeteries slipped by. We went over a monstrous-long bridge above flat rooftops and into the city—*Penn Station*, which I didn't see excepting from inside of the coach.

Through the waste flats of New Jersey, the orange sun up. Gray cities. Under a bridge with a sign painted on it: "You'd be there now by Air-Shuttle." A long haul through truck-farm country broken by developments. I fell asleep watching Lita's hands pick dead leaves from a geranium on a windowsill. The noise of folks getting their belongings together woke me. Off to the right on a river, below a Greek temple on a bluff, were three or four rowers in single sculls. The boats slid through the mirror-like water. We were almost into Philadelphia. Then down the backside of Maryland through the first southern woods. I walked up to the lounge car and bought a sandwich and a cup of coffee. A little past one P. M. we pulled into Washington, D. C., more than two hours late. It was all right though, on account of my next train wasn't due to leave until around seven.

In the waiting room, the noise of the crowd and the scuffle of their shoes soaked into the absorbent tiles of a lowered ceiling. There were magazine-and-candy-bar stands, souvenir stores and fast-food shops offering manna to the masses. Here and there folks who looked like they'd been traveling for years and hadn't got there yet were asleep in rows of armless, plastic-and-metal chairs, amongst their suitcases and packages. They looked so dead to the world it's a wonder everything they owned didn't get ripped off. I found the men's room, shaved and washed up, changed my shirt and socks and put new Band-Aids on my toes.

I had time to spare. I stowed my suitcase in a locker, pocketed the key and walked through a gigantic, high-ceilinged concourse littered here and there with some kind of tourist exhibit and out into blinding sunlight past a leaping fountain and then, in sweat-soaked shirt and sticky boxer shorts, down the long stretch of grimy marble porticos, walls and Corinthian and Ionic columns of the government buildings on Constitution Avenue. The hot pavement hurt my feet. Heat expanded from the traffic and exhaust fumes like to choked me. It was hot even under the trees. Tourists were all over the place, sweat beading their faces and cameras dangling from their necks. Families had come clear from North Dakota or wherever to be in this carbon monoxide and heat. I sat on the granite steps of one of our public edifices. Across the street in a park a pair of lovers were lying on the grass, their shoes off, in their stocking feet. Even here in Washington, D. C., the national capital, that stuff goes on.

> "When a boy falls in love
> with a pretty turtle dove
> he will linger all around her underjaw."

I wandered into a government building where there was a small aquarium and that cooled me off some. I ate supper in a cafeteria.

Southern Railway. The conductor handed out pillows all around. After everybody had settled down I managed to find two seats to stretch out on. I took my wallet and comb and breathmints and other odds and ends I didn't want to sleep on from my pockets, put them in the suitcase and lay down. The one time I woke it was past two in the morning and the train was stopped at some small-town station in nowhere. I sat up and looked out the window. It was raining. Two station attendants were wheeling a long, narrow box to the baggage car. Their rain gear glistened under the single platform light and the top of the crate shone.

I think I dreamed that. That and dark, muddy water. Sometimes I can't hardly get up to the surface, it bogs me down so close. I had a headache when I woke and my back hurt. There ain't nothing worse than coming up out of clambering for air and light and you're in a strange place. It's even worse when the strange place is moving.

We were somewhere near Greenville, South Carolina, and the sun was about to come up. I fished my toilet kit out of the suitcase and walked along the aisle between rows of open mouths and snoring noses to the men's room, where you *really* know the train's moving—you lean toward this wall or that whenever the train's making a curve. If you've got to pee you can barely hit the toilet. I shaved and brushed my teeth and took my brewer's yeast and bee pollen and vitamins and tried to knock the damned swamp mud out of my head. When I got back to my seat I was a little more awake.

Red clay fields.

Mist over peach orchards. The sun will suck it up quick enough.

In the seats all around me folks were beginning to stir. In Gainesville, Georgia, a southern lady got on. First the conductor and a stationmaster came in and sized up the coach. The stationmaster, a white man, touched one of the seats nearby, at the front of the coach, and went on back out. The conductor, who was black, reversed some seat backs so that there were four empty seats facing each other. He dusted them off, went out and came back with a couple of pillows that he placed in strategic places. A redcap came in, carrying two suitcases, followed by another with a third suitcase, a white umbrella, a hatbox and a big Raggedy Ann doll. The conductor had them put the umbrella, hatbox and doll on one of the seats and the suitcases on the floor in front of two empty seats across the aisle. The redcaps left. A little blond six-year-old girl in a frilly white dress ran in. She cried out when she saw her doll, grabbed it and climbed with it onto a seat by the window. Then the lady came in, along with the stationmaster. He and the conductor hovered around her like bees around a queen bee, in low, concerned tones asking this question and that after her comfort. Her answers were laced with smiles and soft, long-drawn-out vowels and the pushing back of a loose strand of her blond hair. She was about thirty years, old, with a jiggly-plump figure in a flimsy, lavender-and-white dress. Her face, pale and powdered, looked like it'd come direct down from a moving-picture screen. When the conductor and the stationmaster had left she took off her wide-brimmed straw hat. Her hair was as soft and mirror-bright as her daughter's. I couldn't keep my eyes off her, which was no problem on account of she didn't pay attention to anyone else in the coach excepting herself and her little girl. They got off the train an hour later, in Atlanta.

I put on a tie and blazer for breakfast, went to the back of the coach, made my way across couplings, shifting iron plates and the rush of morning air and, after a dance with the sliding door, into a coach labeled *Flint River* and down a long corridor past closed doors of roomettes and across another span of air and iron plates into the dining car. It was air-conditioned in here. I was glad I had on my blazer.

One of the waiters, shuffling against the swaying of the coach, led me to a table where an elderly couple were waiting for their breakfast. They looked to be in their seventies.

Whenever I get in a situation like this it's like being in a room with a strange dog: I never know whether I'm going to get my hand licked or my britches tore. But the woman said, "That's a lovely tie." She had the kind of prettiness that happens to some women who maybe never thought they were pretty when they were young, but after years of thinking they're downright plain, come up above a timberline into clear air and snow: their skin draws smooth, gets that thin, white, see-through look like a fine teacup and shows the fineness of their bones. Mrs. Stackbine in Alto Springs was like that. You'd see her face at her window, in the Cape jasmine shade, and it shone like wax. Mrs. Stackbine was a widow woman. She was good to me up until she went and died. She used to tap her window whenever I walked by her place headed home from the third and fourth grades in school and we'd sit on her front steps while I ate the store-bought cookies and drank the bottle of Dr. Pepper she usually gave me. Sometimes it was a slice of store-bought jelly roll. Even up close there wasn't hardly a wrinkle or an age spot on her face. There wasn't on this woman's either. That kind of clearness is likely inside them too.

I said, "You don't mind if I sit here with you?"

The old man said, "We always like company."

Their name was Johnston. They told me about how it was their twentieth wedding anniversary and they were going down to Gulfport to visit his son by a former marriage and then on a railroad tour around the U. S. A.—out to Los Angeles and then up to Canada and back across. They asked me about myself and I told them I was going home for a couple of weeks to Alto Springs, Texas, and they asked me about Alto Springs and I told them about the sheep-and-angora-goat ranches and how the place was miles from nowhere, seventy miles to the next town, no train, no bus—mainly lots of scrub brush and sky. I told them I couldn't wait to get back. Sometimes you tell more to strangers than you do to your best friends.

The waiter put a plate with a cantaloupe-half in front of each of them. There was a sprig of mint at the edge of each plate. I wrote down my order on the slip the waiter put in front of me.

I ate ham and eggs while the kudzu flew by outside. That stuff can sprout up and choke a running horse, it grows so fast.

Back in my seat in the coach I stared out the window at wooded hills, corn and peanut fields in bottomlands, red-dirt backroads, kitchen gardens next to dust-stained, white-painted houses, the backsides of towns with their names on water towers, old, bare-board sharecropper shanties, small, shirtless black boys in shorts staring up from their play in the weeds beside the tracks.

Sometimes, staring out a window like that, everything going by so fast, it wellnigh hypnotizes you. I came to with a start. What I'd been listening to was my daddy. He had a basket on his arm and was reaching up between the leaves of a fig tree to pick ripe figs. It was the fig tree next the garage. I was standing beside him with my arm around one of his legs and my thumb stuck in my mouth. He had just picked a fat, soft, purple one and said, "Here, son, eat this."

I feel sad for my daddy. The Castleberrys used to be *the* family in Alto Springs, way back when. We owned the general merchandise store. My great-grandpa was one of the incorporators of the bank. He held stock in the wool-and-mohair warehouse, which is the main business in town, having dealings with every sheep-and-angora-goat rancher on the Divide. Now my daddy clerks at the warehouse. He works behind the counter selling ranch supplies and during the spring and fall shearings he weighs and tabulates the bales.

Sunlight on the square. Somebody walked through my mind. It was just a ghost. I've never seen a picture of my grandma. There's not a photograph of her of any kind anywhere in the house—not in the old, blue, silk-backed album on top the piano in the parlor or in the shoeboxes of photos that are stored in the crawl space we use for an attic or anywhere. I don't even know the color of her hair. They say she was awful pretty. Her name was Victoria Ann. She died of TB. For the last two or three years of her life she stayed in her room, all the blinds down even in the hottest weather. She stayed in her bed, a fan and a glass and pitcher of water beside, and wouldn't talk to anyone. That's what they say anyway, the few times I've ever heard anybody talk about her . . .

Later in the morning I walked back to the observation car, which had been put on in Atlanta. On the way I stopped in the lounge car and had a Coke. A little boy was sitting with his mama at the table across from mine. He said, "Mommy, what's wrong with that man?" His mother said, "Shush." But I *prefer* the flat-out matter-of-factness of kids. I grinned at the little tyke. He looked away and then turned to me again and stared. After I'd finished my Coke I went on back to the observation car. Man, what a view.

I was in the dining car eating my dinner when we rolled

through Tuscaloosa. A little later we crossed the Black Warrior River and then the Tombigbee River, and before you knew it we were in Mississippi.

Pastures and piney woods, water oaks, Spanish moss hanging from the trees. In the pastures flocks of cattle birds flew up and then lit down to catch bugs stirred up by the snouts of Brahma cows. Here and there a snowy egret stood on one leg. The sun went down. The sky had a green look to it. We headed down into what looked to be a storm front. Piles of purple and orange clouds streamed across, close overhead. We started out across Lake Pontchartrain, floating above water, the flares of refineries off in the distance to one side. On the left, the lights of New Orleans. It felt like hours, getting across that bridge. Then we slid under elevated highways, stopped and backed, stopped and backed and finally stopped for good alongside the white concrete ribbon of the station platform. I'd have to stay in New Orleans overnight: the Amtrak for Texas and points west don't leave until the next day.

I've been in New Orleans before. I took a cab to the place I usually go to, off Rampart Street, where the price of a single for one night don't rob you of every cent you've got. Ate supper at my favorite restaurant, a hole in the wall with four tables, just around the corner. I had a pile of crawdads on a newspaper, lemon and a beer. Then I hit the sack.

It rained hard most of the night. I woke when it quit, about four A. M. After that I couldn't sleep.

The sun came up, sucking the moisture off the sidewalks and streets. I bummed around the French Quarter all morning. There was so much water in the air I could barely breathe. The sun felt like it was about two feet directly above my head. I stayed mostly in the shops, to get out of the sun. I bought a postcard to send to Lita and a little bamboo cricket cage for Pearl. If her mama won't let her have a cricket, leastways she can keep some play-toys in it.

The Amtrak to Los Angeles left at just past noon. My ticket was to San Antonio.

Across the mud-brown Mississippi and for miles on track up on stilts above canals, slues, bayous, swamps. Trees growing out of water. Cattle knee-deep in grass on wide savannahs. Oyster-shell backroads. Rain, cars on wet highways. Morgan City, Lafayette, Crowley, Midland, Jennings, Lake Charles. Rain streaked the windows. Then it came down so hard you couldn't see out. They switched the lights on in the coach at five, and when I went to eat supper in the dining car an hour later the weather was so wet and dark it was almost like night.

I went back to the coach and tried to read a spell. But I couldn't concentrate. The small talk all around me and the weight of the weather outside and the rocking of the coach kept putting me to sleep. We crossed the Sabine River at eight-thirty P. M. and went through Beaumont, Texas, a short time later, headed for Houston. Right up to par, Amtrak was already running an hour and fifty minutes late. That meant I was going to get into San Antonio at about four goddamned o'clock in the morning, when the world's flat out on its ass like a stiff and the only signs of life in the station waiting-room will be the sleeping winos and the goddamned coffee bar will be closed and even if you can get a cab to the bus station there ain't a bus going at that hour anywhere.

Well, if God was to listen to the prayers of crows, there'd be dead horses lying right and left.

I went to the men's lounge to spruce up in order to try to keep awake. It didn't help much. Back in my seat again I picked up my book, a paperback about politics, and there was one paragraph I must of read fifteen times. Everytime I got to the phrase "the determining factor" the book slipped out of my hands to my lap. I finally decided I might as well sleep. My wallet and comb were poking me in the hip, so I took them out of my pocket and put them and the book into my suitcase. Then I tried to get comfortable. But every time I started to doze off, some noise, a voice somewhere in the coach or something, would fetch me back and my eyes would pop open. The coach heaved and rocked. Up the aisle a way a little boy was jumping up and down on his seat, humming, his hands gripping the headrest, his eyes staring around with a bored, half-seeing look. In the seat behind me a young man was explaining something important about his life to the girl across the aisle. He went on and on, like water from a wide-open faucet, and the girl kept saying, "Uh huh. Yes. Uh huh." Pretty soon his voice was a hum, monotonous as a shuttle, and the girl's words quick, bright threads stitched across it. The words hadn't any meaning anymore. If anything, hers got to sound, on the edge of my sleep, like a dog barking from a long way off. I felt the train stop and back, stop and back, in New Orleans, and for a minute the air was so stuffy I had a hard time breathing—smell of close, sweaty bodies and dusty plush. Then I heard Lita's voice again, in sunlight, from the next room. It cut through my heart like a knife.

A bird lit onto my shoulder. It was bigger than a crow and kept shifting from one claw-foot to another on the seam of my good blazer. It shook its feathers, stuck out its head, opened its black horny beak and screeched *pick-it! pick-it!* I woke. The train had stopped: the coach was motionless and quiet, like waking up in a coffin under six feet of earth after the sway of being carried on shoulders, noise of Bible text and sobs, racket of gravel on the lid.

The conductor was leaning over me, shaking my shoulder. "Ticket, please," he said. A bushy mustache hid his upper lip, a goatee was pasted to his chin. Gold braid cluttered the front of his cap, and brass buttons, that looked like planets going through their orbits, shone down the front of his black serge coat.

I said, "Is this San Antonio?"

"Sir, would you please produce your ticket?"

I fumbled around in my blazer pockets and came up with the

envelope with the tickets. I still wasn't but half awake. "Where are we?" I said.

"Houston. Is your final destination anywhere in Texas?"

"I'm going to San Antonio." A headache was narrowing itself down in the front of my skull.

The conductor looked at my ticket. He handed it back to me and said, "Will you come with me, please?"

I wasn't the only one in the coach who'd been waked up. A second conductor or stationmaster or whatever was going down the other side of the aisle, waking folks and looking at their tickets. Some, after their tickets had been checked, were let go back to sleep. They were likely through passengers, as far as I had the inclination to figure it out in my sleep-sogged head. At one end of the coach other passengers, tolled out of their seats like I'd been and about as awake, were huddled like a cluster of stunned, miserable bees outside a hive in a hard frost. The men sleepily straightened their ties and buttoned their coats. The women were trying to push loose strands of hair back up onto their heads. Some of the women, under their jackets and coats, were in their nightgowns, for Christsake—the hems went clean to the floor.

The conductor said, "Nothing to be concerned about. The train'll be held. Please follow me." Somebody said something about a quarantine check. The conductor led about fifteen of us across a vestibule and through the next car—stuffy, narrow corridor between blue, plush curtains. I tell you, I was so god-damned discombobulated it was like walking under water. I saw the far-off ghost of my face in a mirror at the end of the corridor and stubbed my boot toe against a brass vase. It wasn't until I'd stepped down onto the ground that it struck me I'd forgot my suitcase. But I had my ticket: that train wasn't going anywhere without me on it.

My headache was getting worse and my back was starting to hurt.

We were under a big shed. "Out de way, ladies and gents!"

We stepped back. A baggage cart piled four high with trunks crashed by. The conductor said, "Will you-all come this way, please?" We followed him alongside the track, through a warm night fog that smelled of oleanders and bayou water, towards the depot. Wherever I stepped stones crunched under my feet. Frogs and night crickets shrilled in the bushes in a little park nearby. The woman behind me kept saying, "If *this* don't take the rag off the bush," and the man with her said, "I feel worse than he who cometh off a drunk." The woman laughed. The lights from the train windows lit our way. Wet dripped from the sides of the coaches onto the ties. Near the depot the smell, of all things, of horse manure. It was so strong it almost made me sick. Of a sudden I felt panicky. I glanced back at the train. The long row of lights looked like a last view of the *Titanic* before it went down.

The waiting room was bright with electric light. There weren't many people there. Most of them had probably gone out to get on the train. A policeman held the door open for us. Some city winos were wandering around between the benches, their eyes on the floor. They were dressed in the worst rags you ever saw. A timid-looking man sat on one of the benches near the door, beside a tall horse-faced woman with thick black eyebrows. A suitcase, a birdcage and a guitar were on the floor by their feet. A few farmers or businessmen or whatever were sitting around smoking and chatting or reading the paper. They looked up at us as we went past. A depot official in a uniform hurried by carrying a lantern. An old gentleman sat on a bench and in front of him a young woman walked back and forth, holding a baby and humming to it. Her hair was piled on top of her head. She wore a big straw hat with a white bird wing on the side of it. I looked up at the clock on the wall—11:37—and then brushed back my jacket sleeve to check my watch. "*I've lost my watch!*" I stopped in my tracks and the man behind bumped into me. "I'm sorry. *I've lost my watch,*" I said. Then I remembered. I was freshening up in the men's room after supper and I'd taken off my watch and put it on a shelf next the basin.

Jesus H. Christ. And my wallet and aspirin were in my suitcase. "You're holding us up," the man said. I hurried to catch up to the rest, but I felt like a drowner in a bad dream trying to catch hold to a held-out tree branch.

We were crowded past a door marked OFFICE and into a large room stale with the smell of old cigar smoke and—it *smelt* like—formaldehyde. Two unfrosted light bulbs in glass shades hung from the ceiling. They were so naked bright it hurt my eyes. A table covered with a white cloth was in the center of the room, with pitchers of water, towels, wash bowl, soap and thermometers set out on it. A middle-aged man in a white doctor's jacket, close-cut hair and a bushy mustache sat behind the table, peering up at us over the pair of steel-rimmed glasses perched on his nose. He looked tired. By his left elbow, balanced on the rim of a saucer, was a just-snubbed-out cigar. A faint thread of smoke curled up from it. A couple of other cigar stubs were in the empty coffee cup.

The woman behind me whispered to her friend, "They're awful strict." He said, "I got a health certificate in Baton Rouge without any trouble, but ever' quarantine officer I meet makes me sign."

The room was likely the stationmaster's office. The walls were varnished oak. The green shades of the three windows were pulled right down to the sills. A fan blade turned slowly on the ceiling: recirculated air gently rustled the papers tacked to the walls. A big desk was against one of the walls, ledgers, schedules and dispatches scattered all over it. Other papers hung from hooks in front of a rack of pigeonholes over the desk. A Morse code outfit was on the desk and above it, on the wall, a board with a conglomeration of pegs and electric wires. A map of the "Sunset Route" was on the wall.

A police officer and a young man, who also wore a doctor's white jacket, stood near the door. The young man closed the door and said, "There's a few chairs. Won't the ladies, at least, be seated?" Several shiny-bottomed chairs lined the walls, and a few of the women sat in them. Most of the women, under their coats and jackets, had on long dresses, mainly white. One of the women, an elderly lady who had taken off her hat and who was partly bald, wore shiny black. She sat in a chair near me. Her dress rustled stiffly when she sat. She hefted a small satchel that had an umbrella and a book strapped to it onto her lap and said, "This is just about the last straw." She glared at the man sitting at the table. He sighed, looked down at the palms of his hands and then began to tap his fingers on the table. The old woman snorted, opened her satchel, fumbled around in it, muttering something about "—will hear about *this*," found what she was looking for and popped it into her mouth. It smelled like licorice.

I had a chance to look at my fellow travelers. There was a family of four: a plump, round-faced woman whose eyes glistened from deep in her cheeks; her husband, most likely a small farmer or laborer—in fact, you'd of thought he'd just lost his crop or his job, one, he had such a worried look—and their two kids, a little boy and girl, both towheads and both dressed in little-girl dresses. The children were half asleep and the papa held one and the mama the other. Then there was the man and woman that'd been following along behind me. She was a redhead, tall and damned good-looking. She had a pert nose and wideset lynx-green eyes—the greenest eyes I ever saw— that looked like they were taking in everything. When she saw me looking at her she stared me right back in the face. I looked away quick. But I remember wisps of coppery hair and that she wore a flat, shallow-crowned, straw sailor hat perched to the front of her head. The man was a shrewd-looking fellow with a pencil-thin mustache and a pushed-back hat. Another family, of three. A tall, gawky boy and a high-school-aged girl who looked to be brother and sister. The old woman in black. Two or three others. All the men wore dark business suits and, like I say, most of the women, under their coats and jackets, were dressed in white. Some of them had on the damnedest hats.

The first folks to be called over to the table were the family of three. The doctor asked them some questions and then his assistant stuck thermometers in their mouths. When it came my turn the doctor said, "Have you been in any yellow fever district in the past two weeks?"

My back was hurting and my head ached and I was pissed off at the whole business. I said, "The only district I've been in is the District of Columbia."

The doctor looked at me a minute. He leaned back in his chair and pressed the tips of his fingers together. Then he said, "Did you get off the train in New Orleans?"

"Well, yes, I did. I had to. The train—"

"Please just answer my questions. Are you in good health? Have you had any symptoms of illness in the past few days?"

"No."

"And how do you feel right now?"

"Well, if you want to know, I've got a lousy headache and my back hurts."

He looked at me a moment longer. Then he sat forward, stood up and went to the end of the table. He said, "Would you step over here, please?"

I went over to the end of the table. His assistant stuck a thermometer in my mouth. The doctor washed his hands in a basin and dried them on a towel. He took my pulse. He pressed his fingers up under my jaw and then poked and probed my neck. He listened to my heart through my chest, turned me around and listened through my back. With that damned swizzle stick in my mouth I couldn't say a thing. He turned me around again and stuck his fingers into my armpits. I looked over his shoulder. There was a calendar on the wall. It said

K. H. CAWTHORNE & CO.

and underneath that it said

1902   JULY   1902

The assistant took the thermometer out of my mouth. I said, "*Shit*."

It was as still as death in the room. The doctor looked at me. Then he said, "Sir, there are ladies and gentlemen present. *And I am a representative of the United States government*. Please apologize."

I felt so small you could of tucked me under a thimble. The doctor glared at me with his hard blue eyes. Finally I croaked, "I apologize."

"*Go stand over there*." He pointed to where the high school girl, her brother, the family with two kids and one other woman —those he'd separated from four or five others he'd also already examined—stood near the stationmaster's desk. When I went over to them they all moved a step back from me. I kept my eyes on the floor.

Pretty soon there were about ten of us standing near the desk. The rest were let go back to the train. I said, "I have to go get my suitcase," but the policeman motioned me back while he held the door open for them. The doctor, washing his hands and drying them on a towel, said to his assistant, "This is the last train we're going to let in until we've determined the situation. They should have been stopped in Beaumont." He turned to us and said, "This officer will escort you to the observation pavilion." Everyone groaned. The doctor said, "*Ladies. Gentlemen*. For the past three weeks yellow fever has been epidemic in New Orleans. I'm sure you know that. We can't allow it to spread into Texas. Some of you have light fevers. Others show other symptoms. That doesn't mean you have the disease. But we can't release you until we're sure. You're going to have to spend the next five days in quarantine."

The young girl who was with us burst into tears. "But my *folks*! They won't know what-all's *become* of us! They'll be waiting in *Killeen*!"

"You're free to telegraph. We'll take all your messages." The doctor dropped the towel onto the table and began to gather his papers. Everyone rushed over to him and started talking at once. I stood by the stationmaster's desk and watched.

A bell began to clang out on the track.

"Just a moment. Just a MOMENT," the doctor said. He glared at them like they were a pack of Indians. He waited until they were quiet. Then he said, calmly but like he'd about had it up to here, "My orderly, Ensign Parker, will provide pencils and telegraph forms. You may send a message to whomever you wish. There'll be no charge."

I was desperate. While everyone was writing his or her message I went over to the doctor and said, "Excuse me, please, sir. I'm sure there's been some mistake—." He said, "We can't take the risk. Just go with the others." I tried to tell him about my suitcase but no matter how loud I hollered the engine racket swelled up over it and then I noticed that the police officer had begun to sidle over towards me. I went back to the desk and stood there, listening to the clatter fade on down the tracks.

After everybody had written down their messages we were led back through the waiting room and out a front entrance into the night, where we piled into an open, eight-seat conveyance. We started off down the dark, wet street. I was mighty down-in-the-mouth. And if you want to know what made me really glum, well: it was a pair of goddamned *horses* pulling the thing.

I ain't going to go into detail about what happened at the quarantine station. I had all the breakfasts of grits and eggs and dinners of stew I could stand. One thing I learned was to keep my mouth shut. They let me out after five days.

I walked under a row of live oak trees down a sidewalk lined on one side with barrels with planks laid out on them—they were doing some kind of construction on the lot behind—and on the street side watering troughs that men in buggies and wagons had their horses drawn up to, to drink. It was still early morning and it was cool in the shade of the live oaks.

By nine the heat was impossible, worse than in New Orleans. I felt like I was in a sauna bath. My clothes stuck to me so I could hardly move. But every man I passed, might'near, was wearing a dark suit and walked through the heat like he didn't even notice it. The women, in godawful hats and long dresses with full skirits, tight waists and long sleeves, looked as cool as cucumbers. Leastways they made out to be. Some of them carried parasols.

The sun held up over us like a white-hot stone. I could hardly breathe. I walked all morning. One good thing was, mostly folks didn't pay attention to me, mainly on account of I did a lot of standing up close to buildings, looking into store windows. You wouldn't believe what I saw in some of those windows.

I walked under canvas awnings and wooden awnings, past rows of stores. I walked past the City Market House, a conglomeration of Victorian hash if ever I saw it. In fact, everywhere I looked it was nothing but old buildings. Only they weren't old. Not that Houston didn't have its "modern" improvements. There were electric-light poles all over the place, some with as many as six cross-bars, and it was such a raft of wires criss-crossing back and forth above the streets that a bird couldn't of lit down through them. A streetcar went by.

I walked across streets that were shoe-mouth deep in horse shit. The stink was enough to do a body in.

I was in a bad way. My wallet was gone. My Dantrium and my aspirins and my vitamins were gone. I felt like some goddamned lunatic that had got out of the nuthouse up in Austin and if I wasn't careful I was going to pull my pecker out of my pants or stand on my head or some damned thing and get sent right back up. The worst thing was, I was stone broke. Even an idiot, if he's got money in his pocket, is going to be left alone until he's spent it.

Then I remembered the silver dollar in my vest pocket. Jesus Christ, I could of kissed it. I could of bussed the feathers on the eagle's tail.

By that time it was past noon and I was so dry I was spitting cotton. A sign on a brick storefront said DRINK ORANGE CRUSH. But I was hungry too. I went into a place on Congress Avenue called Okasaki Tom Brown's Japanese Restaurant, where I had two beers and some of the queerest Japanese or Chinese food I ever ate. It was what you might call pinto-bean Japanese. It cost me fifteen cents. After I'd eaten and had the two beers, though, I felt some better.

I went back out onto the street. A dog with a brown spot over each eye, brown feet and a brown asshole trotted by, looking as optimistic as if it was certain sure there was a bone waiting for it on the sidewalk up at the next corner. Its tail wagged. *Some* things, at least, never change.

A woman in a white, flowing dress, wisps of dust lifting from the sidewalk where the hem brushed it, hurried by, her head bent forward, a purse dangling from her belt, one hand grasping a handkerchief and the handle of an open parasol, the other reaching up to adjust her hat whilst the sleeve drifted down her forearm to her elbow. It was mortal woman's hand and wrist and elbow. A row of buttons went up her back. Under the movable cloth, the lifting and falling lace, it was the same waist, backbone, breasts and hips.

Men went by with the same looks as ever of strength or weakness in their faces.

Up overhead, the same sun held.

I bought a copy of the *Houston Daily Post* from a kid who was hawking them on a street corner. I couldn't tell what the Hail Mary he was yelling. It sounded like he was talking in Karankaway. Anyway, I gave him a nickel and he gave me the paper and three cents back.

JEFFRIES WON FIGHT

Fitsimmons Put Up A Wonderful Battle, But Lost

THE CHAMPION WAS HIT HARD DURING THE CONTEST

San Francisco, July 25. —After fighting a battle of eight rounds

I turned to an inside page.

THE HOLINESS CAMP MEETING
Big Day Yesterday

CASTORIA

for Infants and Children

Governor of Alabama Endorses PE-RU-NA.

What I was looking for was some way to get some cash into my pockets. A body's got to eat. A body's got to get some kind of passable clothes so he don't stick out like a sore thumb. I found the want ads.

A good colored boy to—.

Sewing Girls.

Good Colored Cook.

100 trackmen at $1.75 and $2.00 per day.

I ain't about to break my back laying railroad ties.

WANTED—A Partner with $2000.00 for good-paying business already established. Address lock box 273, The Daily Post.

I had seventy-two cents left from the silver dollar. That ain't *too* far off of two thousand legal-tender toad skins. Anyway, there's always a fool somewhere near at hand and this might be one.

II

1907

9

They've laid my darling girl in the grave
pine coffin through fog, wet cedar boughs on the lid,
on the flatbed of a wagon through the gate
one whole *week* of this wet! Been here fifteen years and never
seen the likes. And *still* it don't let up
dripping from bushes, quick and heavy as rain
and only three or four to be with her to her graveside, not like
Catherine's funeral. I don't mean the one here, when he had
that box dug up and fetched to Alto Springs
sweet odor of corruption to the box
the one in San Marcos, where the whole town, might'near, followed her up the hillside, covering their eyes with white handkerchiefs.

It's a sin and a shame to leave a family alone with its dead.

Velma pulled the counterpane back from the bed. She stripped
off the comfort and bedclothes and shook her pillow from its
slip. Three saddle-colored hairs and one gone gray
Oh Velma, you're so plain
Mama used to say, said it now. Velma's ears flushed as quick as
if she was still a little girl. She shook her head. She folded the
comfort and put it on a chair and dumped the bedclothes on the
floor. We'll turn the tick at least. And Mr. Castleberry's bed in
the corner. It's Friday. But no use to air things out. Too wet.

"Inéz!"

"¿Sí?"

"Come in here."

Velma turned up the lamp on the table beside the bed. Already an hour past breakfast and you still can't see three feet in front of your face. I'm beginning to hate this wet. Dark enough the roosters've quit crowing, much less any kind of bird to sing. And when it's toted up it won't make one inch of real rain.

Outside the bedroom window fog dripped from the gallery eave. Texas can sure fool you in the spring.

Where's that girl? Velma stripped the bedclothes from Mr. Castleberry's settee in the corner and dumped them with the bedding on the floor.

Yes, a sin to leave a family alone with its dead. It's me the one had to wash her and lay her out. My own Victoria Ann. On her bed, fresh coverlid and plumped-up pillow, the feather wreath of death shook out, an oil lamp at her head. Inéz and old Serafina and I sat up with her. Nobody else came to pay their respects. Not a white person, one. Not even her papa, may he dance in Hell. For two years them two never said a word to each other. Both so stiff-necked. And he used to dote on Victoria Ann, wellnigh like he did on her mother. It's the baby that split the blankets between them.

That's how come nobody else came to see her through her dead-night, either. Or maybe they think I'm too proud for them. But I won't let them talk against Victoria Ann, I don't care what they think.

May the whole town meet in their hats and bonnets in Hell.

Poor soul, all she would do at the last was cough, and barely breath enough to do that. And she had got stone deaf

> hot bath. The first time to cough blood: discoloration
> of the water

to look so healthy for so long and yet be so sick! Even when she was fifteen she had that cough.

I tried to help her up so she could breathe, but she pushed me aside and fell back, working hard to get a breath. Then she laughed, it sounded just like that, and quit. I don't want to ever think on it again.

I was the one had to burn the death sheets. I was the one turned her over, and back and over

blood and sour sweat, yellow stain of iodine on her chest

my poor lamb, and washed her with tar soap. Skin and bones, and I wouldn't hardly of knowed her she was so changed, excepting from the smallpox vaccine scar big as a twenty-five-cent piece on her shoulder and the birthmark reaching a little up under her hair on the back of her neck. The last thing I did, when I'd dressed her and crossed her hands and tied closed her mouth and tied the ruffled collar up under her chin, was take my sewing scissors and trim the hair across her forehead. Still she didn't look right.

The next morning they put her in the pine box with the narrow head and foot. That's six days back! Soon it'll be a year. Then fifty years. I know.

I put a peacock feather from her room and a sprig from one of the pyracanth bushes in the yard in the coffin with her.

And Catherine dead these nineteen years

red roses, white Cape jasmine, singing and weeping, the

organ pumping in the crowded, flower-filled parlor

a hundred years, ten hundred years, on out past knowing or any kind of thought.

You might as well of been sisters, not flesh out of flesh. Two little girls, might'near, barring the years, that could of been laid out in sweet sash dresses side by side.

But *my* Victoria Ann. Mine. My own. Yes, I know, Catherine, Sister: your Victoria Ann. But you surely left her when you died. It was a kind of crime.

"*Inéz!*"

Inéz appeared in the bedroom doorway.

"Where's the baby?"

"*Con mi hermanita.*"

"Well, come help me turn this tick."

Wet branches on the coffin lid, the wagon through
the stone-arched gate

and her papa went to open the store that day just like it was any
kind of work day.

Well, my heart broke long ago. I can't cry.

"Take hold of that corner."

They flipped the heavy tick over on the bed. Then they turned
the pallet on Mr. Castleberry's settee. They put fresh bedclothes
on both bed and settee and covered them with the unaired
counterpanes. They'll have to do.

Velma pointed to the soiled bedclothes. "Take those out to the
wash house." Inéz knelt and gathered the bedclothes in her
arms. When she stood back up she could hardly see up over the
bundle to find her way. Velma picked up the runner and scarves
that she'd taken from the side table and bureaus earlier and
heaped them on the bedding in Inéz's arms.

"If you've finished the breakfast dishes, empty the water from
under the ice box onto my bed of cannas by the back step."

"*Sí, cómo no.*"

She understands might'near ever' word I say, but she just
won't talk it. That's the kind of backwater I get, and from a
thirteen-year-old. But I'm not about to talk Mexican.

Inéz carried the soiled bedclothes into the hall and towards the
back gallery door. It was so muffled outside Velma could barely
hear the screen door slam.

Oh, but the crickets and frogs. Little frogs the size of the end
of a lead pencil all over the ground. Frogs and night crickets.
So much noise at night you can't sleep.

Velma swept the straw carpet, being careful not to raise dust
since the room couldn't be aired yet. She dusted the black walnut
side table by the bed, spread a fresh oval of lacework on it and
put back the lamp and a glass tumbler in crocheted mesh that
held buttons, pins, needles, thread and other such odds and
ends. She wiped the base of the lamp and its milk-glass shade

> gown of white brocade, lace sleeves, high-necked collar
> trimmed with pearls

oiled the wardrobe and the two bureaus with marble tops and spread out fresh runners on the bureaus.

Yes, I was in love with him, from the sixth grade on. Papa used to have him to the house. Then he left teaching at the Institute to go manage the cotton gin outside San Marcos. But he used to come to the house often. Oh he was handsome, no, *beautiful*, with those blue eyes like clearest, richest jewels, I thought, and the distinguished nose and chin, the dark sideburns and mustache. And so tall. I thought he danced the moon up and the sun down. Sometimes I cried, nights in my bed, thinking on him. Alton Travis Castleberry. *Mr.* Alton Travis Castleberry. Mr. *Castle*berry. *Al.* Ton. *Tra.* Vis. *Cas.* Tle. *Ber.* Ry. Al-ton-Tra-vis-Cas-tle-ber-ry. I'd say it over and over, to the ceiling or to my pillow. Over and over, and over and over and over and over till I was numb, like in prayer. If he wrote anything on my school papers I'd blush to the roots, whether what he wrote was good or bad. If it was bad, the grammar or somesuch, I'd want to die. Sometimes when he came to the house to visit with Papa I'd watch from a window while he stepped down from his buggy and tied the horse. It made the blood stop in my throat to see him come up the walk. Catherine and I had to serve the teacakes and coffee, in the front room or in good weather on the back veranda, especially if Mama was at one of her church meetings. I was tongue-tied. I couldn't talk. Catherine, who was four years younger than me, talked a blue streak, till Papa finally'd kiss us both and send us to another part of the house. Catherine hadn't any self-consciousness at all. Even when we were both older, Catherine talked.

> Catherine in lilac, a rose sash to her waist, her bulging
> forehead and round, baby face, her loose, black hair,
> washed and soft, already coming to her waist

I pulled her back as far as I could and pushed her in front of me and ran under the swing to make it go as high as I could, it looked high to me

her hair flies behind her when she goes forward and
gathers around her face when she swings back, her little
fists grab the ropes

she wasn't scared at all

Catherine in the new white princess dress, pearl buttons
and pale embroidered ruffles, a satin ribbon on the back
of her head binding the long fall of tresses, her head
back and her mouth open, down at the rail on her first
communion, taking the crumb on her tongue, sip of
grape juice

nobody could keep their eyes off her. The whole church meeting had its eyes on her when she and the rest of Mrs. Kincheloe's Sunday-school class went down to the front

angel come down to be a twelve-year-old child in a
white princess dress

and she could do needlework and drawnwork, could read French, could play the parlor organ. She could play the piano when she was ten. Ever'body sat and listened to her. Victoria Ann was the same way. And I couldn't, and can't, even sing.

Velma cleaned the window panes with a piece of paper. Fog in the chinaberry tree, wet bushes

walking behind her, carrying lilies or orange blossoms
I don't remember which

white brocaded gown, pearls at the neck, lace sleeves
with pearled wrists, the short train and bridal veil

I didn't hear the music. I didn't see the faces each side the aisle like dozens of sheep or feel the floor under my feet or the flowers in my arms when I walked behind her with my blood stopped in my heart, tomorrow a hole I couldn't even crawl into, and him down there in front of the pews waiting for her to be his bride. She was sixteen years old.

And she didn't even want children! I remember when her and Mr. Castleberry had moved out to Alto Springs—they'd been married three years—and Mr. Castleberry was doing fine with his new store and the warehouse and had a hand in the founding of the bank here too, and Mama and me came out here to visit them. I thought this was the most beautiful house I'd ever seen. It was the prettiest, most up-to-date house in town then, with its curved gallery and the long breezeway and the beautiful bedrooms and front room and parlor and dining room and all the beautiful curtains and fine bedroom suites and teakwood tables and black, upholstered furniture brought down from Chicago or Dallas. And Catherine said to me, "I don't want children. I want to have a good time." It shocked me so. Oh, I was shocked.

Still, she had Victoria Ann. And the next year, at that. But there were complications. She just would get right on up after having the baby, and her health got worse and worse. Finally Mr. Castleberry let her and the baby come back to San Marcos, thinking the trip might do her some good. She hadn't been home two weeks when she took awful sick and died, just like that. It took three days to get the news to Alto Springs. It was August, and so she was buried in San Marcos. He got there the day after the funeral and went out to the grave and flung himself onto it and stayed there until dark. The next year he had her body fetched back to Alto Springs. Victoria Ann stayed with Mama and me for a year.

Well, it's still Catherine's house. He won't let anything be changed. Just my plants. That's the only way I know it's mine.

Velma wiped the leaves of the geraniums and begonias on the windowsill and rotated the clay pots. And she had three dozen geraniums in pots, on the stairstep risers to the front gallery, that she and Inéz had taken out yesterday from under cover in their winter pit along the south side of the house. And there were zinnias and phlox and pinks and purple flag about to come up in the yard, and later in the spring her yellow cannas and showy four o'clocks.

Velma picked up her feather duster and the dustpan and oil rag and broom. She turned down the lamp and blew it out. The bowl was one-fourth full. Inéz'll take all the lamps to the kitchen later, to be filled. I hope I don't have to tell her. She doesn't remember anything. Or she doesn't care. Velma closed the bedroom door and went up the hall to the front room. Inéz was, for a wonder, already there, starting to take down the curtains. Her younger sister was with her, playing with Earl Leroy. Velma said, "Take him out of here." Inéz said something in Spanish to her sister, who picked up Earl Leroy and carried him off somewhere.

Even in the front room, with three big windows that went clear to the floor, it was dark, and Velma lit the lamp on the marble-topped table at the end of the day lounge. While Inéz was taking down the curtains, Velma swept the ceiling and corners of the room. Inéz piled the curtains outside in the hall. Then she and Velma rolled up the Brussels carpet and put it out in the hall. Velma swept the floor and dusted, and Inéz cleaned the ashes out of the stove. She started with the ash bucket out into the hall. Velma called after her, "Fetch back some hot soap and water."

Sharp nose, thin mouth and narrow upper lip. Velma unlocked the glass doors of the bookcase. It's Papa's mouth. It doesn't look so cold on a man. She opened the pair of doors and commenced to take out each book in turn and wipe it with a cloth. *St. Elmo. Quentin Durward.*

Even on our wedding night he went to his own bed
       one end is tied to a tree. Catherine holds the other end
       of the rope and swings it, and Velma skips—

> *"What shall I wear on my*
> *wedding day?*
> *Silk, satin, calico, rags,*
> *silk, satin, calico, rags"*

and said to me, "What comes after the first love is the rose when it's withered and lost its perfume." That was so cruel! Oh, there were times. And still not to have any little ones of my own
       the pain, the water and the blood
to see that thing in the chamber pot! To see it three times.

Velma's hand shook. She managed to shove the book into its space between two others.

Well, I believe in the Christian stars.

Inéz came back with a bucket of suds and hot water and one of rinse water. They moved the furniture to one end of the room and commenced to scrub the floor. Velma dipped her rag in the hot rinse water and wrung it and wiped up some suds. Inéz sneezed.

"What on *earth*!"

"*El diablo nunca descansa*." Inéz sneezed again and laughed.

A puredee child. If I could just get decent help. But the good help left long ago.

When we came home from our wedding Mr. Castleberry was good to me. But I saw soon enough he wasn't really interested. He just wanted company. All I had was Victoria Ann
                        through the stone-arched gate
no, don't think on that. Just keep working
                        head on the pillow
I trimmed the hair across her forehead with my scissors
        closed eyes, one sprung partway open, edge of milky
        gray behind the slit
it just wouldn't close
        cotton in nostrils, the nose already losing its shape, going
        flat, lifted chin, lips drawn apart for all there was a
        napkin brought up and tied in a knot on top of her head,
        white muslin shroud coming below her feet and, towards
        morning, fresh trickle from her mouth, stain by her ear
        on the pillow

                "Mother, Mother, I am sick.
                Call the doctor quick, quick, quick

stop

                Mother, Mother, I am sick"

stop, I said. "Stop!"

Velma looked up. Inéz was staring at her.

"Get back to your work!"

Inéz recommenced scrubbing.

Oh, leave her be. It's no use to go around feeling mean-tempered. We have to love the Lord Jesus and do as He did.

Velma and Inéz moved the furniture to the other end of the room and commenced to scrub the remaining half of the floor

> Victoria Ann climbing up the stile in front of the house,
> lifting the hem of her riding skirt out of the way of her
> feet. Jésu, the gardener, holds the reins while Victoria
> Ann puts her leg over the double horn, eases onto the
> saddle, gets her foot into the stirrup. She adjusts her
> riding habit and Jésu passes the reins up to her.—*Oh*
> *Auntie, I've got sense enough, it's just it always turns*
> *up too late to help*

about something I'd scolded her for

> beaver hat, hair cut across her forehead, done in a bun
> at the nape of her neck

she just wouldn't put up her hair like her schoolfriends did, she had to do ever'thing her own way

> light-complexioned face, quick gray eyes, dark eyebrows
> and dark lashes, laughing, half-parted lips, dark-blue
> riding habit wellnigh skintight, the tiny feet in low-
> heeled, high-topped shoes

wanted so much starch in her petticoats they rattled like news-papers

> fifteen years old. Victoria Ann gives Badger a rap with
> her whip and the horse bolts down the street for all like
> a fox has hold to its tail.

She rode him so straight-backed! And you could tell where she was by the dust. The most reckless, light-hearted, self-reliant thing I've ever seen, bar none.

Won the prize in the fourth grade in school for having the best posture in her class

> nostrils stuffed with cotton, stain by her ear on the pillow

Oh, it's so dark outside it makes me want to die. It's like a bad

dream. And it's going to fester flies, all this warm wet. Need a
norther to clear it away.

   Velma scrubbed
      riding a stick horse with a plumy chinaberry tail
music lessons from Miss
                  perched on books to the piano . . .
   When Victoria Ann was thirteen ever'body thought she was
sixteen. She thought so too. But I knew better
      dinner table. Serafina reaches over Victoria Ann's
      shoulder to put some food on the table. She screams
      and drops the dish: pet green lizard hanging from
      Victoria Ann's ear
squeeze its jaw, its mouth'll open, you can catch it to your ear
lobe
      white belly, pink throat, long, dangling tail
and Mr. Castleberry never gave her a licking for anything. He
always gave her three-days' grace and by that time he'd forget.

         I'll never marry. —Child, ever' young
      girl says that
I had to laugh
      —I don't have any friends. —You don't have girlfriends
      because you don't have little secrets and pass notes like
      other girls do. You don't have anything to hide. —I want
      to go to San Antonio and be a great singer. I want to go
      to Chicago and learn to play on something besides this
      old moldy upright thing. —It's your mother's piano.
      —I love Alto Springs. I love the sky. I love the night
      breeze. It's given me good health and lots of color
and then turn right around and say
      Might's well be living in a desert. I'd like to shave my
      head so as not to have to all the time be putting up my
      hair. —Victoria Ann! —What if nothing ever happens
      to me? What if I just live and then go ahead and die

I swear, trying to keep up with her was enough to give a body the fits.

And then she went through her "simple" phase, when she wouldn't wear anything but dark clothes
Two Havana waists and two black skirts are all I need
a year
insisted on washing her own change of linen ever' Saturday and putting up her own hair and keeping her room and eating the plainest foods
That's all I want or need
only she'd be furious if she found onions in anything. Sweet, silly thing. "Where's she get that foolishness?" Mr. Castleberry'd say, as if it was my fault. And in the next breath tell me a certain amount of tomfoolery's as necessary for a child as a certain amount of air is to breathe.

When a baby's put on a bottle instead of nursing its mama, it's certain sure to be hardheaded. Victoria Ann didn't give up that black rubber nipple till she was five. I'd try to break her of the habit and he'd always tell me to leave her be.

Victoria Ann was born with a victory cap on her head.

The rest of us were born bald-headed.

Click of the front gate. Velma heard *that* through the fog. Up onto the gallery and through the front door. *Tap tap tap* of Mr. Castleberry's bootheels on the hard pine flooring as he came down the hall. He didn't look in when he went by the front room, though the curtains and the rolled carpet were in the hallway, and anyway he knew they were there, it being Friday housecleaning. He went into the bedroom, the next room down, and Velma heard him moving around in there. He's forgot his spectacles again. Or that medicine he keeps in the drawer. Mr. Castleberry came back out of the bedroom. He came by the front room again and went out the front door. And—Velma listened real hard—the front gate clicked.

He hates to stay here and he hates to go to the store.

—Shut the door to her room and never came out again. Closed

the shutters and pulled the curtains to, burnt an oil lamp night and day. You could hardly breathe in that place. If I tried to ask her why all this, she wouldn't say anything. I was afraid if I kept after her she wouldn't let even me in.

Mr. Castleberry never went in to see her or to speak to her. Not for two whole years. He'd hardly even talk to *me*, after that. I said something about it. He said, "Have something to say. Say it. Quit talking."

I fetched her her food. She got to coughing worse and worse. And when she had that baby—her health was so poor by then I don't know how-all it was bornt alive—she said, "Its name's Earl Leroy." She insisted on that, as if it weren't already shame enough to fill all four corners and then some. After it was born she said, "I don't want to look at it. Take it away."

> *To think a nice young man like that*
>> in the new dress Mr. Castleberry had got her for her
>> ninth birthday, and she sits on the window seat, twisting
>> and untwisting the ribbon-end of her sash around one
>> of her fingers and looking downhearted. —*What's all*
>> *this about?—I hope I never have smallpox but grow*
>> *up to be pretty and have a beautiful voice and get*
>> *married*

I laughed and went over to her and kissed her and told her not to be morbid. "You've had a lovely birthday party, and all your friends are out in the yard. Go play."

> Came home one evening from the eighth grade in school
>> *boys aren't worth the trouble it takes to try to get 'em*
>> *to understand. I'm only going to love dogs. Boys and*
>> *cats're fools.*

flung a book onto the floor

>> *I'm tired of reading. I want to do*

went out and climbed the fig tree and stained her dress.

Velma and Inéz oiled the furniture. They replaced the needle-work on the backs of the lounge and Morris chair. They cleaned the windows and put up fresh curtains. They fetched in the rolled-up carpet from the hall, to be left against one of the base-

boards till the floor was dry. Inéz picked up the curtains that
were in the hall and took them out to the wash house. Velma
followed her down the hallway towards the kitchen. At the ell,
where the hallway turned to the left, she saw one of the curtains
on the floor. She picked it up and got to the door just in time to
catch Inéz. The fog dripped from the gallery eave. Wet spider
webs laced the rose bushes down below the gallery rail. A wagon
went by, like a wooden ghost, somewhere out in the street. Velma
closed the door and started back up the hall towards the kitchen
        brushed hair and closed, white face, the crossed hands
the hands that pushed me away! Velma stopped in front of the
door to Victoria Ann's room. *Oh, I don't care! If she could be
here. If I could bring her back to her room. If she could hear and
I could talk to her and she was my own little girl again.* Velma
pushed the door partway open, half expecting to see Victoria
Ann. *My dear. My child. My own.*

Smell of Creo-Carboline and formaldehyde solution, though
the room had been airing for a week. Stripped-bare, disinfected
walls, brass bedstead with empty frame, empty clothes press,
empty chiffonier
        peacock feathers, crepe-paper roses, collection of fancy
        candy boxes stacked in the corner, a horse's blue-and-
        yellow fly net stretched out on the wall—cabinet photos,
        postal cards, invitations and valentines tucked in the
        meshes—books all over the place
Mr. Castleberry spoiled her by buying her any novel she wanted
        fan of pink curlew wings, pyramid of pillows in slips
        decorated with embroidered red peacocks and fluted
        ruffles, the fancy wash stand and mirror
it's cold and dismal in this place as a tomb.

Two serious beaux and it both times came to grief. Victoria
Ann was happy as a June bug when Mr. Gilstrap proposed to
her. I thought she was young
        *Mama married you when she was sixteen, didn't she,
        Papa*

ran over and kissed her father. And of course he just went along
with everything. For certain sure he was *proud* of the match.
Carson Gilstrap had fourteen sections of land along the breaks
of the West Nueces, a few miles out of town. He had a good
run of stock. He was the most eligible bachelor in the county.
And when the engagement was final he went and built a lovely
new ranch house, just for Victoria Ann. He'd of gave Victoria
Ann the sky if she'd asked for it. The ranch house had a long
gallery and a cedar-stake fence around it to keep out stock and
he planted pecan trees in the yard. Victoria Ann and I drove
out there lots of times for her to make up her mind what kind
of furniture and all was going to go into it. Mr. Gilstrap was a
sweet-tempered man who stammered a mite. He came of good
family, from over near Johnson City. Then he was killed the
week before the wedding day by that Mexican they caught
     dust in a cloud from off the street, the noise
the whole crowd of them went right by the house, in broad daylight, some on horseback, most afoot, I saw it. There was nigh
a hundred of them, even little boys. Otis Twelves and Buckle
Satterwhite pushed him in front of them, he was just a young
thing
     arms tied, blood coming out of his nose and mouth,
     gun-blue hair tangled with blood and sweat
stumbled in front of the house, crying hard. He wasn't but about
twenty years old
    Mrs. Castleberry, get back in the house
somebody yelled. They'd made the sheriff hand him over. They
took him out to the edge of town where some of the men had
already built a brush pile. I saw the smoke go up to the sky.
Later the sheriff and his deputies went out to the spot and held
an inquest: death by burning at the hands of parties unknown.
    Inéz came back up the steps from the wash house. Velma
went down the hall to the kitchen. In the kitchen Earl Leroy
was sitting on a chair up to the table, eating a piece of dried
fruit. His eyes came just to the edge of the table. Inéz's little

sister Graciela was sitting at the end of the table playing with one
of Earl Leroy's toys, a string of thread spools. She wasn't all that
much older than the baby. Earl Leroy squinched up his face and
tried to crawl down from the chair when Velma came in.

I can't stand to look at him. He ain't a pretty baby. And I see
those St. Clair eyes ever'time I look.

And her and Mr. Castleberry both so prideful stubborn

       The gray suit moving back down the front walk,
   the head bent over in that puzzled way

       Victoria Ann's face to the wall, refusing to budge
       Mr. Castleberry's lips stretched tight behind the
latched screen door *I no longer* have *a daughter, sir.*
It's a wonder he wasn't bornt dead.

Velma went to the stove. She opened the draft and slid a
saucepan of sweet boiled cocoa-and-water onto the heat. The
coffee, at the back of the cookstove, was already hot. When the
cocoa-and-water was about to come to a boil, Velma went to the
icebox and got a jar of milk. The drip from the icebox peedled
into the pan. Velma said as she crossed back to the stove, "I told
you to take that icebox water out."

"*Lo siento.*"

"Do it *now.*"

"*Ya me voy.*"

Inéz got down on her hands and knees and pulled the pan
from under the icebox. It was about to spill over. Graciela ran
to the kitchen door and opened it and ran out onto the back
steps and held the screen door open for her sister, who staggered
down the steps with the pan of water. Of course Graciela let the
screen door slam.

I can't get help. Even Serafina quit. "I'm too old, *Señora,* and
I have my own family."

Velma poured half of the jar of milk into the saucepan. She
stirred the cocoa and let it heat. She stuck a finger into the
saucepan. When the cocoa was warm she slid the pan away
from the hot stovelid and got three cups from the kitchen safe.

Put the baby to nurse with a Mexican woman. For certain sure I wasn't able to tend to him. I had my hands full with Victoria Ann.

Velma poured cocoa into the three cups.

You *wanted* Victoria Ann to be sick. You wanted her to yourself.

That's not true.

You were *glad* Mr. Castleberry wouldn't have anything to do with her, or with that man.

"*Inéz.*" But Inéz was standing right by Velma's elbow. In a calmer voice Velma said, "Give this to the baby. The other two're for you and Graciela."

"*¡Ay, qué bueno!*" Inéz's face was high-cheeked, brown as a parched coffee bean. Her eyes were an Indian's. Already plump, already turning into a woman. She'll be hitched by the time she's fourteen and that's the end of this help, such as it is.

Button by button and thread by thread the whole world's coming apart.

Velma shut the firebox draft. The flame in the box roared, then choked. She took her cup and saucer down from the warming-shelf and poured hot coffee into the cup. "I'm going to the dining room. We'll start in in there directly. Drink your *choco-láhtee.*"

"*Gracias, Señora.*"

In the dining room, Velma sat to the table. She breathed in the steam from the hot coffee

> head under a newspaper, face red above a pan of boiling
> onion, petrolatum and water

Mama treating the chest colds Catherine and I got three times a year, sure as the cat had kittens.

The fog collected and ran down the outsides of the windows. Velma sipped her coffee. I talked to Mr. Castleberry, after the awful thing that happened to Carson Gilstrap. I wanted to get Victoria Ann away, send her to San Marcos or to visit her cousin in Corpus Christi, and for once he agreed with something I said.

But Victoria Ann wouldn't do it. "I'm going to stay here. I'm going to be gay despite ever'thing."

Fourth of July picnic. After the picnic and speeches, Mr. St. Clair and his son Earl Leroy, who was managing his papa's campaign, came to the house. We had a cold supper, fried chicken and deviled eggs and green onions. The senator loved my fig preserves and my pickled-peach-and-black-walnut pie. "Mrs. Castleberry, too many folks pass through life not knowing the *humanizing* effects of a good meal," and laughed that way he had like you were his oldest, best friend. I liked him. I liked his son too. And anyway, how many folks get to have a state senator to the house at the peak of the primaries? They stayed three days

> in the orchard, walking back and forth between rows
> of peach and plum trees

I saw them when I came out of the kitchen onto the back steps
                        laughing and talking

Victoria Ann

> white lawn dress, waist with Irish lace on the sleeves,
> the China-silk fan that she sometimes used, sometimes
> let dangle by a colored ribbon from her wrist

and the young St. Clair

> dove-gray suit coat, white silk vest and white cravat

taller'n her by a head. I saw him bend to her

> stops, and he puts something in her hand and she laughs.

Junior partner in his papa's law firm.

And her engaged to Carson Gilstrap! It makes me heartsick.

Inéz came into the dining room. Velma handed her the coffee cup. "Take this out to the kitchen." Velma got up and went to the sideboard. She took the silverware from its drawer and laid it out on the table for Inéz to polish. While Inéz was polishing the silver, Velma took the platter and commemorative plates and the covered soupbowl off the sideboard and ran an oil rag over the veneer. She emptied the cabinet and cleaned the cabinet shelves and windows and mirrors. Then she wiped the things she'd taken out and put everything back in its place. When Inéz had finished polishing the silver, Velma sent her to the kitchen to clean the lamp chimneys and refill the half-empty bowls.

> Fever powders in small papers on the table by
>> the bed

hot and cold by turns. Fever ever' evening and the middle of ever' night. Went from her bed to her chair to her bed and back again. Almost'd fall out of the chair with her cough. I tried to read to her. I tried to fix her interesting meals and fetch her cheery things

> *I wish someone'd cut the head off of ever' body I know.—*
> *Even me? —Oh, not you*

was barely able, finally, to sit up and eat

> *I never had a childhood*

pushed away the food

> *I'm tired of life on account of I'm tired of it.*

Inéz returned with the freshly filled oil lamp. Earl Leroy was standing in the doorway. He had cocoa on his face and the front of his dress, and his thumb was stuck in his mouth. He had cocoa in his hair too. He was a mess. Graciela caught him by the hand and led him away.

Velma and Inéz put a fresh linen cloth on the table and Velma sprinkled water on the feathery asparagus fern she used for a centerpiece. She put clean napkins at the two places. —I don't know what-all for. *He* won't notice it. He never notices anything anymore. He doesn't care about anything. He's quit the board of directors of the bank. When they bought out his share at the mohair warehouse he didn't put up any kind of fuss. And the store: folks come in and he doesn't pay any attention to them. He leaves it all to the clerks, who're robbing him blind. He doesn't care what he eats or how-all he dresses and I'm ashamed to see him go out into the street.

I'm sick to death of this slow wet. I want a blue norther to come blow it away. I want to hear the windmill pumping again.

Aisles between dark, varnished display counters. Smell of yard goods, harness and new rope. Barrels of vinegar, coal oil, sorghum, flour. Shoes. Hats. Buckets, kegs, tubs. Canned goods on shelves. Saddles and chamber pots hanging from the ceiling

---

A. T. CASTLEBERRY

• WHOLESALE & RETAIL •

GENERAL MERCHANDISE

---

but it was best when Junior Luckett ran the store. That man had a head for commerce. It freed Mr. Castleberry to give all his time to the warehouse business. And honest? The Devil could of run a herd of steers with golden horns and dropping diamond cow plops and Mr. Luckett would of walked right on through them and slapped a twine on the one piece of honest business on hoofs. Pretty soon he was running the place.

He used to bring the account books to the house ever' Friday evening. I'd watch him come up the gravel walk with that nod he always made to one side as he limped, swatting a hand in the air to fight off the two scissortails that flogged at him whenever he came under their nest. I had to laugh. Those birds flogged at cats and dogs that came in the yard, and crows and hawks and him, but never anybody else. When he got to the back door he'd be in a sweat. But he was always nice-mannered. He had a queer look to one side of his face the way that if you were to hold a breadboard or somesuch up to the one side and then the other, it'd be two different faces. He was short. But wiry, not fat. It looked like his waist came right up under his armpits. He could laugh, though. At himself, too. "A feller with my good looks, Mrs. Castleberry, has got to be able to laugh." Just about ever'body liked him, from the first day he set foot in town. The only one who didn't cotton to him was Victoria Ann.

He was mighty handy, and he did a lot of things for us around the house. He was a good churchgoer, too.

But once I heard Victoria Ann calling him down. They were out by the front gate

What's your business

she stamped her foot

*I said, what's your business? —Your papa sent me to
fetch you this. —Good. Now you can head on back.*

It was the only time I'd ever heard her be rude to anyone. It shocked me to hear her talk like that. I said something to her about it

*I'd as soon see a cow full-up of wood ticks as look at him.
—That's no way to behave towards anyone. Mr. Luckett's
a gentle, good-natured young man. Ever' body else likes
him. —He's ugly as homemade sin*

went in a huff to her room. I didn't even try to call her back. The very thought that a one I'd loved and raised would look down on anyone, would behave towards anyone like that, fetched tears to my eyes. She must of took what I said to heart, though, on account of I never saw her act like that to him again.

Velma left Inéz to scrub the dining-room floor and went up the hallway to the parlor. Can't see the cast-iron fence or the street even from in here, for all the fog. Can't even see the front-yard rose bush.

I am so *tired*. It don't seem like I ever get my rest anymore, nights.

And poor Mr. Luckett dead, finally. They found him face down in the Nueces River, at the first crossing. Oh, it seems like ever'body around here dies in a hard way. There was young Jesse Zoeller who got knocked off his horse by a tree branch. And Gus Haines who shot Billy Bob Quarternight while they were hunting turkeys down on the Agua Fria a couple-three years ago. And Alva Pryor, on a picnic, who got stung so bad by bees she couldn't breathe. And even the bones the Mexican sheep-herder out to the Altonsall place found under a cedar bush, that

Sheriff Taylor was called out to see about and nobody ever knew
the name or reason for.

I'm so godawful lonesome. It's so far out here from anywheres
it's halfway to Hell. And Mama dead. And Papa dead. *Mama,
where are you? Catherine*

in the swing
*when we fought so and played with our dolls and made doll
clothes*

the upstairs balcony above the privet-shaded alley,
locusts in summer shrilling in the trees, the veranda,
the parlor, the streets of San Marcos
Papa, who used to trot me on your knee!

The man leans over the child's shoulder
that's *me! I've got Papa all to myself today*

Shows her how to bait the hook, the curve clear through
the innards. The worm, color of mud, twists and untwists
its free end in a gut-like tangle. Then he shows her how
to swing it out onto the water and let the cork plop, pole
so long it's hard to hold
cool under the trees, and the coolness off the San Marcos river.
The water goes so fast

transparent, muscular. Water weeds wave through shades
of green and blue
but I'm not afraid. Papa has his arm around me
bluegills and sunfish and Rio Grande perch hover in
the space between the weeds, above the white gravel.
—*Papa, I can see them!* The cork floats on the water
and then bobs again. The man has an arm around the
child. He helps her hold the pole. Out in the middle of
the river the water glitters like mirrors. Above the willows
and moss-hung oaks is brightest sunlight, but here under
the trees it's shady and cool and the man, who has taken
off his coat and slung it across a limb of a live oak a little
way back from the riverbank, kneels beside the child.
He keeps an arm around her, being careful not to muss
too much her white summer dress, and helps her hold

the pole. His chin almost touches the top of her head.

He kisses the top of her head.

A fly buzzed in the room. A leaf of dried abelia broke from its bouquet and ticked onto the mantel. Hot tears sprang to Velma's eyes and before she knew what was happening spilled and ran in burning streaks down her face. She sat blindly in her chair, leaning forward as if she had a pain in her gut, and put her apron to her face. She didn't make any sound. Her shoulders shook. The grief was so great it knocked every thought out of her head. She commenced to rock back and forth in a kind of madness of grief. It was the first time she'd cried since Victoria Ann's death.

Finally she quieted. She dried her face on her apron and sat up straight in the chair, took a handkerchief out of the apron pocket and blew her nose. Something made a sound over near the parlor door.

It was Earl Leroy. He was standing in the doorway, staring at her. He was barefoot and wore a loose, waistless dress with cocoa all over the front of it. Somebody'd washed his face but he still had cocoa in his hair, which stuck out every which way. His face was thin and pointy-chinned and his ears stuck out like jug handles on both sides. One of his fists was on the door knob, the other was bunching up the front of his dress.

Velma said, "Come here, child."

Earl Leroy stepped back and fell. He began to cry. Velma went over to him. Graciela came running from the kitchen and Inéz stuck her head out of the dining-room doorway. Velma gestured to them both to go back. She picked up Earl Leroy. He screamed and fought. It was like she had a trapped badger in her arms. She said, "Shhh. Shhh. Shhh." She carried him kicking and squalling into the parlor and sat with him in a rocking chair. She said, "Stop that. I ain't going to eat you." Earl Leroy grabbed hold of Velma's apron bib and wailed. Velma rocked back and forth. "There, there, there, there." He kept his face pressed to the bib and his sobs went through Velma's breastbone. "Now shush. Rude little thing! You've been raised from pillar to post." She held him away from her and looked at him and he let out another red-faced wail. Well, he *is* ugly. I don't know as I've ever seen uglier child from fairer parents.

Of a sudden she laughed. Oh, we can't all of us be bornt pretty! She held him to her again.

She rocked back and forth. The chair under her creaked like it had a cricket in one of its rungs. The longer Velma rocked, the quieter Earl Leroy became. There was a sour, baby-smell to him.

I've been so wrong, little Earl! I won't hate you anymore. The front of her shirtwaist was wet from his runny nose and his tears.

Fifty years. A hundred years. A hundred thousand years.

If this fog don't let up we'll have catfish swimming in the pyracanth bushes.

Velma heisted Earl Leroy higher, so that his head was up under her chin.

She rocked back and forth. She commenced to hum.

III

1904

10

> *"Delightful Wyoming! beneath thy skies*
> *The happy shepherd swains had nought to do*
> *But feed their flocks on green declivities*
> *Or skim perchance thy lakes with light canoe*
> *From morn till evening's sweeter pastime grew,*
> *With timbrel, when beneath the forest brown*
> *Thy lovely maidens would the dance renew,*
> *And aye those sunny mountains, halfway down,*
> *Would echo flageolet from some romantic town."*

Crisp, orange sunlight—the evening sun about to hit down behind shinnery and mesquites in the vacant lot across the street—struck in through the dining-room window. It lit the fork on Victoria Ann's plate, next the piece of cake she hadn't touched yet. After the declamation everybody laughed and clapped, and Victoria Ann, might'near laughing her ownself, brushed her skirt under her and sat back down to the table.

Declivity. Flageolet. But of course that's what old Miss Carruthers in school—black shirtwaist and black skirt, streaked-gray hair done up like a cowpaddy on top of her head and every day a different, little gold pin stuck like a crawly, shiny bug on the front of her "bust"—had you to say out an assigned poem by heart each week in class for, the old coot: to make you look

up in the dictionary every blessed word you didn't know, and
you'd better know what it meant and say it *right*, too, or you'd
be up there the rest of the morning, front desk, middle row,
under her eagle eyes and hawk nose.

"And-that's exac—that's exac—that's just the way it was!"
Carson said. When Carson was seventeen, he'd gone up to
Wyoming to work for a cousin who had a ranch there. He'd
stayed there four years.

Carson's forehead was shiny with sweat. Even his hair was
beginning to look wet, like a boy up from swimming in a stock
tank. For the past hour he'd been acting a mite silly. *Everybody*
was getting a mite silly, the men especially, even Papa, who
sat up there at the head of the table looking at Victoria Ann like
he thought she was funny as a crutch. It must be Papa's Old
Forrester, that the menfolk had been sipping at off and on since
dinner and right on up to supper. Of course Auntie and Victoria
Ann hadn't been allowed to touch it. It was the company that
made Victoria Ann excited and breathless. It likely showed in
her cheeks.

Victoria Ann cocked her head and peered across the table at
Carson. "Lovely maidens?"

Carson grinned. "Them poor gals danced their sh-shoe soles
through. The woods were full of 'em. It got so's a body couldn't
s-sleep for the noise."

Victoria Ann sniffed and said, "Not that you wanted to."

Everybody laughed. Weldon, Carson's brother, who was
twenty-two, six years younger than him, said, "Look out there,
Gip." That's what Carson's two brothers called him—"Gip."
They'd been calling him that all day. Victoria Ann couldn't
get used to it. She'd never call him that, and she didn't mean to
let *them* do it either, leastways not in her presence, once she
and Carson were married. It just didn't set right.

Hollis, Carson's other brother, said to him, "Don't dig up
more snakes than you can kill."

"Oh, foo," Victoria Ann said. "Thunder ain't rain." Hollis
blushed. Hollis had sandy hair like Carson's, but a thinner,

sharper-nosed face, strong mouth and chin and the Gilstrap family eyes, blue and a mite sleepy-lidded. There was a tiny black mole at the edge of his lower lip, and another, even smaller, just below his left eye. He was going on nineteen. Victoria Ann had already made him blush twice, earlier today, just by looking him straight in the face.

But it's true, she *had* been jealous a minute ago, when Carson had got to teasing her. It'd surprised her that she'd felt that. She'd told herself a long while back (when she was thirteen and was in love with Brother Dement, the new Methodist minister, and he'd finally gone and married Ora May Crooms, who taught piano and sang in the choir: Victoria Ann's ears reddened with the silly thought of it) that she'd never let herself feel jealous again. It blinded a body to too many things. And anyway, she knew Carson was hers, as safe as if he was her ownself and as gentle in his love as a lamb sucking milk-wet fingers. He never said much, maybe partly on account of his stammer, which Victoria Ann couldn't figure out rhyme nor reason for: he knew his own mind, lord knows. Everybody she knew looked up to him. Papa most of all, and as far as Victoria Ann could figure out, Carson's own mama and papa and brothers and sisters well-nigh adored him. But there was no curing that stammer, she'd tried. They'd worked hours at it, out on the side gallery or when they went riding or to take a walk, away from everybody else. But there was no snaking it out. It was like witch's fire in the brush that you can't put your hands to, and she'd end up stammering her ownself till they'd the both of them be laughing so hard they couldn't quit.

The whole east wall of the room was on fire with the light of sundown excepting where feathery shadows of mesquite tree tops were beginning to move on up it. For a minute everybody's face was orange and the talk seemed feverish. But it'd be dark before they knew it, the sun goes down so quick, and Auntie slapped the tea bell for Serafina to come in and light the lamp.

They say tickling a baby's feet might-will make it stutter.

Victoria Ann looked across the table at Carson and he saw her and smiled, then turned back to listen to whatever-all it was Papa was saying. Of a sudden Victoria Ann felt tingly and trembly. She wanted to reach across and touch Carson's hand, but of course you don't do that in company.

What was he like when he was seventeen, that year he'd gone up to Wyoming—one year older than she was now? The same sandy, curly hair, large forehead and tipped-up, boyish nose, the reddish-blond eyebrows and serious blue eyes, the same little *declivity* above his upper lip that sometimes she just wanted—Victoria Ann looked down at her plate so nobody could see her face—to put her *tongue* to, of all things, just like that!

> Here I stand on two little chips.
> Come and kiss my sweet little lips.

Victoria Ann might'near laughed. She concentrated on poking her fork at her chunk of coconut cake. Her throat of a sudden felt ticklish, but she didn't let herself cough.

But he was just a boy then. Boys don't grow up quick like girls do.

"That—that little old bitty rain, that rain we had last week wasn't a p-patch to what we need."

"Fourteen-inch rain. Fourteen inches b'tween drops."

Well, she knew the menfolk'd get serious, if the talk got around to the weather.

Weldon Gilstrap said, "The last time me and Hollis were out here, three years back—it was in May then, too, just about now, weren't it, Hollis?" Hollis nodded. "We rid seventy miles on a bed of flowers. This year it's nothin' but limestone rocks."

Hollis said, "Grass is all browned off."

The last time Weldon and Hollis had been out to Alto Springs was when Carson had bought his ranch. Victoria Ann hadn't met them. She hadn't hardly even known Carson then: she was just a schoolgirl, and Carson, the new bachelor in town that every marriageable female on the Divide had her eyes on, was as far off into his own speculative interests as if he was in another county. But this time the two brothers had come out to meet their new soon-to-be sister-in-law. And for certain sure when they got back home they'd be telling the whole Gilstrap connection what she was like. Well, she was wearing her new summer dress, the one from Bowling Green, Kentucky, made special for her—white lawn, full-gathered skirt with rows of insertion and tucks at the hem, perpendicular tucks with lace insertion on the waist-yoke, large bertha tucked and edged in lace—and as far as Victoria Ann was concerned, when she was wearing this dress she was perfect.

Weldon and Hollis had come out from Johnson City by way of Krugerville, a two-day ride. Dry, drouthy country. "Hot enough to sunburn a horned toad. Even the mesquites ain't hardly put out yet." They meant to stay a week, out to the new ranch house, and then head on back. They'd been into town several times since they'd got here, and today, Sunday, they were the Castleberrys' special guests.

"Had us a good winter. Streams full. The whole Plateau green as a new wheatfield. I didn't feel uneasy till January."

"Clou—clouded up and begun not rainin'."

"It don't look thrifty."

"This keeps on, ever'body'll be sellin' off their stock."

Darkening leaves of Aunt Velma's jasmine bush outside the window nearest Victoria Ann. Smell, through the open windows, of horse droppings in the dusty street, faint, rich smell of Auntie's flowers, alongside the gravel walks, that she kept watered even if she had to use dishwater. Smell of dust, of still-hot leaves on miles and miles of cedar and scrub brush. Sound, from over on the other side of the square, of Mrs. Nettleship's belled cow. The curtains commenced to stir at the windows: the first of the night breeze.

"If it thunders to the north, it's just dry thunder."

"The clouds go right on over and d-down to the coast."

The ceiling of the dining room was fading to pink. Serafina

came in and lit the lamp. Auntie told her to light the lamps in the parlor.

Aunt Velma was still fanning herself with that tacky fan from the drugstore. She said, "The deer come into town ever' night. They get into the vegetable gardens and flower gardens. They ain't at all scared."

Victoria Ann had seen three of them outside her bedroom window two nights back—a buck and two does. They didn't make a sound when they stepped. Their legs were thin as sticks, their ribs showed. They moved along the edge of the gravel walk, noses down, and only looked up if they thought they heard a noise. Their eyes when they did look up were ruby-red in the light of the three-quarters moon. They ran off when Auntie came out onto the gallery, banging a fry pan.

"Tiltin' quarter-moon last week."

"Water so scarce the Baptists are like to quit turnin' up their noses at the rest of us and go to baptism by sprinklin'."

Carson and Weldon and Hollis laughed at Papa's joke.

Aunt Velma said to Carson, "Mr. Gilstrap, can I help your plate?"

Carson said, "I won't ar—I won't argue. That cake tastes like more." Auntie put a fresh slice of coconut cake on each of the three brothers' plates.

Victoria Ann put her fork on her plate. She said, "Somebody drove an automobile clear from San Francisco to New York. It took fifty-two days."

Papa said, "What'd they do for fuel?"

"They fetched it with 'em. Or had it sent ahead by rail." A long, black machine with buggy top and ruby sidelights and bicycle wheels drove around the square. Victoria Ann thought she saw herself in it.

Carson said, "They'll never get one of them things out here. It'd never make the f-first crossin'."

Hollis said, "There's this doctor back east started a crazy house. Had one ward for motorists. A friend come through the buildin' one day and the doctor showed him the auto-mo*bile* ward. He looks in and says, 'Ain't nobody *here!*' 'Oh,' the doctor says, 'they're all under the cots fixin' the slats.'"

Everybody laughed. Hollis blushed.

Jacinta came in to clear away the things. Serafina fetched in the coffee.

The men got to talking again. "—'ll last till it rains." "Business so bad I may have to close the store." Auntie was sitting there nodding at their talk like she thought if she didn't give them all the support she could they'd flat quit. Victoria Ann closed her eyes and willed Carson to look at her. When she opened them he was doing just that.

She loved the blue of his eyes. All the Gilstrap brothers had the same color eyes.

Carson said, "Are—are you tired?"

"No. Just happy."

She loved to hear him tell her that he loved her. Sometimes when he'd say it over and over—say, out by the horse pen after they'd been walking through the orchard—she'd put her elbows on the fence and her head between her hands and just plain *think*.

It's so *delightful* to be engaged! There's nothing in the whole world as nice as that. Everybody looks at you. Everybody admires you, and if it's your high school girlfriends they think you're something stepped down off a cloud. You feel your whole self open up like a flower in spring rain under the sun.

Carson said, "Victoria Ann, you make a p-picture any artist would be p-proud of. Don't she, Weldon?"

Weldon was sitting at Carson's right. He said, "All wool and a yard wide."

Victoria Ann said, "Her head was like a kettle. Her nose was like a spout. Her mouth was like the fireplace with the ashes shoveled out."

Weldon and Carson laughed, and Weldon said, "Not so's a body'd notice it." Weldon was the best-looking of the three brothers, Victoria Ann had to say it. He was the only one who was dark-haired, with a smooth, dark complexion that made his eyes seem bluer than they were, long, regular nose, small mouth with might'near perfect teeth—excepting that two of his upper teeth were a mite apart, like hers—and a big mustache that made him look like a whole lots older man. He had a soft, deep voice.

Fingers poking through rust-brown cedar needles. Now why did she think of that?

Victoria Ann tossed her head. She brushed back a loose strand of hair from the side of her face. She remembered that Carson had said once, just after they'd first met, "Blue ribbons against black braids're lovely." That was when she was wearing her hair braided back, the last two months of school last year, her junior year, just to keep it out of her face. Now she wore it cut across the front and done up close in back.

Papa, up at the head of the table, said, "Well, how do you feel, missy?" Drops of coffee clung to his longhorn mustache.

"About what, Papa?"

"It's only ten more weeks."

"I think I'll be very happy." She looked across at Carson. "Provided he don't change his mind."

Carson leaned back in his chair and laughed.

Auntie said, in her nervous, glancing way, "More'n likely it'll be *you'll* be the changeable one. About three days b'fore the ceremony."

"Were *you*, Auntie?"

"Oh, I had all my eggs in one basket."

The menfolk laughed.

Victoria Ann felt tiny beads of sweat prickling her upper lip, and her hair of a sudden felt sweaty. She said, " 'Women should beautify themselves and spikenard themselves for their lions.' "

Hollis sang out,

> "Flo was fond of Ebenezer—
> 'Eb,' for short, she called her beau.
> Talk of 'tide of love'—great Caesar!
> You should see 'em, Eb and Flo."

Everybody laughed. Papa leaned across the table and said to Carson, "Look out for her, young man. She's flighty. One day a new dress, next day a piece of furniture, next day a cat."

"Oh, *Papa*! It's not like *you* and your horses." Papa was always swapping around for a new horse, and it was might'near always something wrong with them—excepting, of course, Blue, their buggy horse, and Victoria Ann's own horse, Badger. But Victoria Ann had picked out Badger her ownself. But Papa would fetch home a new horse pret'near every First Monday, and it'd turn out the horse was colicky or foundered or would balk kick or somebody'd dosed it with Dr. Legrar powders until the horse looked good. Once he fetched a beautiful gelding, a four-year-old blood bay with black mane and tail and not an off mark on it. They put it in the shafts and it choked and fell down. Everybody was always joking about Papa and his horses, even Papa joked about it, but Auntie let him go on, it was as close as she'd let him come to gambling. Sizing up horses was the one thing Papa wasn't good at. If Papa'd owned the livery stable in town instead of his other dealings Victoria Ann would likely right now be herding goats.

But sometimes, yes it's true, when Victoria Ann put the wedding out of her mind, she wellnigh forgot it was going to happen.

Maybe, after the wedding, after they were all settled down and had got used to each other, she and Carson would travel—maybe to New Orleans or St. Louis or maybe even to Europe.

She already had a ranch house waiting for her.

Auntie said to Weldon and Hollis, "Would y'all like some more coffee? It's still hot."

"No'm. I'm just fine."

"No, *gracias*. I'm full-up as a tick."

"Mr. Gilstrap?"

"May—maybe just a mite-dab more." Velma poured Carson some coffee. Carson waved his hand. "That's f-fine, Mrs. Castleberry."

"Mr. Castleberry?"

Papa waved his hand. Auntie poured a little into her own cup and sat back down.

Victoria Ann's throat of a sudden was pestering her again. Dr. Hodges had looked at her last week. He had tapped her back and her chest through a sheet, but hadn't found anything. Her cough was purely nervous, he said. Victoria Ann sipped some more of her warm coffee and that helped.

Her auntie had been bothering her all week about "arrangements"—which corner of the garden to put the dance floor in, what flowers to go in the parlor, which salmon dish to serve—until Papa finally stepped in and put his foot down. Now the wedding was to be in the schoolhouse, followed by a dance there, and a midnight supper at the hotel.

Papa and Carson and Weldon and Hollis were talking about the explosion that had happened at the waterworks last week. Mr. Satterwhite, who owned the waterworks, had put two dynamite charges in the hole for the freezing vat in the engine house of his new ice plant. Papa said, "It worked right well. It broke up that stone and knocked about seventy dozen holes in the tin roof. It fetched up a scantlin' a mile high that lit back down onto the engine and broke the governor castings. You can run it without the castings, though."

It was going on dark outside the windows. There was a cool night breeze, and the flame in the lamp fluttered, blackening the chimney. Auntie turned the wick down a mite. When everybody had finished their coffee Auntie said, "Let's go into the parlor." She rang the tea bell for Jacinta and Serafina to come clear away the coffee things. Papa and Carson and Weldon and Hollis stood. Papa, of a sudden humming "Sugar Lump" under his breath, led the way. Carson gave Aunt Velma his arm and they followed. Hollis was about to help Victoria Ann from her chair. He knocked a piece of silverware from the table and the next thing Victoria Ann knew he was down on his hands and knees looking for it. Victoria Ann laughed. "Oh, leave it," she said. She stood and shook her draperies. She and Weldon started for the door.

Weldon stopped to let Victoria Ann through the doorway into the hall. He was tall and slim. All the Gilstrap brothers were tall. Victoria Ann stopped for a moment and said, "Did you fetch your clarinet, Mr. Gilstrap?" He nodded and said, "I stashed it b'fore dinner in the parlor." Actually, his eyes were a whole lots bluer than Carson's. Victoria Ann touched his sleeve and said, "You and Hollis've got to come visit more often. Why don't the two of you come out and ranch here? Anyways, when me and Carson've got moved into our place, I want the both of you to come visit us ever' minute you can."

He stared at her in the queerest way. It was like his eyes went back and back, and it was the coldest look at the back of them. A thin smile was at the corners of his mouth, but the muscles hadn't moved. Victoria Ann took her hand from his sleeve like she'd been burnt. Hollis came up to them. He was even taller than Weldon. He said, "Hair of the dog." That's what Victoria Ann thought he said. The three of them went out into the hall. It was dark in the hallway. The only light was from the parlor doorway, up towards the front of the house. Victoria Ann and Weldon and Hollis walked up the hallway towards the light. She felt like she was being conducted by two dark, hovering, sword-in-hand angels.

Both lamps were lit in the parlor and the room was bright and cheerful. Papa was sitting on the settee with Carson. "They just l-lay down onto their b-backs and . . ." "Well, you know how it is with sheep. Their favorite pastime's dying'." Auntie sat in one of the straight-back chairs nearby. She already had her drawnwork out and was busy working the cross-threads for a new table scarf. Auntie never wasted a minute. There was always a piece of yet-to-be-finished drawnwork or needlework close at hand wherever-all she sat—on the gallery or in the front room or in the parlor. All she had to do was reach out her hand. "Idle hands, idle minds." But it seemed like whenever Aunt Velma got to doing her drawnwork or needlework all her thinking was in her hands. You couldn't hardly get her to say a word. Oh, she'd nod like she was listening, but sometimes a body wondered. Victoria Ann had noticed plenty of times that whenever Auntie *did* talk her hands quit moving and the needle-work lay on her lap like a stopped life.

Victoria Ann went over to the piano to see what music was laid out. Weldon followed her. Auntie's potted plants were all around the room—geraniums, begonias, rose moss and baby blues. Auntie had had them fetched in especially for the company. Weldon said, "Them plants're so darned *thrifty*." Victoria Ann turned several sheets of music and said, "Oh, Auntie talks to 'em."

It was dark outside the windows. Already, outside, it was night and distance and likely the first stars. Victoria Ann said, fast as she could, " 'Peter Prangle, the prickly pear picker, picked three pecks of prickly pears from the prickly pear trees on the pretty, pleasant prairies.' Say it, Auntie."

Aunt Velma looked up, surprised. Victoria Ann said, " 'Peter Prangle, the prickly pear picker . . .' "

"Peter Prangle, the prickly pear pricker—oh, *bother*!" Victoria Ann and Weldon laughed. Auntie took up her drawnwork again. Victoria Ann sounded E♭ on the keyboard.

Papa and Carson and Hollis were still talking about the weather. Papa was telling them about the drouth of '93. "I tell you, *ever*'body was leavin' the county then. The Nueces went dry clear down to Bird Springs. Dust so deep 'round the stock tanks the cows were in it halfway up to their knees. I had teams on the road from Krugerville and Ugalde all the time, haulin' cottonseed hulls for feed. Coyotes killed the sheep right in the pens."

Victoria Ann listened. What she remembered most about that time—she was seven years old then—was the bugs in the cistern. There were little white bugs in the drinking water that they had to strain through a cloth. And the time the grasshoppers lit down like a cloud off the sun. They crowded the sky and hit down like bullets—so thick on the orchard trees and the bush beans in the garden you couldn't see the leaves. Auntie's zinnias and cannas and four o'clocks broke under the weight of them. Victoria Ann remembered the chickens running around in the yard gobbling up grasshoppers till they couldn't hold any more. Then they stretched out their necks, squawked and fell onto their backs.

Papa said, "That drouth didn't quit for eighteen months."

Victoria Ann said, "Auntie says when I heard the first drops of rain onto the roof I didn't even know what it was. Ain't that so, Auntie?"

"What?"

"I said, when we had that first rain in '94 after the drouth I didn't know what it was, did I?"

"No. You heard it hittin' the roof and you said, 'What on earth's *that*?' "

The men talked. Papa looked so *distinguished* over there on the settee. He sat up so straight. Even when he stood, his back was ramrod straight, and whenever he sat a horse he looked like a soldier. It wasn't only that he was tall—might'near as tall as Hollis—but he was broadshouldered and strong-looking, too. He had a short, reddish beard and handsome longhorn mustache. He looked like King Edward, the new king of England that Victoria Ann had seen a picture of once in the *Pictorial Review*. Everybody in Alto Springs looked up to Papa. He owned the store and was a partner in the bank and part owner and manager of the wool-and-mohair warehouse and he was county treasurer and a trustee in the church. But it wasn't just that. It was half of it the way he *looked* whenever you saw him in the store or the bank or somewheres around the square. He looked to be a judge or a general or maybe even a state senator. And when he talked he talked like a man who knows what's what.

"Right now the conservative business element's fetchin' the gospel to the brush arbor," Papa was saying, "so you *know* the legislature'll enact that bill. Anybody with a hand in land or business is going to be mighty happy to see it, too."

"But what about L-Lanham?"

"Oh, he'll carry on like an old granny, but when it's there on his desk lookin' right up at his face he'll sign it quick enough."

Weldon said to Victoria Ann, "We want you to meet the folks."

"I want to. I wish they were here today."

"It come on us kinda sudden."

Victoria Ann pinched a leaf from a red geranium that was on top the upright piano. She crushed the leaf and held it to her nose. Sharp, pleasant, okra-like smell. She said, "I feel like I know 'em already, just from what Carson's told me. I want to meet 'em soon. I'm sure when we meet I'll love 'em just like my own."

Weldon had his back to the rest of the company. He said, "I reckon you know he was wellnigh engaged to a second cousin back home."

Victoria Ann didn't say anything for a moment. Then she said, *"Please hand me those papers."* Weldon took some papers from the top of the piano and handed them to her. They were notes for next week's Methodist League programs, for which Victoria Ann had to read the closing scripture. She put them on a pink-marble–topped table nearby and came back, sat down to the piano and commenced to sort through the sheet music in front of her. She said, in an angry half whisper, "Our friend is twenty-eight years old. I expect that's old enough a body can honor his decisions."

Get out before I kick your two eyes into one.

Victoria Ann lit right into the piece of music in front of her—"In the Mansion of Aching Hearts." She wasn't playing it any too good, she knew. She was too angry and her blood wasn't keeping the same time. Leastways she hit all the right notes. She played the song through a second time, a whole lots gentler and quieter. It helped to soothe her, and when she was done Papa and Auntie and Hollis and Carson clapped. Weldon was still standing there at the end of the piano. Victoria Ann proceeded to play something fancier, from memory, phrases from Schubert.

Weldon leaned down to her and said, "I'm sorry. I feel like twenty-nine cents at a thirty-cent bargain counter."

Victoria Ann played a mite longer, letting her fingers ramble over the keys. Finally, without looking up, she said, "I don't even remember I heard it. If we took ever'thing ever'body said to heart we wouldn't have *any* friends."

Papa, from the other side of the room, said, "Play something pretty, missy."

Victoria Ann spread out a fresh piece of music and played Mendelssohn's "Songs Without Words." She knew Papa would be settled back on the settee, eyes closed, foot lifting and falling, and she played it especially for him. How good it felt to be able to play well—without thinking, even! The procession of songs was like sunlight in the room: now bright and direct, now a haze, now a sudden streak through clouds. What was on the page, dumb as pieces of stone, translated instantly into sound. The playing took Victoria Ann out of herself. She hardly felt the keys, it was so natural, like sitting in a puddle of sunlight.

When the last note had died out, the parlor was as still as death. Victoria Ann's hands were on her lap, but in her nerves and mind they were still playing. Then Weldon stomped his foot. "Whoo-ee!" he said. Somebody whistled and everybody clapped and Hollis and Carson came over to her. Carson said, "That was *perfect*." Victoria Ann looked up at him and said. "Ever' sausage knows whether it's made out of beef or cat," and threw back her head and laughed.

They chattered and laughed, and then Weldon took his clarinet out of its flannel and he and Victoria Ann did a duet. Outside, the night breeze moved across the Plateau: Victoria Ann felt it on her neck and face. After the playing everybody got around the piano to sing, even Papa. Only Aunt Velma wouldn't join in. "I've got a voice like a screech owl. I'd rather listen."

They sang "Bedelia," "Sweet Marie," they sang "I'm Trying So Hard to Forget You" and "Come, Thou Fount of Every Blessing." Victoria Ann sang the top part. Hollis and Carson sang tenor and Papa and Weldon came in on the bass. When he sang, Carson didn't stammer at all.

> "Thou wilt come no more, gentle Annie.
> Like a flower thy spirit did depart.
> Thou hast gone, alas! Like the many
> That bloomed in the summer of my heart."

> "I'll be all smiles tonight, love,
> I'll be all smiles tonight.
> Though my heart may break tomorrow,
> I'll be all smiles tonight."

> "Teasing, teasing, I was only teasing you."

When they were done, Serafina came in with brandy and fresh coffee. At the windows the lace curtains lifted and fell. The tongues of flame flickered in the lamps. Crickets and other bugs were making a racket outside the windows. For a minute they stopped, then started up again. Victoria Ann shivered. Carson touched her on the shoulder and said, "Are you cold? Let—let's get away from the window." She looked up. She felt a rush of feeling for him, a press of joy in her chest and throat. He *was* handsome, and sweet, and for certain-sure he was the go-gettingest of the three brothers: *he* was the one who had the ranch and the seventeen hundred head of sheep and two hundred grade-goats he was hoping to breed up and had had the lovely new ranch house built for her. He'd done it all with might'near no help from his family in the way of money either, which was saying a whole lot. Victoria Ann leaned her head to the side so that her ear brushed Carson's fingers and he gently squeezed her shoulder.

All I want is to be a good wife.

She got up from the piano and she and Carson went over and sat in a pair of straight-back chairs near the settee. Old Serafina, her wrinkle-skinned brown arm reaching over their shoulders, served them coffee with a dab of brandy in it. Papa and Hollis and Weldon were talking about sheep and angora goats. Victoria Ann said, "I love the way the new lambs're bright orange sometimes, when they're first dropped."

Carson joined in the talk. The four men got to discussing the price of mohair—fifty-five cents a pound last fall, but, Papa said, likely to drop by two or three cents this year. Victoria Ann said, "Blair and Sons up in Sonora sold some eighteen-inch staple for three dollars a pound last year."

Hollis said, "What?"

"They did. They paid sixteen hundred dollars for a purebred South African buck, two years back. It shears nineteen and a half pounds."

Weldon said, "How d'ya know that?"

"I like to read the Association report. Papa gets it in the mail."

The talk got around to kidding, which had just gone past. Almost all the ranches on the Divide used the Mexican method, staking out. Victoria Ann stopped listening. She put a hand to the back of her neck, where the birthmark was. She felt a headache coming on her. Of a sudden she was restless. When a polite place came in the talk she said, "Excuse me, please. I'm going out onto the gallery for a spell."

Victoria Ann stood. The men stood. Hollis said, "You all right?"

"It's nothing. I think I've got a slight headache coming on. I just need a breath of fresh air."

Carson came with her. She knew he would. Victoria Ann's shawl was on the coat rack in the hallway and Carson got it and put it across her shoulders. They went out the front door, but light was shining from the parlor so they walked around to the side gallery.

The moon hadn't come up yet. The stars, flung like chipped ice through the black, were so bright you could wellnigh see by them. There were so *many*, scattered thick as limedust. The brightest ones, Arcturus and the bright star in Virgo, might'near hurt to look at, they were so close and bright. Victoria Ann knew some of the clusters, from what she'd learnt in Natural Philosophy. The assignment had been to stand outside at night with the science textbook in your hand and try to pick them out. Virgo. Boötes. Serpens. The Crown, with its forty-year-old new star that Miss Carruthers had told the class about. Scorpio, rising, its red star spitting and twitching just above the edge of the Plateau. Victoria Ann could even make out Libra, halfway between Virgo and Scorpio. She pointed them all out to Carson.

He said, "Many's the night I've laid on my s-s-sugan, out to the ranch, and fell asleep tryin' to count 'em."

All along the south and east, down low, the Milky Way was a powdery cloud.

The night air and the clean, cool brightness of the stars did wonders for Victoria Ann's head. She said, "I already feel a whole lots better. I don't know why, I don't seem to have much 'pep' tonight."

"I thought you were wonderful."

"You're just prejudiced."

They laughed, and Carson took hold of her hand. They looked up at the stars. The crickets were going lickety-split, near and far, their chirps like pieces of light. Booming noise of a bullbat swooping for bugs overhead. Out in the barn Blue or Badger kicked against a stall.

—Brown needles. Fuzz of a peach against her cheek, cleft peach that spits out juice. Tonguing the split, sucking the juice, her chin wet. Victoria Ann felt the queerest laugh lift in her. It made her vexed and irritable. Carson gave her hand a squeeze.

How she used to have to lie on her tummy at the edge of the gallery to eat a peach when she was little—whenever Papa or Aunt Velma gave her a peach—so as not to get the juice on her dress.

That's better. And the tickle in her throat quit.

She said, " 'The fair, the chaste, the inexpressible she.' Ha!"

They looked up at the stars for a spell. Of a sudden, in a low, choked voice that sounded like it was coming from a long ways off, Carson said, "God A'mighty, it ain't right how I l-l-love you! It'd make an ordinary man sick."

Victoria Ann smiled.

"Well, it's s-so! You're so blessed pretty I can't *sleep* for thinkin' on you!"

Victoria Ann felt almost sad. She said, "I don't know as that's a real reason to love anyone. Besides, there's *scads* of girls prettier'n me."

"If that—that's so, they're all hidin' under the rocks somewheres." Carson squeezed her hand again. Victoria Ann felt the longing go up like electricity to her armpit. Of a sudden she wanted to take his hand and smother it with kisses.

A girl doesn't do that.

She turned to him. She could just make out his face in the starlight. Behind him Aunt Velma's hanging plants made dark, globby shapes. Victoria Ann raised Carson's hand to her lips and kissed, just once, the tips of his fingers. She held his hand between her two hands and said, "It feels like we've always known each other."

He leaned to her and kissed her on the cheek, near the eye.

The crickets quit. Somebody was coming up the walk, from the front of the house, bobbing past Aunt Velma's zinnias and the dark mound of the pomegranate bush. *What's he doin' here?* Victoria Ann pulled away quick from Carson Gilstrap, as if she'd been about to be caught doing something wrong. Right off she was angry and ashamed she'd done that. Her whole body shook.

Junior Luckett stood at the foot of the gallery steps. Victoria Ann couldn't make him out too well in the starlit dark and that's just the way she wanted it. She'd as soon she never had to look at his face—the mussed-up hair he's always brushing back from a cleft forehead, dark, heavy-lidded eyes, the way the one side of his face is so fish-*flat*, the heavy chin and queer, baby-looking teeth that she couldn't stand to see whenever he smiled. *So ugly he'd turn sweet milk to clabber.* And his *body*, if you want to call it that—all arms and shoulders and no waist and that little winglike-looking thing sticking out of his back. Victoria Ann took a step towards him and said, *"What do you want?"*

He said in his strange, soft voice, "Is your papa to home?" It sounded to her both close and distant, like in a dream.

She said, "Of course he is."

"I know it's late."

"Late enough the chickens're gone to roost."

"I didn't know y'all had company."

"What do you *want?*"

"I wouldn't of come by if I'd knowed you had company." He coughed.

Victoria Ann stamped her foot. "Do I have to stand here and listen to *this* all night?"

Carson said, "Excuse—excuse me, Victoria Ann . . ."

"He's welcome as the flowers in May. I'm sure he knows."

"I've fetched your papa the store inventory."

"On a *Sunday night?*"

"I figured he'd want to see it. I been workin' all weekend totin' it up."

Victoria Ann gave a queer laugh.

Carson said, "I'll take it. We'll see Mr.—Mr. Castleberry gets it when we go in." He went down the gallery steps. Victoria Ann could see Junior Luckett shifting from one foot to another in the half dark. He must of handed over the ledger, though, on account of Carson came right on back up. The next thing Victoria Ann knew, Junior Luckett's head was bobbing towards the front of the house. For a minute he was part of the pomegranate bush. Then he was gone. Of a sudden her legs felt weak. She grabbed hold of the gallery rail.

Carson said, "You're all in a lather."

"I don't like him. He won't stop pestering me. Oh, I know every'body gets along with him fine, and Papa calls him his right-hand man at the store. But as far as I'm concerned he wouldn't make up into first-class fertilizer."

"I don't expect there's a one of us ain't got a right smart p-passel of f-faults."

Victoria Ann shivered. The dark shapes—trees in the yard and the wandering Jew in hanging baskets—seemed to be pressing in at her. She said, "I'm sorry. I ought not to carry on like that. I don't know why it bothers me. It ain't a body's fault, what face and all they're bornt with. Maybe it's just, what some folks cotton to others shy off from like it was a live rattler."

"What's tamales to some's hogs' lips to another."

"I've always liked ever'body. I've always seen the good in ever'body, but I can't stand him."

"He ought to keep quit of you then, if he knows it."

"He knows it. I've told him often enough." Of a sudden Victoria Ann stopped talking. Her whole self strained, listening. Carson started to say something. She said, "No, don't! I don't want to talk about it. Please! *Please, please, please!* I don't want to *talk!*"

The night wind pressed through the leaves. A windmill banged and creaked somewhere. The light from the stars clicked like machinery.

Victoria Ann listened. *Yes, there it is. Over by the fence, right next the road. The* crickets. *They were carrying on a minute ago. Now they've* quit.

11

The small, blue-backed novel with the red poinsettia on its cover lay face down beside her on the bedclothes, her hand still on it.

"You know, don't you, Sybil, darling?" Maitland murmured . . .

The curved brass rail arching across the foot of the bed shone bright as the polished handle of a coffin. Oh, it ain't all so bad as *that,* silly. Just the same simple throat problem you had last year. Still, when she coughed her chest hurt, especially under her right shoulder blade. And she felt feverish, damp with a light sweat. But not *bad,* really. Mild laryngitis, Doctor Hodges says. You'll get over it. She hadn't wanted to stay in bed this morning—she'd finished all her lessons and in her dream last night she'd solved the trigonometry problem that the whole class two weeks back and even Miss Carruthers herself hadn't been able to, it'd been on her mind all week and come to her in the dream just like that—but Auntie had made her stay in bed. The whole day was wasted. She *could* of gone to school. Already she felt some better—the pain was letting up and the faint stickiness of sweat had disappeared. If she could keep from coughing. The small tickle was like a piece of fur in her throat and she hated it. She only let it have its way when she just couldn't hold it back. Likely, if she wouldn't *think* on it, it'd go away.

It made her so restless, to have to stay in *bed* all day!

*In the clear light her eyes shone lustrous, pools of tawny
flame; her hair showed itself of a rich and luminous
coppery hue, spun to immeasurable fineness; a faint color
burned in her cheeks, but in contrast her forehead was
as snow; while her lips . . .*

Victoria Ann glanced up over the top of the book. The mid-morning sunlight was coming in through the window as harsh as brass. It would be beating down onto the courthouse and barbershop and Dimmity Dress Shop and Kyle's Drug Store and all the other shops and stone business buildings around the square. It would be pounding the tin roof of the schoolhouse, making the tin pop, poking in through the windows and making a glare of the open pages of Bensen's spellers and Monteith's geographies in the primary grades downstairs and upstairs the *Selections from Caesar* or Dole's *American Citizen* or Wells's *Essentials of Geometry*. The heat itself was as solid as a stone. It was so solid and still, not a windmill anywhere in town could move in it.

To have a *fever* in this hot weather! It was just plain stupid.

    *. . . tossed her flower-wreathed head, wound
    the lovely pearls around her slender throat . . .*

The little scaly-backed dove that had waked Victoria Ann before daylight and had been carrying on in the heat all morning like it was taking a bath in it picked it up again outside the window *you-too you-too you-too, you tuck-a too you tuck-a-tuck, you tuck-a too you tuck-a-tuck* and flew from her flat twig nest in the box bush at the corner of the house into the pecan tree over by the fence. Victoria Ann could see it shifting from one direction to another on the branch, checking the yard and the glare heat of the road and then picking it up once more.

    . . . a red damask rose drowsing on her breast . . .

Of a sudden sweat prickled her chest and her throat and broke

out again on her forehead. She closed her eyes. She couldn't
tell if it was the midmorning heat or the heat of her blood was
making her sweat so. She hated the way the sweat stuck to the
flannel outing-cloth across her chest that Auntie had pinned
inside her nightgown earlier this morning. Auntie had rubbed
Victoria Ann's chest and back with Warner's Safe Cure and
pinned on the cloth and it was an oily mess. She could just about
cry, she was so vexed. Even her hair felt damp. If Auntie found
it out Victoria Ann would likely have to spend *another* day in
bed, and it was just too much.

> *An idiotic impulse seized Thrall to take her head between*
> *his hands and bury his face in the warm darkness of her*
> *cloudy hair.*

Why didn't Carson come *save* her, show up at the house and
say to Auntie and Serafina and everybody else who was fussing
over her, "*Get thee hence*"? Yea, say unto Victoria Ann, his
face serious, vague with ethereal light, "Take up thy bed and
walk." Victoria Ann giggled. She saw Carson in a long white
robe and bobbing tin halo like in last year's primary-grades
Christmas play, and then she watched him climb up onto a
cross and all he had on was a white diaper, just little pins holding it together. *That is no way to think on your fiancé*, it ain't
right, it ain't even Christian, and she watched him up there in
his white diaper and, well, a pair of cowboy boots, and she
flat-out commenced to laugh.

The laugh turned into a cough. The first cough made it hurt
again under her shoulder blade, a round spot of pain. Victoria
Ann sat up to ease the pain. Serafina opened the door partway
and stuck her head in. "*¿Mi hijita, estás bien?*" Her little fist
of a face was so wrinkled and brown and leathery it minded
Victoria Ann of one of those formaldehyde frogs she'd had to
dissect in Natural Philosophy class. Serafina was stooped and
tiny, her gray, braided hair done up in a coil on top her head.
Her eyes were little watermelon seeds of black. They were so
dark Victoria Ann never could tell what-all she was thinking,
no matter how deep she tried to look into them. But she knew

for certain sure in a minute Serafina would be hobbling right on off to Aunt Velma to tell her about the coughing. Victoria Ann held her breath and the coughing quit. She said, "*Estoy bien. Trae me aquel libro, por favor.*" Serafina went over to the chiffonier and fetched Victoria Ann the Williams's *Rhetoric* from the pile of schoolbooks over there. "I was just clearing my throat. *¿Es necesario practicar mis oraciones, verdad?*" Aunt Velma didn't like for her to talk to the servants in Spanish, but she did it anyway. Serafina looked at her a moment and then went out. Victoria Ann flung the *Rhetoric* onto the floor. Auntie'll be in here in a minute and I'll have to stay in bed another day. I hate ever'body.

The thing to do is to look fresh and rested. And don't you *dare* cough.

Privy. Hockey. Chicken do. I'm sick to death of ever'thing.

She flopped back onto the bolster and picked up the blue-backed novel.

> . . . *a room full of the scattered riches of rare books, of carved miniatures, of bubbles of Venetian glass, beautiful as jewels and as precious, a room for study, for dreams, for love* . . .

I want to go into *society*, in Chicago or New York. I want to be a famous singer, to be the center of a "brilliant circle," riches, pictures, lovely rooms, jewels. She watched the Emperor of Russia propose to her. He was young and handsome and had deep brown eyes that were helpless with passion and tenderness. The wedding was a brilliant success, just like the drawings of the wedding of that English duke in the *Pictorial Review*. She watched herself moving in jewels and a white gown amongst her people, explaining her political views to them. The people and the emperor were moved to tears. The emperor had come to America to hear the famous singer sing, he had been introduced to her . . . you are so *stupid*. Here you are in your silly little room—tasseled fly-net with its valentines and post cards and peacock feathers, the yellow counterpane with red embroidered peacocks, the satin pillow with the bulldog on it with the real glass eye—it's a *child's* room, stupid. I'll make Papa put in bird's-eye maple, a *pretty* chiffonier and clothes press, paint all the walls and ceiling white and the floor black, put down a blue rug, and white curtains and a white counterpane and Howard Chandler Christy pictures on the walls.

It was all done in her mind and she lay back on the bolster, satisfied. The Emperor of Russia—*shush.*

Her breath was fragrant upon his cheek.

You-too, you-too, you-too. The dove flew back across. It made a creaking sound when it flew.

He did not speak to Sybil, but she knew he was claiming her for all time.

Victoria Ann swallowed against the tickle in her throat.

Two raps on the door. Victoria Ann brightened up quick as she could. She sat up straight in the bed. "Come in, Auntie dear."

Velma came into the room. Her mouth looked grimmer than usual, like there were two clothespins pulling it at the corners. She had on a black skirt and waist and black lace fichu. She almost never wore anything but black, no matter what the time of year.

"What's this I hear about a cough?"

"It's nothin'. I swallowed a bug or somethin'. I'm all right. I'm feelin' a whole lots better."

Auntie came to her and felt her brow. Velma had her hair done close, pitched up high on top and combed over a rat, like always. It was the way they used to do their hair fifteen years ago. Just to look at it made Victoria Ann peevish.

"It don't feel quite normal."

"Poo. It's this drouthy heat."

"Yes, and I reckon ever' other child at that school is in bed with the drouth today."

"I prob'ly just caught somethin'. It'll be gone by tomorrow."

"Let's hope."

Serafina came in with a cup of hot broth. Velma took it from

her and set it on the bedside table, next to Victoria Ann's tuck-
ing combs. Serafina looked at Victoria Ann for a moment with
suspicion and then went back out.

Victoria Ann said, "Why does ever'body keep *fussin'* at me?"

Velma said, "You didn't even brush your hair this mornin'.
You must *not* be feelin' good."

"Oh fiddle. I like to leave it like it is onct in a while. Anyway, you moved all my things."

"What do you mean?"

"You moved my mirror and you moved my hairbrush and I
can't find anything."

"They're on the chiffonier."

Victoria Ann bit her tongue. She'd begged Auntie *time and
again* not to touch her things or put her room in order, and she
does it all the same. It's a *disease*. If Auntie only knew how
exasperating it was and how Victoria Ann had to fight back
saying sharp things.

"Well, *I* didn't put 'em there. I think I'm gonna die. In about
three days."

Velma's nose got thinner. She said, "From the way you carry
on I don't doubt you will."

"So much the better for you. Then you and Papa won't have
to spend so much."

"Oh, I swear. You push a body to the limits."

"Then quit all the time straightenin' up my things and puttin'
'em where I can't find 'em. I can't find half my books. I can't
find last week's *Home Companion*. No wonder I'm half the
time sick. It's puredee frustration."

"Not only do you have a fever, you're might'near delirious."

"I am *perfectly* all *right*. And I'll get up when I feel like it.
Don't you *dare* say I got to stay in bed tomorrow."

"Please don't shout at me."

"I'm not *shoutin'*. *Not. Not. Not. Not.*" Victoria Ann broke
into tears and beat the bedclothes with her fists.

Of a sudden Velma sat on the bed. "Poor sweet *dear*! It *scares* me when you carry on like this." She took hold of one of Victoria Ann's hands and Victoria Ann decided to let her keep it. Velma covered it with kisses. "I *know* you're not really sick."

"I've only been in bed one day. Doctor Hodges says it's just a nervous cough."

"Of course it is."

Victoria Ann looked at Velma. There were tears in Velma's eyes and her hands were trembling. Victoria Ann scooted half out of the covers and flung herself into her auntie's arms. "Oh Auntie, forgive me! You're so *good* to me and I'm all the time so mean."

Velma kissed Victoria Ann's forehead and eyebrows and ears and nose and eyes. She smothered her face with kisses. She likely would of kissed Victoria Ann's feet if Victoria Ann had let her do it. Victoria Ann said, "I know you love me tenderly, just like I love you."

"I do. I do."

Velma held Victoria Ann and rocked back and forth with her. There were long, crinkly hairs on the underside of Auntie's chin.

"Auntie, *do* you forgive me?"

"Ain't nothin' *to* forgive. You're just high strung and spirited." Velma gave Victoria Ann a peck on the forehead and said, "*Well*. You'll be quit of this thing b'fore you know it."

" 'Course I will. It'll be gone in a day, just like last time. It's likely somethin' in the air."

Velma stayed with Victoria Ann a spell. She made her drink her broth. She brushed and combed and did up her hair. She fed her a spoonful of Dr. King's Discovery. Then she gave her one last kiss and went back out to the kitchen to tend to dinner.

As soon as Velma was gone Victoria Ann let down her hair again. She could just *see* Velma frowning about it.

Leave me be. I'm the one that's sick, I'll do my hair the way I want it.

You're spoiled.

Well, why shouldn't I be spoiled? I'm intelligent. I'm good.

The only thing I have is a bad temper. Besides, she'll forgive me. Auntie always forgives ever'thing.

Victoria Ann shook her head and lay back, letting her hair spread out on the bolster. Chicago or New York sunlight came in through the window. There were tall stone buildings outside the window, and down in the street carriages and motor cars went back and forth. Victoria Ann pulled a strand of hair through her teeth.

> *. . . cloudy hair . . .*

A man's face was above hers, the clear gaze of the manly eyes troubled now with longing, the warm lips trembling, the closeness of his breath onto her face—somebody walked down the hallway outside Victoria Ann's room, a screen door slammed, the harsh sunlight of the Plateau poured in again through the window. Out in the yard the dusty leaves of the pecan tree hung caught in the heat and light. *You tuck-a too.*

She picked up the book—

> *He hurried to the expectant, throbbing Sybil.*

pulled the strand of hair again through her teeth.

> *Raising big, tear-brimmed eyes to Maitland's face,*
> *she said . . .*

Look at my fingernails. I've got to *quit.* Oh, but she'd told herself that a hundred times before and still she bit them, mostly when she wasn't thinking, nibbling at the nubbins, sometimes tearing into the quick. But *otherwise* you're pretty. No, I'm too exacting to believe that. I don't have a "wasp waist" or a large bust. All I've got is this soft, black, wavy hair—long clear to my waist if I let it—and my eyes. *That's* what ever'body means when they say I'm pretty.

I want somethin' to *happen* to me. *Ever'body* gets married. You can be *ugly* and get hitched. Verdie Ruth Hudspeth got married, and she's ugly as sin. I want to travel, to see the capitals of the world, ride in motor cars, dance! Carson in black tie and tails whirled her, they spun around and around, marble floors, crystal chandeliers, and he was glad they'd sold the ranch. Velma frowned, watching them from the crowd of stickin-the-muds along the wall—oh, all you snippy-nosed Methodists and Baptists and Church of Christers can go straight to the Hot Place, you're just like dead anyways, it's no fun at all.

It shocked her that she'd thought that, especially since she was due to lead songs nos. 84 and 108 at midweek prayer services this Wednesday.

Well, I can't help it, I'm *sick*. I'll think anything I want.

Maitland bent over her, his face all passion-pale, his heavy, drooping lids betraying their girl-like length of lashes.

"Sybil!" he breathed.

What's the use to be the most important family in town when ever'body's watching you and you can't *do* anything?

So love comes, strangely masked.

I'd be happy if a simple twister'd come along, just so's somethin'd *happen* onct in a while.

Brown cedar needles flung by the wind. She was on her hands and knees in the brush, hidden by the bent, whipping branches, her hair loose and flying, her naked body bristly with goosebumps, sniffing the air, the way dogs do.

12

E·v·e·r t·h·i·n·e, and the whole gathering sat, tents of rustling tulle and white lawn and velveteen over crisp petticoats, crush of men's summer serge, coughs, rear ends shifting on the pews to settle down for the edifying, the Quarternight and Van Zandt babies crying, scared half out of their wits, hymnals slapping shut. Victoria Ann was even more shocked than the babies by how *loud* the singing had been. She hadn't ever really heard it before, since she'd always been right in there with them, as loud, likely, as the rest, trying to keep on top of the surf of song around her, her voice light and delicate as a silver boat. But Victoria Ann had strained her voice, injured it might'near, that's how come she'd had that cough, and she'd promised God she wasn't going to sing anymore until her throat was rested and until Papa, or Carson maybe, somehow someway got her *proper* lessons—Mrs. Murchison, the one so-called voice teacher in Alto Springs, wasn't any good.

The singing had been so loud it still seemed to be bouncing around up there on the ceiling. The chimneys and glass shades of the coal oil lamps still rang. Elder Kyle, who usually pitched the tune, had pitched it sky high and the men singing the lead part had had to come up onto it brass-lunged. The women had placed one octave higher, up around high C, and didn't even know they were doing it. Victoria Ann had never heard the likes.

Red and green and blue and purple light poured in through the triple stained-glass windows of paisley-like vines, leaves and flowers at the front of the church, stars of Solomon's seal, onto the back of Preacher Mayhew's bald head. Colored light poured in through the two side windows of stained glass—Christ complete with lambs and shepherd's crook in memory of Grandma Throop, who had suffered the little children and cared for the sick, and one of the Cross circled by a crown paid for by Orphus Buckelew, rancher, just before he went under with a case of late mumps. Heat, and flies from backyard stables and the town's wagon yard, poured in through the other, plain, opened windows, and everybody's cardboard funeral-parlor fans—"The Last Supper," Jesus praying in Gethsemane, Jesus knocking at a door—were going, trying to keep both off.

It hurt to sit on the hard bench, especially since Victoria Ann's corset steels were printing themselves on her ribs and back. Brother Mayhew called for the prayer of confession, during which he wanted "ever' head bowed and ever' eye closed." A fly was tangled in Alva Pryor's hair in the pew in front of Victoria Ann. It buzzed its own prayer. *Our Heavenly Father who by Thy love hast made us, and through Thy love hast kept us* Alva Pryor's pile of golden-brown hair was something to dream on *and in Thy love wouldst make us perfect, we humbly confess* it would make a good mattress, in fact *have not loved Thee with all our heart and soul and mind and strength, and that we have not loved one another as Christ hath loved us. Thy life is*

A spider dropped onto the lap of Victoria Ann's white mull skirt. She wasn't at all surprised or scared. The spider's body was a tiny button of yellow and black. Its shiny, black, hairy-footed legs were bunched together toward the center of its belly. It wasn't dead—move one of its legs and it'll fold slowly right on back to the center, alive and numb. Victoria Ann knew where it came from. There was a mud dobber's nest overhead.

It was one of Victoria Ann's favorite fixtures in church. She
never told anyone. The dobbers came in through a crack at the
point of the arch of one of the plain windows. Victoria Ann had
knocked a mud-dobber's nest from the eave of the privy at home
once. She had broken it open. In some of the cells were baby
wasps, in others, spiders of all kinds and colors, each dead to
the world but alive and perfect like a memoried saint. She
brushed the spider from her lap.

*that Thou mayest come into the full glory of Thy Creation, in
us and in all men, through Jesus Christ our Lord. Amen.*

Everybody bowed their heads in silent meditation. What
made Victoria Ann so blessed *peeved* with Carson Gilstrap was
that he'd gone to Johnson City on account of his mama had
the flu or somesuch. He had more loyalty to his folks than he
had to her. It was like his folks had a collar onto him and whenever they took the notion they just pulled on the string. She
hadn't met his folks *yet.* They hadn't come out here to visit her
and Carson hadn't taken her to Johnson City. He kept saying he
would, but "things out at the ranch . . ." Of course Victoria
Ann wasn't about to go now, with *her* throat, when Carson's
mama and God knows who-all else had the flu in Johnson City.
Carson was going to miss the Fourth of July picnic tomorrow
and everything.

Anybody who gets sick on the Fourth of July ought to have
a firecracker put under their bed *no, dear God, forgive me that
unsightly thought, make me good, take the meanness out of my
heart.* Victoria Ann felt a whole lots better, having decided that.

The palm of her right hand of a sudden commenced to itch.
She scratched it through her glove.

The fly buzzed in Alva Pryor's hair.

Brother Mayhew said the words of assurance and everybody
went through the responsive reading. It was right after the
affirmation of faith, when they were about to light into "Blessed
Assurance," that Victoria Ann and most of the rest of the congregation looked back over their shoulders towards the church
door. The door had opened and closed, and it was like an angel

in a gray-and-white broadcloth spring suit, white vest and white cravat and fresh celluloid collar had stepped in. He looked to be about twenty years old, so clean-shaven you'd of thought his skin was firmed-up light or smooth ivory, his fine, brown, brushed-back hair parted to one side in the new style.

And just like Victoria Ann figured, like she *knew*, right from the start of the service—like *ever'* Sunday—there sat Junior Luckett in a back bench, directly behind her. Slanted nose. Head too big for his body. The left side of his face looked queer even from here. Right now he wasn't looking at Victoria Ann but sort of up past her to the chancel rail or whatever. Victoria Ann turned right back around.

Hunched-up, toad-looking thing that ought to be under a rock. He ain't got no *right* in this place. He gave out to be Baptist when first he come here, but as soon as he started workin' in Papa's store he turned Methodist.

No, I don't intend to think on it. Still, she couldn't help it, she slid a gloved hand onto the back of her neck, as if to protect it.

Alva Pryor was still craning around, trying to see past Victoria Ann to the stranger at the back of the church. Her eyes were hazel, with flecks of yellow and red in them. Her mama had to rap her with her fan.

Some folks think Alva's pretty, but it ain't so. She's stuck up. She can't play the piano, either.

What Victoria Ann had written in Alva's last-year's memory album was

> *May you and I in heaven meet*
> *And cast our crowns at Jesus' feet.*

What Alva had written in Victoria Ann's was

> *Voyager upon life's sea,*
> *To yourself be true.*
> *Whatever your lot may be,*
> *Paddle your own canoe.*

She *is* stuck up. And she's wearin' a downright *silly* hat.

Head tones, chest tone, throat tones. The Porter family, Mr. and Mrs. Porter and all five daughters, were scouring their lungs in the pew behind Victoria Ann. It sounded like they were cleaning out their insides. Auntie, next to Victoria Ann, held the hymnal for the both of them but neither of them was singing, Victoria Ann on account of her throat, Auntie on account of she never sang. "No need to mar the parts. God'll hear me right enough in the pearly chambers of His Home." Auntie's lips moved, mouthing the words. Papa's deep bass sounded from the other side of her. The whole congregation did their best for the visitor, working slurs and melodic variations into the notes, raising their eyes towards heaven, hefting the hymn up to their Redeemer through the stenciled ceiling, the roof peak, the pitched spire, into the atmosphere.

This is my STO-ry, this is my song,

The fly had got loose from Alva Pryor's hair.

Praising my Sav-IOUR all the day long.

Smell of Florida water and lavender. Ember Crozier was wearing a pink, flat-brimmed hat with a pair of outsized bird wings. Mrs. Nettleship was in her widow's black, black lace, black hat, black fingerless mitts. The only thing white was the lace handkerchief tucked in her hymnal. She'd been a widow so long Victoria Ann used to think she was born one. The McKennon woman from out towards Devil's River was in the same pew. She had on a tobacco-colored one-piece dress and a plain black straw hat. She was the one everybody said rode a burro on her place, butchered her goats her ownself for meat, dug postholes and fixed windmills with her own hands. She hardly ever came into town excepting for church and groceries. She never said much to anyone, and when she smiled it was an off smile, not quite in the middle of her face. Her daughter Willie was with her.

Mrs. Stackbine, two rows down, had on a frilly-looking maize-

colored toque with a crown of chiffon topped with pink rosebuds and wiry green leaves. The rosebuds shook as she sang.
Lutetia was standing next to her, fatter even than her mama,
her blue velveteen dress just about the ugliest thing in sight.
It was Lutetia who had gone into hysterics one day at school.
She claimed she had seen Jesus coming down the hall, light
shining out on all sides, leading a little black dog with a pink
nose and three white feet. Her brother "Snooter" was between
her mama and papa where they could keep an eye on him.
Snooter always came up with the most interesting answers to
"Fill in the Scripture" in Sunday school. Miss Moriss would
call out "Love" and Snooter would pipe up with "Canticles 1:2
—Let him kiss me with the kisses of his mouth: for thy love is
better than wine." *Animals*." "Numbers 22:21—And Balaam
rose up in the morning, and saddled his ass." Sister Moriss's
face would get redder and redder. *"Sports*. Who can tell us
about Bible sports?" "Genesis 26:8—Isaac was sporting with
Rebekah his wife." Nobody ever could figure out why Miss
Moriss didn't just quit the game, but she was stubborn. Right
now Miss Moriss was over on the other side of the aisle, singing
so fierce it looked like it might-would paralyze her soul.

Calabria Wright's dress was pretty: white lawn, lingerie
waist, puff of point d'esprit on the back of her collar. She
looked to be the bee's knees in that dress.

The hymnals slapped shut. The hats of velvet, satin, silk,
lace and soutache braid sank down into confusion under the
weight of the song's end.

A slight breeze sent essence of wagon yard through the room.

Everybody bowed their heads through the pastoral prayer.
Then Papa got up and went to the chancel rail with Mr. Satterwhite to get the collection baskets. Papa looked so *handsome*
in his tall collar and silk tie and gray worsted suit. He looked
strong and manly: stern, commanding eyes, handsome, close-
trimmed beard, fine head and large mustache. Even the
wrinkles at the corners of his eyes were strong and manly. He
and Mr. Satterwhite walked to the back of the church.

"To the preaching of the good tidings of salvation"
"We consecrate our gifts."
"To the teaching of Jesus' way of life"
"We consecrate our gifts."

Whatever the stranger dropped into the collection basket, Victoria Ann couldn't hear it. What she did hear was Junior Luckett plopping his fat silver dollar, like every Sunday. Every time Victoria Ann heard that dollar plop into the collection basket it made her back twinge. It put her in a rage. Where does he *get* it? Papa only pays him twenty dollars a month. He's showin' off, that's what it is. For certain sure it ain't Christ's humility, like Christ asks for. Nobody else puts a silver dollar in the collection basket *ever'* Sunday, not even Papa. "Seems to get a dollar and half's worth out of ever' dollar he earns," Papa said, one night out on the front gallery. Still, she didn't like it.

She concentrated all her thought on the cross sewed to the blue velvet in front of the pulpit. She watched Christ climb up in His diaper and cowboy boots *oh dear God, dear Jesus forgive me, save me from myself* and her face flushed, her innards turned over in her belly, she was so filled with shame. *At home sick in* bed, *maybe, but not here.* Brother Mayhew, his Bible open, a white ribbon dangling from the text he was soon to deliver, seemed to be looking right through her. She lowered her eyes, clasped and unclasped her gloved hands in an agony of shame.

Half blinded with tears, surprised by the collection basket, she fumbled in her reticule and found two dimes, dropped them in with the rest of the coins.

"We consecrate our gifts."

She watched a teardrop widen and darken on the wrist of one of her gloves. Of a sudden she felt some better. She knew her tears were token and proof of a deeper humiliation and love. She wanted to go down onto her knees, writhe on her belly, anoint Christ's feet with spikenard, wipe them with her very hair like Mary of Bethany, in gratitude for His grace come upon her. She thanked God for this gift of humiliation and tears. She lifted up her head, proud now in Christ, her face wet, likely transfigured, radiant with joy. Brother Mayhew read out the morning's text—"The flowers appear on the earth; the time of the singing of birds is come, and the voice of the turtle is heard in our land"—and she felt flowers springing, heard birds singing in her own soul.

Victoria Ann put her whole mind to the sermon, how the voice of the turtle dove is heard in *our* land. Well, not exactly here, on account of that particular bird is found only in Europe, but it is heard in the land of our *hearts*. "Its melodious voice, cuttin' through the world's thorny brush of grief and sin, reverberates"—Brother Mayhew said that word like he was tipping and swinging on a branch his ownself, making like a bird— "in our hearts through confession, prayers and praises. Its notes're wonderful and enchantin'. It sings upon a thorn." Brother Mayhew thumped the Bible. Sometimes he was up on his toes, cooing, sometimes he leaned towards the congregation, his nose sharp and eyes fiery, like a white-tailed hawk come down onto them. "Some folks don't *hear* that song right. But, dear sisters and brethren, there's a *world* of difference between 'Shibboleth' and 'Sibboleth.' That seeming *trifle* marks the friendly Gileadite from the rebellious Ephraimite." Victoria Ann was proud of Brother Mayhew. She hoped the young visitor was listening close. Likely he had slipped into a pew. In her mind she saw him leaning forward in his handsome gray-and-white suit and white cravat, his eyes—were they brown? blue?—serious, his face rapt, amazed to of come on a preacher as fine as this way out in nowheres, right here in Alto Springs. Brother Mayhew invited the congregation to take a nearer view of the turtle dove. "As the Son of God chooses the lamb for His symbol, so the Holy Spirit selects the dove for His." He led the congregation on to discover the full meaning of the symbol, how the Spirit of God brooded over the face of the formless deep (the Spirit here compared to a dove with wings outspread, covering her eggs. Victoria Ann thought of the time Auntie's little speckle-spotted

bantam had twenty-six chicks put under her: they lifted her up
into the air like she was on a bed of caterpillars), how the
Spirit moved over the waters of the De-luge and, again, over
the waters of Jordan. "Why was the dove chosen as the symbol
of the Holy Ghost?" It was on account of how the dove was
tender and faithful, "emblem of constant love" (of a sudden,
Constant Love plastered itself like a bunch of feathers inside
Victoria Ann's breast. She wished worse than ever that Carson
was here beside her), how of all birds the dove is the cleanest
and most delicate. "In filthy places they will not abide and
rest." Well, I don't know about that. Jimmy Satterwhite keeps
pigeons, and they make an awful mess.

Victoria Ann got tired of thinking about birds. She smoothed
a wrinkle from her skirt. Once she had sneaked to the Alto
Springs Church of Christ to hear Early Arceneaux, the na-
tionally famous boy preacher. Most of her school girlfriends had
been there, and some of their folks too, it didn't matter if they
were Methodists or Baptists or whatever. The boy evangelist
was a little butterball with pudgy face and plumped-in raisin-
looking eyes. His cheeks were puffed out like he had hard
candy inside them. He wore a tie and long britches just like a
man, but if he got behind the pulpit all you could see was the
top of his head. He preached a hellfire-and-brimstone sermon.
Everybody was amazed that a little boy could know so much
about sin.

. . . as the Spirit like a dove brooded upon the face of the
waters, so the . . .

Louie Thallman, over on the other side of the aisle, was get-
ting more and more good-looking every day—in particular this
Sunday, what with his haircut and new sack suit. Sweet on
Mozelle Peters. And half the time she don't even come to church.

. . . speaks through the children of God, though not always
in the same notes. Sometimes . . .

The sun had shifted enough that a patch of blue and white
light from the Throop window was touching Gus Haines's head.

His head was bowed. In the past six months Gus had changed from being the biggest cut-up in school to not talking at all, suspicious of everyone. He had killed Billy Bob Quarternight in a hunting accident last fall (they were both fourteen at the time). Now Gus walked around like he thought any minute the ground was going to open under his feet and he'd drop into a bottomless pit.

. . . is *heard in our land. God be praised, the time has come when these words have application to the land in which we dwell. The droopin', expirin' church of our Christ begins to revive and put forth blossoms*

and the sermon was snubbed down, cinched, saddled and rid. Feet scraped, babies waked, coughs played over the gathering like chips and scraps of thunder. Fans were tucked into the racks on the backs of pews. Everyone stood. The Doxology.was forced up through the roof and the benediction laid out over grateful heads.

Outside the church the sunlight was so bright it stunned Victoria Ann, wellnigh blinded her. Her irises tightened and hurt and the shock of the light seemed to paste itself on the inside of her head. She might'near had to *push* through the heat, it was that thick. Her whole body broke out in a sweat, sweat prickled her upper lip. She pulled a handkerchief from her reticule and dabbed her face and forehead.

Folks poured past her out of the church. Calabria Wright touched her elbow as she went past and said, "That's a pretty dress."

"I'm like to suffocate in it."

Calabria laughed.

Some of the folks went right to their buggies and wagons, across the street. Others stood around in little bunches on the caliche walk or burnt-grass lawn, discussing the sermon or whatever. Most of the women's dresses were white—white lawn, white silk and summer linen—and it hurt to look even at that. The darker dresses seemed so heavy and to soak up so much heat you'd of thought their wearers would sink to the ground directly.

Here and there clusters of girls whispered and giggled, glancing at the stranger, who stood talking with Mr. and Mrs. Satterwhite down on the walk.

Papa and Auntie came out of the church with Brother Mayhew. Brother Mayhew's hands and face were paste-white and his eyes were pink. It took a lot of concentration not to be troubled by that. It was like the body of Christ blenched white in the tomb and all but a ghostly red drained out of the eyes. Mostly Victoria Ann didn't look at his eyes. It minded her of white pigeons. Brother Mayhew opened an umbrella over himself as soon as he came out of the church.

The sunlight bore down from directly overhead like a white-hot stovelid. Victoria Ann opened her parasol. Others had gathered around the young visitor down on the caliche walk, she saw out of the corner of her eye.

Mrs. Nettleship came up next to Victoria Ann, her black taffeta hissing. She said, "Oh, Brother Mayhew, I was so *moved* by your message. In particular the part about Sacred History as our guide and what you said about Noah as a type of the Christ. It seems so *true*. I'm going to go home to Cousin Anice and tell her it all. She still can't hardly get around." Louisa Stackbine, who was holding Snooter by the elbow, said, "We surely wish you didn't have to go to Harmony ever' other Sunday."

"One must minister to all of God's children."

Mrs. Stackbine sniffed. "It makes for a power of backsliding here, I can tell you."

Brother Mayhew laughed and said, "Well, you don't want a tribe of heathen for neighbors, do you?" There had been bad feelings between the citizens of Alto Springs and those of Harmony ever since they moved the county seat up to Alto Springs in 1879. It had taken a court order to get the county records, stored in the old courthouse in Harmony, freed. They had been fetched up to Alto Springs in a safe on a wagon, and men on horseback had ridden along ready to shoot if necessary. Folks in Alto Springs had it in mind the ones in Harmony weren't but half Christian, if that, and off-horse to boot.

Papa shook Brother Mayhew's hand and said, "Remember, we want to go fishin' down to the canyon this week. I've already got the supplies in the wagon." About every three or four weeks Papa and Brother Mayhew and Mr. Satterwhite and Mr. Dupree from the bank and sometimes Doctor Hodges went down on the Nueces or Agua Fria rivers overnight to fish. They fetched back bass and bullheads and perch.

Auntie shook Brother Mayhew's hand and said something in her soft, nervous way. Others came up to congratulate Brother Mayhew on the preaching. Papa tipped his hat and nodded to a number of them. He said, "That's the St. Clair boy down there, ain't it?" Mr. Satterwhite said, "His papa's sent him on ahead." Papa went down the steps. Victoria Ann shifted and fidgeted while Auntie adjusted her hat and opened her parasol. Papa was talking to the young visitor. Why don't they get out of the sun? There was one live oak tree in the churchyard, but everyone was standing out in the sun like a bunch of sheep. Finally Aunt Velma headed on down the steps, and Victoria Ann went with her.

The caliche walk threw back the white sunlight. The young man was looking at her. He glanced again at her as she came up. Papa said, "This is Mrs. Castleberry, and this is my daughter Victoria Ann. Velma, this is Mr. St. Clair's boy. You remember the senator. You met him in San Antonio once."

"Of course I do."

"Earl Leroy, is it?" Papa said to the young man.

"Yes, sir." He had quiet, assertive, brown eyes, clear, completely unblemished skin and little, soft crinkles on his lips. He was might'near as tall as Papa.

Auntie said, "It's so good to meet you. I remember your father quite well, though I only met him once. Mr. Castleberry knows him much better, of course."

"The pleasure's mine, I'm sure, ma'm."

Victoria Ann took off a glove and held out her hand. Earl Leroy gave it a firm, brief shake. "A pleasure to meet *you*, Miss Castleberry." Their shadows on the ground touched.

Papa said, "He's come ahead to prepare for tomorrow's ceremonies."

Earl Leroy laughed. "Papa felt he had to stay behind and do some heavy politicking down in Privilege. Not in church, of course." He laughed again. Victoria Ann's heart took a hitch at the way his smile made tiny parentheses at the corners of his mouth.

So this is the son of a state senator!

"Your papa and I had some business dealin's once," Papa said. "It was a speculation in cotton and it looked like we were both goin' to go under."

Earl Leroy said, "He told me about that."

"I figured I was goin' to have to go back to school-teachin'. But he pulled us through."

"He told me *you* were the real fox in the brush."

Papa laughed. Victoria Ann pinched his sleeve. She said, "We're goin' to dry up and blow away if we don't get out of the sun."

She moved towards the live oak tree. Like cockleburs to fleece, the others came along with her. Little puffs of dust rose from the dry grass where she stepped.

It wasn't all that much cooler in the shade. Victoria Ann pulled out her handkerchief again and dabbed at her neck. Of a sudden she had the whole sense of herself, the blood in her standing up off the ground, pounding in her neck like some kind of wild blossom, the strength of her legs and back, the brief miracle of her face and neck and arms. She felt the queer iciness of her thoughts like secret water in a well, the calm and clearmindedness that must be in her eyes.

He was looking at her neck. Yes, it's a pretty collar (there was a pattern of tiny vines and leaves embroidering the tucks).

Earl Leroy looked down at the ground. He said, "I think what your Preacher Mayhew said is right. There *will* be a revival of our churches and all our other great institutions in the South." Victoria Ann thought she saw him blush.

Ember Crozier and Lutetia Stackbine and a couple other girls had edged near the group and stood at the rim of the shade, trying to listen. Victoria Ann noticed Junior Luckett standing behind Papa, a little ways back, next the trunk of the live oak. The bulging forehead and slanted nose, the queer flatness to one side of his face. Hasn't that toad of a thing gone *yet*? I can't *stand* him. Why does Papa keep him on at the store? Victoria Ann shifted so that she could get him out of her sight. But still she felt him standing there like an out-of-sight sun burning through an overcast against the side of her face.

Papa and Auntie and Earl Leroy St. Clair were still talking about the sermon. The crowd in front of the church had thinned out. Folks were driving away in their wagons and buggies. Brother Mayhew and two others had gone inside the church to close up. The Porter family were walking over to the square, the five girls strung along behind like a line of ducks. Towards the square the business buildings stood up into the heat, behind Victoria Ann the church loomed. It would of blinded her to of looked at that stuccoed white.

The shade under the live oak tree didn't give any comfort at all. Heat and light held over everything, and for miles around section on section of stones and cactus and brush burned under it. Victoria Ann was in a box of heat and light, the lid coming down, it felt like, and if she didn't get hold of herself right quick she'd scream. She swallowed, jabbed the point of her parasol at the dirt.

". . . impressed by the parallel he drew between the Lamb and the Dove," Earl Leroy was saying. A little vein stood out at the top of his collar. He was talking with an assurance that was somehow boyish and at the same time as if out of the experience of a much older man. He was good-looking, that was for certain sure. His white silk cravat was so smooth and care-fully tied it looked like it'd never been worn before. Victoria Ann said, "Why don't we have Mr. St. Clair to dinner, Papa?" The young man flushed and looked again at the ground.

Papa said, "I was thinkin' the very thing. It's no problem, is it, Velma?"

"No."

"We'd be delighted to have you, if you ain't otherwise occupied."

Earl Leroy's eyes avoided Victoria Ann's. "I wish I could. I'm engaged to have dinner with Colonel Lowry over to the hotel." Colonel Lowry was an eighty-year-old, bald-headed, white-bearded coot who'd sold his ranch years ago and moved into town, and when his wife died he'd moved into the hotel. He mostly sat all day on the hotel gallery, a cane between his legs, and more than half the time asleep. Just the thought of him irked Victoria Ann. She said, "Well, you can come to supper."

Auntie said, "Do. We'd love to have you."

Papa said, "Fetch your bags over too. No use to stay at the hotel. We don't mean for your papa to stay there either, to-morrow night."

Somebody said, "If you don't leave the hotel on your own the bugs'll carry you out." It was Junior Luckett. Papa stepped back and said, "So there you are!"

A piece of sunlight down through the leaves of the live oak made the knowledge bump on Junior Luckett's forehead shine like it was oiled. He grinned and blinked. The teeth in his mouth were so tiny and far apart it was like somebody had stuck seed corn in his gums. He said, "I know. I spent three weeks in that place once and the night visitors took so much blood out of me I was beginnin' to look like a locust hull."

Everybody laughed except Victoria Ann.

Papa said, "Mr. Luckett, Mr. St. Clair."

Junior Luckett made it to the young man in two limping steps. He shook his hand. It was like a dwarf working the handle of a pump. "Pleased to meet you, sir. You've met the best folks in town to pass butter back and forth with. They'll do you up proud."

"Mr. Luckett's my right-hand man at the store."

"The left-hand one's out back chasin' the store cat."

Papa laughed.

Victoria Ann felt the blood rush up her neck. He's got a lot of brass. *Why does he always have to turn up somewheres around?* Victoria Ann wanted to get away from here. She had the hardest time not to show it.

The churchyard was empty. Even Ember Crozier and Lutetia Stackbine and the other girls had left. The hot ground in the churchyard seemed to pulse under the heat. The weeds were dry ghosts of themselves. In the street, fresh horse droppings were already turning crusty. A blue-and-green butterfly drifted across like it was lost.

Papa said to Earl Leroy, "We'll walk you to the square." They started across the lawn towards the street, Junior Luckett tagging along behind, and Victoria Ann dropped her glove. Papa said, "You dropped your glove, missy. Mr. Luckett'll pick it up." He and Auntie and Earl Leroy went on over to the road.

Like some chicken rushing to peck a bug, Junior Luckett picked up the glove. He turned to her, a kind of dog-like look on his face.

"*Here* you are, Miss Castleberry." Once again he grinned.

Victoria Ann hissed under her breath, "*I* didn't ask you to pick it up." She pulled off the other glove and pitched it onto the ground. "There! You can have that one too. You can blow your nose on 'em, for all I care."

She hurried after the others on the road. She almost stumbled at the curb, just missed stepping on a horse biscuit. She was might'near like to cry. She pushed her forehead and her hat through the heat.

Ever' time I *see* that man, I'm scared. He's goin' to *do* somethin', I know it. The next time Papa's in a good mood I'll see he's fired.

The blood pounded in her throat. She drew up to the others. Their backs were towards her. It was like they'd forgotten her completely, like she hadn't anything to do with them. It scared her even worse. She slowed down a minute to get hold of herself. The sweat was pouring down her back, it was even sliding in the ugliest way between her buttocks.

I just hate all of it. I don't want dinner and I don't want supper and I don't want to see anybody.

But later, after she had had a chance to freshen up and change into her new lawn dress with the Irish lace and Eaton waist, she felt some better. She looked at herself in the mirror. The trimming of pale-blue ribbon was pretty. She went again to the wash basin and wet a handkerchief in the cool water and touched it to her face and neck.

The eyes *are* pretty.

The heat seemed not so bad now that she was in her room. Maybe it was the way the pecan trees and the huge live oak tree shaded the house. She went over to the chiffonier. She looked at her hands a moment. You're goin' to *quit* bitin' your fingernails, and I mean *right this minute*. She turned the engagement ring on her finger. It was a diamond solitaire mounted in platinum prongs attached to a thin gold hoop. She slipped it off her finger, opened a chiffonier drawer and stashed it under a stack of lace-trimmed handkerchifs.

At supper the young Earl Leroy was fine company. Sometimes he teased. Sometimes he was serious. Victoria Ann could tell that Papa had taken a liking to him right off. Victoria Ann mainly watched and listened. But Earl Leroy kept turning to her and saying, "Don't you think?" "I believe the human race is gettin' better, not worse, and someday the ones who come after us'll reach a kind of greatness way past what we know, don't you think?" and he looked at her with warm, brown eyes—brown as a butternut—between soft, almost silky lashes. Victoria Ann didn't know what to say. Mainly she smiled and nodded.

She kept her hands under the table.

Earl Leroy's face was the smoothest and clearest complected she'd ever seen in a man. His hair was soft and brown and wavy. He had—of all things—beautiful ears. It made her heart beat to look at them. And she loved to hear him talk. His voice was wellnigh musical, but manly, with not a childish note in it. It was pret'near like an angel *had* stepped in at the church-house door.

Again and again he would touch things with his hands—his cup, the edge of his plate, the damask tablecloth, his fork—he would touch her sleeve, "Don't you think?" He had been to the University in Austin. He was a junior partner in his papa's law firm. He was the son of a state senator! "It's been my experience." "You bet." He wore a dove-gray suit coat, white silk vest and fresh white cravat. He was from another world.

After a spell Victoria Ann took a turn in the conversation. Earl Leroy listened to her with such seriousness she saw that he considered her his or anybody else's equal. She felt so certain sure of it, it like to've made tears come to her eyes.

Earl Leroy praised the food and the table setting and Aunt Velma blushed.

Once Auntie started to say something about the engagement and Victoria Ann said, "What's that on your collar?" Flustered, Velma fingered her collar with her rough, red fingers and tried to look at it. Victoria Ann said to Earl Leroy, "Did you see it?"

"No, I didn't."

"It was a ladybug. It's likely somewhere in the room."

"My goodness, I was afraid it was a spider or something."

"No, Auntie. If it'd of been that I wouldn't've said a word. I'd of just leant over and brushed it off."

After supper Victoria Ann and the young St. Clair went out for a turn in the orchard. They stood for a moment on the gallery. They just caught the tip of the sun before it sank out of sight: the whole west was a spread of dusty red with not a

cloud in it. The light colored the courthouse and the jailhouse
and the three tall water cisterns over on the square. The moon
in its first quarter was going down in the west. The sky, metallic
with a windblown haze of dust way up high, held over everything, clear to the edge of the Plateau. The town was quiet, not
a wagon in the streets in the late Sunday evening light. Only
the night breeze. Back behind the house the windmill creaked,
its sucker rods fetching up water with a wet, strangled "pop."
Victoria Ann could hear the water spilling into the cypress tank.

She flicked her China-silk fan.

Smell of the town wagon yard, of dry dirt streets, odor of
dusty fig trees. Victoria Ann said, "It's so dry I haven't seen or
heard a mosquito yet."

The lightning bugs were already out.

They walked over to the orchard, over near the barn at the
back of the lot. Aunt Velma's pinks and bouncing bets and
four o'clocks were on each side of the gravel walk. In the late
light, down close to the ground, it looked like the flowers' colors
were all drained out. The pink and yellow pinks were might'near
white and the bouncing bets hadn't any color to them at all.
Earl Leroy knew the names of all of them. "My mother keeps
flowers," he said. "Her and your Aunt Velma would get along
fine."

They walked out past the kitchen garden, with its irrigated
rows of onions and okra and mustard greens, tomatoes, Kentucky Wonder beans and blackeyed peas and lady peas. Water
was trickling down a ditch right now, rolling and dissolving
the black limestone dirt. Evening's the best time to wet the
ground.

Wash house, canning house, summer cook house, barn,
chicken shed: it was like a small village out here.

Victoria Ann said, "Do you have any brothers or sisters, Mr.
St. Clair?"

"I'm the only one, like you."

"When you're the only child you wellnigh have to look after

your own upbringing, don't you think? It makes a body grow up so fast."

Earl Leroy laughed. "Sometimes I feel like I was *born* in my papa's law office."

"I don't think I even had a childhood. But let's don't talk about that."

"I know exactly what you mean, dear girl."

They walked past the horse pen. Victoria Ann felt the miles and miles of Plateau, stones and scrub oaks and brush, pounding like an ocean sea around her, or maybe it was the blood pounding in her ears.

Earl Leroy said, "Your papa's a fine man."

"He's a *great* man, I think. He could of been in law or politics. Instead, he devoted himself to business and the church and his family."

"I like your Aunt Velma too."

"She suffers awful from catarrh. Sometimes there're seventy or eighty washed handkerchiefs spread out on the bushes or woodpile. 'Specially in December."

To the west the sky was plum-colored. The evening star showed. Victoria Ann and Earl Leroy walked in the orchard, between peach trees and plum trees. A bullbat boomed in its stoop overhead. The tops of the orchard trees to the east shone purple and pink, the leaves of the trees to the west were silhouetted black. Victoria Ann felt like a ghost in her summer white.

The night breeze was delicious on her face and neck. It was the first time today she'd been able even to breathe without breaking into a sweat.

They walked back and forth in the orchard. Close and far off, between the trees and sometimes even down in the grass near their feet, lightning bugs blinked. The breeze stirred the leaves of the trees, all over town windmills were picking up. Over near the house, likely in the big live oak, a katydid commenced its long-drawn-out *chirrr*.

Once Victoria Ann and Earl Leroy were parted by a bush

at the edge of the orchard. She said, "Bread and butter." He said, "Come to supper." They laughed and came together again.

Victoria Ann said, "Sometimes the world seems so flat-out *good* it's like you're walking in a miracle."

"You take the words right out of my mouth."

She said, "Up to the age of twelve I was spoiled. I saw it wasn't going to do me any good. I made myself *work*. I took piano lessons. I set myself up a readin' program, a lots more than what they make you do in school. I even did my own sewin' and mendin'."

"We could as well of been brother and sister. Oh, *not* brother and sister! But there ain't a thing you say, dear girl, that ain't like it'd come direct out of my own life. We're so alike in the way we think I might'near have got to use your words to say my own thoughts."

Victoria Ann laughed and said,

> *"I asked her would she have some talk.*
> *Her feet covered up the whole sidewalk."*

Earl Leroy laughed. He said, "Well, I don't go for the charlotte-russe types, all whipped cream and sponge cake, without any filling qualities." Of a sudden he stooped down to the ground. He said, "Look at this!"

"What is it?"

He stood. "Give me your hand." He took her hand and put a stone snail shell in it. It was a thin spiral, small and delicate.

"It's a fossil! It's lovely. I've never found one like that before."

He didn't let go of her hand. In the gathering dark his face was awful serious. He said, "I mean to marry you." Victoria Ann was shocked. Earl Leroy held her hand even tighter. "When I saw you this mornin' in church it was like I'd seen you before in my mind, in the same white dress, with your hair done up just like that, and I knew right off who you were. Oh, Victoria Ann, God moves in mysterious ways. Don't you think

He made us to meet like that, in church, and that's where He means it to end?"

Victoria Ann closed her eyes. She felt like if he hadn't had hold of her hand she would of fainted dead away.

He said, "I would always honor you. I believe in the richness of your heart."

She opened her eyes. Earl Leroy still had hold of her hand. She managed to laugh and say, "Poo. You've probably got as many sweethearts as I've got white spots on my fingernails." She got her hand free.

He laughed. "Yes, dear girl, but they're all back home!" Then he looked at her again and said, "Victoria Ann, you don't know how determined a man I can be once I put my mind to a thing."

Victoria Ann stared at him. Then she touched the cuff of his coat sleeve and said, "Don't you know? Such things have got to *grow* on a body."

"Well, there's a world of time. I'm only twenty-two years old."

They laughed. He offered her his arm. She took it and they started back towards the house. All up overhead the stars were coming out. Victoria Ann said, "Let's be friends. It's better to be good friends like this."

"I'll go for that. I've said my say for now. After a good night's sleep I can always make a fresh start."

What Victoria Ann figured was, he was just teasing. She put it all out of her mind. Outside her bedroom window, way up in the live oak, a treefrog was piping, *pip pip pip pip pip*, like water hitting into a half-filled bucket. Everything else was quiet. Everybody else was asleep. *He* was likely asleep, in the bed they'd made for him in the spare room.

To think of him asleep in that bed, his brown, wavy hair on the bolster, his closed eyes under the fine, girl-like length of lashes.

To think of him asleep in the same house!

13

She was the favorite of all the teachers and of Professor Bird, the school principal. When she walked down the hall, her schoolbooks against her breast, all the teachers smiled at her. She was the best girls' basketball player and the best declaimer and she always turned in the best book reports and papers. In the schoolyard at recess the first and second graders would crowd up to her and dance around her. The teachers smiled to think of her brilliant future, especially for a girl. All her school girlfriends were shy around her for the promise that was in her.

Now Miss Carruthers would not speak to her. She had called in Professor Bird.

Victoria Ann had turned in a book-length report, expecting praise. She had copied out a whole book to pass off as her own. She wept and said she had written the paper her ownself. Even her papa had not helped her. Neither teacher spoke. She could tell from Professor Bird's eyes how all his suspicions were roused —all the other papers she had turned in, all the reports she had fudged up out of books.

Victoria Ann stamped her foot and said, "*I wrote it!*" She turned away as if to walk out on them in anger at their unjustness, but she knew it wouldn't work. What hurt most was that Professor Bird and Miss Carruthers were so *pure* and *good*, so upright and honest. It made her own soul show out like dirt, and Victoria Ann longed to either die or have their forgiveness.

What if she told the truth this once (out of a life of lies and sneaky little deceits)? They might respect *that*. Maybe in their goodness there was also forgiveness. Oh, they'd never respect her again, actually. Professor Bird would likely pass her in the hall without even a look. But at least she might-could stay in school. Then it would be others who would be praised, the ones who were truly virtuous—Alva Pryor with her messy hair, that fat dummy Lutetia Stackbine, ones who hadn't anywhere near Victoria Ann's brains and looks. Victoria Ann would walk through the school hall like a ghost of herself that no one would talk to, truly without any kind of future.

She turned back to them, to the blind blackboard, the varnished wall locked in angled sunlight, the pink and blue and yellow map of a lost world and their stone faces. She wanted to get down on her hands and knees, crawl on her hands and knees to them. She knew it wouldn't work. She tried to reason with them: Lutetia Stackbine had done it, Alva Pryor had written it for her. There was no way she could get a prise on it. The world just simply stood still. Then in a rush like the opening of the gates of destruction she told everything. Yes, she had copied it. She had not turned in an honest paper in years. She was the one who had stolen the money out of Professor Bird's tin box. She was the one who had put the horse turd in Miss Carruther's desk drawer. It was her had had the dead baby, two years back, and buried it in a quart Mason jar in a hole under the pyracanth bushes.

A bad dream told before breakfast will come true. Well, *she* wouldn't talk, for certain sure not about *that*. Victoria Ann rinsed her face in the wash basin and felt some better. She combed her hair, trying to get the webs of the dream out of her head. Only after she thought of the young visitor and heard the dove outside the window and laid her Fourth of July picnic dress out on the bed was she able to forget.

14

 They met on the front gallery. Some of the night's coolness was still caught in Aunt Velma's hanging plants and morning glories, though the sun was well up. The two big pecan trees shaded the gallery. Earl Leroy smiled and said, "How *are* you, dear girl?" Victoria Ann looked around quick, afraid Papa or Auntie might of heard him. But he must've known they weren't anywheres near. She went down the steps, through the musk of Auntie's dozens of potted geraniums, onto the gravel walk and he followed her.

Already, across the street, the heat was beginning to lift from the vacant lot. Victoria Ann turned to Earl Leroy and said, "I hope you slept well." The way his eyelids covered the top part of his pupils made her heart beat and her head a mite dizzy.

He said, "You couldn't of waked me with a brass band."

He wore a handsome, summer-weight gray alpaca suit, a fresh white shirt with wing collar and a four-in-hand tie. His hair was soft and brushed back. Unlike Papa, who only shaved every other day, he was fresh-shaved. He said, "I like the way the veins in your hands are like little rivers in a field of snow."

Victoria Ann flushed. She said, "It's hard to keep a pink-and-white complexion in this country."

"You have the prettiest eyes. I could look at 'em all day."

"I don't think this is what I meant."

"How's that?"

"When I said yesterday let's be friends."

"Oh, the world's in a constant state of flux. You can't depend on anything."

Victoria Ann said, "Why don't you quit teasin' me?"

Earl Leroy took hold of her hand. "Listen, dear girl. I love you dearly."

The sunlight shaping his face was so clear and clean and bright it hurt, it made Victoria Ann's throat choke. She got her hand free. *It's just like last night.* She started to giggle and said, "You just like the way I look."

"I can't say as I haven't noticed it."

Victoria Ann laughed. She said, "You don't want to believe ever'thing your eyes tell you. Sometimes you lift up a rock and it's got a bug under it."

"I'm serious. Yesterday I saw a pretty woman. Today I see a way more than that. You ain't at all spoiled. Even your manners are simple and engagin'."

"I just might grow wings."

"I mean it. You've got so much life in you. Besides, you're flat-out fun!" He took her hand again and said, "*Will* you marry me?"

Victoria Ann didn't know what to do. It had got to where she couldn't tell trees from bushes. She managed to say, "There's my folks."

"I'll take care of that. Or Papa will."

"I mean, they just might see us. If we keep standin' here like this we'll look like fools." Her legs were trembling. She felt the sweat in her armpits. Of a sudden she said, "Listen, I *believe ever'thing you've said!*" She hardly recognized her own voice, it sounded like a wood rasp. She pulled her hand free again, looked down at the ground. "Only, I've got to have time to think."

"I know that."

She started towards the house, her skirts rustling. "If we don't go in now, they'll come out and get us."

At breakfast Papa was in fine form. He told all his favorite stories. But Auntie hardly said anything. She passed the biscuits and rang for Serafina to serve a second round of coffee. She didn't smile once. Her mouth was pinched tight, even thinner than usual. She kept looking up from her plate and across the table at Victoria Ann. *She's been* spyin' *on us.* Of a sudden Victoria Ann wanted to get up from the table and walk out. *Why does ever'body keep* spyin' *on me? You'd think I was five years old. I'm grown up. I'll do* whatever-all I want. The biscuit she was chewing tasted like a piece of dry wasps' nest in her mouth. *You can't do a blessed thing in this town without in two minutes ever'body and his brother knowin' ever'thing about it.* Victoria Ann was like to have a fit. *I'm goin' to live my own life.* But she knew it wouldn't do to lose her temper. It might be just what Velma wanted. Victoria Ann put her fork down beside her plate. She said to Papa, "Tell him about the time those two cowboys goin' to the dance got hold of the shirt starch, Papa," and she laughed when Papa told the story. After breakfast she teased Auntie about something or other. She helped Serafina clear away some of the breakfast things. Then she went back to her room to freshen up and put on her riding skirt.

They put the picnic baskets—boiled ham; salmon salad pressed down in its big bowl and decorated with sliced pickles and hard-boiled eggs; sliced, smoked turkey; fresh-baked bread; pecan pie and a coconut layer cake—in the boot of the buggy. Papa and Auntie and Earl Leroy St. Clair rode in the buggy and Victoria Ann rode Badger. They rode over to the square, down the wide dirt street dusty with pulverized horse dung, past the limestone courthouse standing up into the air like something fetched out of Egypt—picket fence around it to keep out stock, spindly, new-planted pecan saplings and cedar elms bush-high on the lawn—

past the jailhouse, little stone Pharaoh's tomb its ownself, and Papa's store and the meat market and the Buckhorn Saloon. They rode past a row of telephone poles just going up for the new telephone company in town and then two blocks east towards the schoolhouse, a long stone building at the edge of town like a ship at the edge of the sea. At the schoolhouse they turned northeast on the high road, towards the town picnic grounds. The whole town, on horseback or in wagons, hacks and buggies was headed to the picnic grounds. Victoria Ann saw Calabria Wright with her mama and papa in their new Spaulding hack, and the Stackbines and the Haineses and the Satterwhites, all of them dressed up for the Fourth of July doings. The sun bore down like it was going to bake their brains under their hats. Already most of the womenfolk had their umbrellas up.

The picnic grounds were out on a flat near the old seep springs, a tumble of rocks and a dip in the ground that every three years or so, if there was enough rain, had water in it. The seep springs were how come the town of Alto Springs to be here: the first settlers thought it was water under the rocks. It was just bugs clicking. If it weren't for windmills, there wouldn't be a town here at all.

Some folks from out to the ranches who didn't want to stay in the hotel or hadn't a second house in town had pitched tents over near the seep springs, under the live oaks. They had likely come to town to church yesterday and then put up their tents. Tables had been set up, a long row of them under canvas awnings, and a big freight wagon had been pulled up and decorated with red, white and blue bunting and an awning put up over it for the speakers. There was already a crowd, and lots of others were driving up in their buggies and wagons. "Mornin', Mr. Castleberry. Mornin', Miz Castleberry."

"Mornin', Mr. Crozier. Goin' to be hot as blazes, I reckon. Mornin', George."

"Mornin', A. T."

Little Charlie Kincheloe was running across the flat after

Wesley Murchison like he was about to tackle him. Charlie's mama, who was standing by one of the tables, called out, "*Stop that!* You're already a mess."

Most of the women had on slat bonnets or carried umbrellas for sunshades. The men had already begun to shuck back to their sleeves and vests.

Papa and Auntie and Earl Leroy drove over to the tables to leave off the picnic baskets. Victoria Ann rode Badger into the thin shade of a stand of mesquite trees where some other horses were tied, lit down and hitched him to a tree. Old, last-year's mesquite-bean hulls crackled under the horses' hoofs. Victoria Ann loosened Badger's saddle girt. There was a shadow of sweat on Badger's withers and rump, pasting down the hairs. Victoria Ann loved the cinnamon color of Badger's coat, the way it shaded into brown. She rubbed the horse's neck. "Sweet thing," she said. She took off her riding skirt and flung it across the saddle.

Elgia Slate, who was in the fifth grade at school, was standing at the edge of the stand of mesquites. She had on a white sailor suit with peppermint-stripe trim and a new leghorn straw hat. She kept shifting from one foot to another, her patent-leather shoes filmy with dust and the sweat already collecting dirt around her stocking ankles. When she saw that Victoria Ann had noticed her, her face lit up. She was a pretty little thing, for all her nose was so freckled. She blushed and said, "Hi, Victoria Ann."

"Hullo, Elgie."

"That's the purtiest, purtiest dress."

"Thank you, sweetheart."

"When I get bigger I'm gonna have a dress just like that."

"I think what you've got on's the cat's whiskers."

"Foo. It's a baby's dress. Mama made me wear it. But when I have a dress like that I won't never take it off."

Victoria Ann laughed. "It won't last long that way."

Elgie pouted and said, "I don't care."

Victoria Ann laughed again. She said, "Here, give me your
hand." Elgie brightened right up. She took Victoria Ann's hand,
as proud as she could be, and they started across the flat to the
picnic tables, Elgie talking a blue streak. Earl Leroy came out to
meet them.

"I see you've got a friend."

"This is Elgie Slate. She's in the fifth grade at school."

After greetings all around Earl Leroy said to Victoria Ann, "I
can see you're mighty lucky in your friends," and Elgia followed
them around everywhere.

They walked over to the shaded picnic tables. Two big pots
for coffee were on a fire nearby, steaming. Auntie and Mrs.
Murchison and Mrs. Satterwhite were arranging the food on the
table. Cloths were spread over the food to keep off flies. Victoria
Ann said, "Can I help, Auntie?"

"Did you put the big serving spoon in the basket?"

"No, Auntie, I forgot."

"Oh, you never listen!"

"Should I ride back and get it?"

"No no no no. There's plenty of spoons. It's just I wanted that
one."

"I'm sorry, Auntie."

Mrs. Murchison said, "We've got a-plenty of spoons."

Velma turned to Victoria Ann. "Oh well, it doesn't matter. I
only asked you to put in the spoon because I knew Serafina'd
forget." She looked at Victoria Ann a minute, a worried look in
her eyes. Then of a sudden she smiled. She touched Victoria
Ann's hand and said, "I'm all in a fret. I know you *mean* well,
dear, and you wouldn't *really* do anything to trouble me.
Now run along. Enjoy yourselves. Leave the fussing to us old
folks."

Without thinking, Victoria Ann kissed Auntie on the cheek.
She was surprised she did it. She whispered in Velma's ear, "I
love you," where no one else could hear it. She caught Elgia by
the hand and walked away quick. Earl Leroy followed after.

Earl Leroy said,

> "I know I must be wrong,
> But I cannot love Ping-Pong.
> I cannot sing
> In praise of Ping.
> I have no song
> for Pong."

Victoria Ann laughed, and Elgia skipped alongside.

They walked over to where Papa and Mr. Satterwhite and Mr. Crozier and some other men were looking at a horse. It was Mr. Altonsall's Bess, that was going to run in the races this afternoon. She was a blooded mare, a light bay with a star on her forehead and half-stocking feet. She had a long, narrow croup, sound legs and good chest and belly. The horse was nervous and danced upon her shadow. What Victoria Ann liked was the look in her eyes: they were soft and clear but very wide awake.

After a while the men got to talking about politics. The first primary was in one more week, with the runoff in August. Victoria Ann left Earl Leroy with them—he couldn't, if he had good manners, follow her—and went over to where some women— Mrs. Crozier, Mrs. Kyle, Mrs. Thallman, Mrs. Slate and Mrs. Crump—were standing in a circle under the shade of their umbrellas. They greeted her and opened up the circle to let her in, and Mrs. Kyle gave Victoria Ann a kiss and told her how good her singing was at prayer meeting last Wednesday night. Mrs. Slate said, "Go off and play, Elgie."

"Oh, Mama."

"Go on. Don't keep pesterin' Victoria Ann. Besides, this is grown-up talk."

"Oh, all right." Elgia went off, sulking. She looked back at Victoria Ann. Victoria Ann smiled at her and blew her a kiss. "Don't worry. You and me'll stand together at the ball game to-night." Elgia brightened up again. She skipped off.

The talk was about patterns, cures, gardening, canning and cooking. Victoria Ann looked down at her shadow to see if her appearance was correct. She felt hot in her dress, like the threads in the cloth across her shoulders were about to pop into flame. She opened her parasol. Up overhead a hawk circled under the sun.

Of a sudden somewhere somebody let up a shout. A buckboard with two men in it had just turned in from the high road onto the picnic grounds and everybody started moving towards it. Mrs. Crump said, "Looks like the senator's done got here." The circle broke up and the women went over to join the crowd. Another cheer went up for the senator. Before Victoria Ann knew it Earl Leroy was at her elbow. "That's my papa," he said.

The two men were stepping down from the buckboard. One of them, a stout, heavy-set man with shrewd, close-together eyes, a thin nose and reddish beard, Victoria Ann recognized as Mr. Honeycutt from down in Privilege. The other, who was tall and lean and wiry, lit down from the buckboard like he was stepping down off a porch. As soon as his foot hit the ground he started shaking hands all around. He was wellnigh the tallest man in the crowd and he bent forward to whoever he was talking to when he spoke. He was a handsome man, for all he was going on sixty or so years old. He had eyes the same color as Earl Leroy's, a firm, lean face with wellnigh no signs of age in it at all, and a strong, hawklike nose above a gray mustache. But what struck Victoria Ann most was the *sureness* that seemed to shine out of him. It was a light that lit up everything he looked at or touched. He wore a fine black Stetson that Victoria Ann could tell was awful expensive, but the rest of his clothes were plain, a black broadcloth suit and a standup collar with white lawn tie. His brushed gray hair curled up off the top of his collar. When he shook hands with Papa his smile made little laugh wrinkles at the corners of his eyes. Earl Leroy introduced Victoria Ann to him. He gave her hand a brief squeeze, looked at her a moment and said, " 'Thus did they speak of duchesses and queens.' "

Papa introduced Mr. St. Clair to the folks nearby. Mr. St. Clair's hand darted in and out of the crowd like a fish in water. He praised a woman's hat, said something good he had heard about the man he was just being introduced to. To one man he said, "I might swear to it, but I wouldn't bet on it," and all the men around him laughed. He took off his hat, wiped his brow with a handkerchief and said, "I believe the Republicans are up to some mischief: they're down there right now stokin' up the infernal fires," and everybody laughed.

Mr. Dupree, the picnic chairman, said, "Well, folks, let's start," and the crowd moved toward the bunting-covered wagon. Victoria Ann took Papa's arm and Earl Leroy escorted Velma. Mr. St. Clair kept on shaking hands all around, talking and laughing, handing out campaign cards and cigars. He greeted folks like he'd lived here all his life. The queer thing was he knew so many of their names by heart. He knew things about their crops, their ranches, their families. And Victoria Ann didn't remember *him* from the time he'd been here four years back. But likely that was the time she'd been gone to San Marcos. Anyway, she'd just been a girl then, with no more interest in politics than she would of had in dipping goats.

Dust lifted from the ground and mingled in the folds of her skirts. She felt Earl Leroy behind her, staring at her back. She hoped the sweat in the small of her back didn't show.

If I could just wipe out the last four months! Her finger stung where she'd worn the engagement ring. *What on earth did I see in Carson Gilstrap? This is the one meant for me, I know it in my heart. And to think he should come so close and just miss!* She could wellnigh weep. She stumbled. Papa said, "What's the matter, sweetheart?"

"Nothin', Papa. It was just a rock."

There were straight-back chairs set up on the wagon. Everybody who was running for office climbed up onto the wagon. It was a good thing it was a big one. There was Orphus Taylor, the County Judge, Mr. Crooms, Mr. Satterwhite, Ira Hance, who had been Sheriff and Tax Collector from before Victoria Ann could remember, Mr. Holly and Mr. Alsop, both running for Commissioner, and Mr. St. Clair. Earl Leroy sat in a chair behind his papa, and Croften Mabry, chinless, rubber-lipped,

prissy little fool with a pimply face and hips like a girl, who
spent all his time collecting beetles and World's Fair postal cards,
sat beside him. Croften Mabry was to deliver the high school
declamation. Every year the graduating senior who wrote the
best patriotic essay got to give it for the Fourth of July declamation. Victoria Ann hoped Croften was scared stiff. He looked to
be. Victoria Ann's essay had come in second place, but poo, it
was always a boy, a girl never got to deliver the declamation
anyway.

Mr. Dupree introduced the speakers and the high school declamation came first, thank goodness, at least we'll get *that* over
with. Croften wellnigh tripped and fell off the wagon as he
came forward, but he got there, all dressed up and soaked in
sweat, a drooping carnation stuck in the lapel of his clay worsted
jacket. He put one foot in front of the other just like Miss Carruthers had taught him and slung his arm across his chest—you
could might'near *see* Miss Carruthers pulling the strings—and
commenced to pitch the whole declamatory mess out over the
heads of the crowd, his eyes squeezed shut like he hoped they
couldn't see him—*The citizen is the most valuable product of
civilization. He is the result of an evolution in human progress
in which*—and already Victoria Ann was flat-out bored.

Croften went on and on, it was endless, the sun swirled overhead, flies swirled around Victoria Ann's face and hat, the earth
swirled in its held sphere in space. Victoria Ann was like to be
dizzy. "I mean to marry you." She stared at Earl Leroy, who sat
behind his papa, his hat off, looking so cool you'd of thought the
heat wasn't touching him at all, his soft brown hair brushed back
from his forehead, his face shaped of the light—dark eyebrows,
dark, piercing eyes, fine nose and strong, gentle mouth. He sat
so tall-up-and-proud in his chair. *He's handsomer even than his
papa*. It was only his being there that kept Victoria Ann from
flying off the face of the earth. It made the whole world hold.

Junior Luckett stood at the end of the wagon, near Earl Leroy.
He stared out over the crowd like it was a herd of cattle. Even
he didn't look so queer this morning. "—*bearing aloft the honor*

and glory of the nations," and the declamation was ended. It looked like Croften Mabry's clothes were going to slide off him, he was so wet with sweat. The shadow of the hawk slid across the heads of the crowd.

Mr. Dupree introduced the local candidates. Each said his say, most of it full of deep flounces and a double row of fluting up the back. It looked like they'd never quit. Only Sheriff Hance got his over quick. He said, "You-all know me. I been doin' this job the best I know how for goin' on fifteen years. If reelected, I aim to keep on doin' it thataway." Then he sat down.

When the senator finally got up to speak it wasn't what he said—"investigation of the Waters-Pierce Oil Company," "corporate property tax for the Republican corporations," "the Hogg progressives"—that took hold of Victoria Ann, so much as the way he said it. He had a rich, deep voice that rambled like some slow, powerful river between banks: it would of been bass in a choir. He didn't talk loud or sling his arms. He stood still, leaning towards the crowd, talking lower and lower and them leaning towards him like they were telling secrets together. Sometimes Victoria Ann couldn't hear all that he said—"a matter of public moment," "the fine Italian hand of Republican opportunism"— but she was carried on the current of his voice. The whole crowd was caught up in it. Sometimes they clapped, sometimes they laughed. It was his voice that did it. *He's not like other men. Neither is his son.* Victoria Ann saw them in the state capital, she saw them taking tea in huge, shaded houses, she saw them in a brass-lamped automobile up Congress Avenue. To be a state senator's wife! Someday Earl Leroy would be a senator his ownself, or maybe even governor, she just knew it.

Earl Leroy was looking at her. She glanced down at the ground. The senator finished his speech and everybody whistled and cheered. When Victoria Ann looked back up the speakers were climbing down from the wagon. Folks crowded around the senator and his son, congratulating them.

Papa waited a spell, humming "Lorena" under his breath. Then he went forward and shook Senator St. Clair's hand. He

invited him and Earl Leroy to sit to the picnic with them. "And
we want to have you to the house this evenin', Otis." The senator said, "A body can't go wrong in that company, A. T. May I
have the honor, ma'm?" Auntie took his arm and Earl Leroy
offered his arm to Victoria Ann. They walked over to the picnic
food, the senator talking to Papa and Auntie about Austin. The
senator and Earl Leroy had their law office in Austin. Victoria
Ann was worried about what the rest of the town might think,
the way Earl Leroy kept sticking to her like a cocklebur. *I wish
Carson'd never come back. I wish he'd get the sun stroke or catch
whatever it is his mama has and go down.*

Elgia Slate and Laura Kyle were playing "stiff starch." They
stood toe to toe, leaning back, their hands hooked together by the
fingers, spinning around and around, laughing and dizzy, going
faster and faster and faster, up on tiptoe churning a cloud of
dust. If one of them let go, they'd both fall.

At the picnic tables, Earl Leroy said, "Papa, I mean to stay
another day or so in Alto Springs. There's lots to do, and I can
come on after you."

For a minute the senator looked surprised. Then he looked at
Victoria Ann. "No," he said, "I reckon Rome wasn't built in a
day. Nor even a swallow's nest." He laughed. Victoria Ann
blushed. She let go of Earl Leroy's arm.

Victoria Ann filled her plate with a little of what everyone
had brought. There was so much to eat! Calabria Wright, who
was taking some of Velma's salmon salad, said, "Mama never
makes it as good as this. I'm goin' to eat till I'm sick." She was
wearing French stockings and a good pair of Rachael shoes.
Victoria Ann said, "I just take a little taste of ever'thing. That
way you don't get fat." She carried her plate over to where
Auntie had spread out a picnic cloth in the shade of a live oak.
Earl Leroy followed after her, but Victoria Ann sat down beside
her aunt. Auntie said, "Goodness, look at all the flies," and
swooshed her hand back and forth above her plate.

The senator didn't do much eating. Folks kept coming over
to shake his hand and talk with him—Mr. Crozier, Mr. Alton-

sall, Mr. Holly, Mr. Crump. Finally he said, "Here, son, hold this," and Earl Leroy had two plates in his hands. Victoria Ann laughed. Earl Leroy grinned and said, "I'd make a good sideboard." He was might'near beautiful in his gray alpaca suit and wing collar and white pongee four-in-hand tie.

Junior Luckett was standing a little ways off, looking at her and Papa and Aunt Velma and Earl Leroy. *Well, I don't care. Charge it to the dust and let the rain settle it.*

After the picnic was the matched horse races. In the first race Haze Kirchner's sorrel Beauty beat out a roan horse owned by Mr. Prentice from down on the Agua Fria. Mr. Dupree's Cold Deck won the second race. In the third race a black horse named Skillet, whose coat was so smooth it shone like silk, came up on Victoria Ann's favorite, Bess, and won by a nose. There were seven races in all. The dust was so thick you could hardly breathe.

After the races everybody went to their tents or back to their houses in town to rest and get out of the heat. Later in the evening would be the watermelon feed and the baseball game.

Everyone took a nap. They put a cot in the parlor for the senator. In her room Victoria Ann took off her dress and hung it by the window to air. She rinsed her face and neck and shoulders in the basin on the washstand and then lay down on the bed. There was only the slightest breeze and she lay in a fresh sweat. Finally she began to feel cooler. She shifted onto a cool part of the counterpane. Time seemed like it was standing still. Then she was in her new lawn dress with the Irish lace and Eaton waist again, walking in the evening orchard with Earl Leroy, a night breeze through the orchard leaves, and she really was cool. "I mean to marry you."

A fly woke her. She rinsed her face and put on a fresh, two-piece dress of white lawn with flounced skirt and lace-trimmed shoulder cape. She brushed her hair and did it up again with a few pins. How wonderful to be on the earth! How wonderful to have clear gray eyes with such a—briskness to them, and the clearest, whitest skin! No, it's not good to think like that. Better to be your plain self and depend on goodness and kindness and turn your thoughts to others, like Auntie says. But still, how lovely I am! and the whole room was filled with a kind of loveliness like it was a part of herself, even the combs and brushes and nail scissors and pins on the chiffonier were lovely and right, it seemed like everything on earth was good.

She brushed the wrinkles from her bed and propped up the pillows and went to the dining room. They were all there already, and Victoria Ann blushed. "I overslept," she said.

They had cold fried chicken, potato salad, radishes and tomatoes and onions from Velma's garden, light bread and fig preserves, donuts and peach-and-black-walnut pie. "Mrs. Castleberry," the senator said, "too many folks pass through life not knowing the *humanizing* effects of a good meal." He laughed and had another slice of peach-and-walnut pie. After supper they all went out onto the gallery.

The menfolk had coffee and Auntie and Victoria Ann had some more ice tea. Later Auntie took up her embroidery and Papa and the senator lit up Virginia cheroots. Victoria Ann loved the tangy smell of the cigars. It hung a short spell in the air before it drifted away. A mite breeze moved the leaves of Auntie's yellow climbing rose and those of the wandering Jew and rose moss in hanging baskets. The senator, in loosened tie and silk vest, sat in a wicker chair by the table with copies of *The Christian Observer* on its undershelf. He waved his cigar in reply to something Papa had said. "Well, at times one *is* politically or diplomatically impelled to jump over, go around or turn one's back on a blundering, mischief-making truth, but I revere truth as an abstract proposition in all its amber-like purity." Papa laughed.

Victoria Ann said, "Does Mrs. St. Clair ever go with you when you're out campaigning, sir?"

"Yes, she does. And a fine companion she is, too. She makes me toe the mark, let me tell you." He took another puff on his cigar. "But at the moment she is not well."

"Oh, I'm so sorry to hear that."

"Indeed we are," Auntie said. She let her embroidery rest on her lap.

"Some sort of summer cough," Mr. St. Clair said. "It seemed to be improving when we left. I notice you have a slight cough yourself."

"Oh, it's nothing," Victoria Ann said. "I mean to live to be a hundred years old and then turn into a white mule." The senator laughed.

Earl Leroy, who was sitting on the gallery rail near Victoria Ann, said, "The doctor says Mama just needs rest."

"That's what I keep telling Victoria Ann," Auntie said, "but she flits around like a meteor. She has so much get up and go it makes me tired to watch her."

"It's just the fever of life," Papa said.

Auntie said, "Let's hope that's what it is, and not the St. Vitus." Everybody laughed.

Now Papa and Mr. St. Clair got to talking about the chartering of state banks by constitutional amendment. Earl Leroy said, "I like your Maréchal Niel rose, Mrs. Castleberry. The only other place I've seen 'em grow like that is down on the coast."

Victoria Ann said, "I've never been to the coast."

"Galveston before the storm was a beautiful city. Oleanders and fine houses and wide, oystershell streets. Our family used to go there in the summers to catch the breeze."

Auntie said, "Wasn't that storm a terrible thing?"

"It will never be the same city again. But the ocean is something," Earl Leroy said to Victoria Ann. "Someday you'll visit it."

"No, I'm just goin' to be stuck here all my life."

The senator, who apparently had been listening, said, " 'More true joy Marcellus exil'd feels, than Caesar with a senate at his heels.' "

"Marcellus likely had six automobiles and his own theater company," Victoria Ann said.

The senator burst into laughter. He said, "Alto Springs is a little too small for you, is it?"

"Oh, I love Alto Springs, Mr. St. Clair. I love my home and

my family. I have a dear papa and a dear aunt and lots of friends here. But I can't even get a decent voice teacher." She looked at her papa. "My mind's about to shrink down to the size of a coat button."

"Victoria *Ann*." Auntie's embroidery went down onto her lap again.

The senator laughed. He said, "I was raised in a small town my ownself. I have to admit there *are* a few more oranges of pleasure to be sucked dry in a place like Austin, Texas." He shook with silent laughter.

Auntie said, "Well, you'll soon have enough to keep your mind and hands busy, both, Victoria Ann."

A door swung open onto a room filled with doom. Victoria Ann had tried so hard, she had worked so hard to keep the still-born monster out of sight.

Papa said, "Settle your mind, missy. Just a few more weeks and you'll have your husband and your home."

Earl Leroy stood up from the gallery rail.

The senator looked at his cigar. He said, "And who's the lucky man?"

Papa said, "Mr. Gilstrap. He has fourteen sections of land south of town, down along the breaks."

"I hope the gentleman's as handsome as his spread."

"Oh, he's a fine young man. He comes of the Gilstrap family over in Johnson City. Already he's built up his stock to where it comes near matching up to anyone else's in the county. I wouldn't change him as a prospective son-in-law for any other young man hereabouts."

Earl Leroy said, "I'm sure he's much obliged to you, sir."

Victoria Ann said angrily, "Well, I'm not in any hurry to get married. Not to anyone."

Papa chirped, "End of this month! I won't be satisfied till the knot is tied. I don't hold with these long engagements."

"Papa, I'm only *sixteen*." You'd think *Papa* was going to marry Carson Gilstrap. But I'll have my own way, I *will*.

She didn't dare look at Earl Leroy. All she noticed, out of the corner of her eye, was his hand to take a stick of gum from his pocket, finger it, then put it back.

I didn't *see* before. What I thought was love was like a cheap glass diamond you get in a racket store. And I don't care who Papa likes. I don't love Carson Gilstrap.

I *won't* marry him. She heard Carson stutter and it made Victoria Ann sick with rage. Hot tears blinded her eyes. She couldn't even make out the boards on the gallery floor.

The senator said, "I don't believe Earl Leroy and I have had the pleasure of the young man's acquaintance, A. T."

"He's gone to Johnson City. His mother took sick. Nothin' serious, we hope. We expect him back in a few days."

"Such a fine young man," Auntie said.

Earl Leroy walked over to his papa, his hands in his pockets. He sat in a chair beside the senator and leaned back, one knee across the other, pursing his lips like he was whistling. He stared up at the gallery ceiling. Victoria Ann was filled with shame.

Earl Leroy said, "Papa, we're invited to spend the night with these good folks. But there's a dozen things needs tendin' to, before we take off tomorrow mornin' for Vinegarone. It'll take all hours. I'm goin' over to the hotel tonight and leave the bedroom to you."

"I understand, son."

A grief came on Victoria Ann like she was standing at the edge of her own grave. To die like this! Because it is a kind of death. She wanted to tear her hair, she wanted to tear open her shirtwaist and cut her breast with knives or stones. It would of been a terrible show. But she kept herself still. She stared down at her hands, squeezed her eyes shut. Her blood pounded like it was going to break open the front of her head. Even the press of the weave of the wicker chair she sat in felt harsh and cruel. No no no no. I *won't* give him up. I *won't* let go.

A locust shrilled in the live oak like a hellish buzz saw of doom.

Papa said to Earl Leroy, "Oh, but you'll come with us to the baseball game tonight, I reckon."

"There's lots needs tendin' to."

"There won't be nobody in town to tend it *with*. They'll all be out to the game, young man. Last year Junction City mopped up the ground with us at baseball and we don't mean for it to happen again."

Earl Leroy said (and Victoria Ann could hear the bitterness), "Of course. We mustn't miss that."

"If you-all were goin' to be here, we'd have you to the weddin'."

I will kill you, Papa.

The locust buzzed in the live oak tree again.

Victoria Ann managed to get through the rest of the afternoon. Earl Leroy didn't say pea turkey to her. He and the senator and Papa talked and Auntie did her stitch work. Victoria Ann felt like she was in the middle of a desert, with nothing around her but dust and sky. If only Earl Leroy would look at her! But he had shut her away from him as certain sure as if he'd put her behind a door. During the long, slow move towards evening her heart broke several times.

The day heat settled. The sun moved overhead. More bugs commenced to sound in the grass and trees. There was the start of an evening breeze. Finally Papa pulled out his watch and said, "Looks like it's about time."

Everybody went to their rooms to freshen up. When Victoria Ann came back out Earl Leroy and his papa were already in the buckboard. Victoria Ann and Papa and Aunt Velma drove to the picnic grounds in the buggy.

The sky held all around. The cedar and mesquite grass and prickly pear and scrub oaks at the edge of town seemed like they were trying to keep hold of the heat, like they didn't want to let go. The whole country seemed to be grieving over something.

Papa hummed "You're my hon-ey, hon-ey suck-le, I am the bee" under his breath.

At the picnic grounds, folks crowded around the shaded tables, where the watermelons had been cut up and spread out.

They laughed and talked and sank their faces into the slices of watermelon. Charlie Kincheloe spat a watermelon seed and it skipped right across the table past Victoria Ann. Charlie's mother slapped his head. It didn't seem to faze little Charlie. He grabbed his slice of watermelon and ran off. "I declare," Mrs. Kincheloe said, "I don't know what I'm goin' to do with him. He's wearin' me to a nubbin with his stunts." "It's all right," Victoria Ann said. "I can out-spit him any day." Mrs. Kincheloe laughed and said, "Well, at least you're good-natured about it."

Victoria Ann considered aiming a seed at Earl Leroy. He was across the table from her. He hadn't said two words to her since they'd got here. She tried, concentrating hard, putting all her mind to it, to get him to look at her. He wouldn't do it. He kept talking to Calabria Wright, who was standing next to him. It made Victoria Ann sick at heart. The watermelon she was eating tasted like wet paper. Aunt Velma, beside Victoria Ann, was picking at her piece of watermelon with a fork. Victoria Ann wanted to knock the fork from her hand.

Finally Earl Leroy did look at her. Victoria Ann was so sunk into herself that at first she didn't notice it. Then she looked up. Earl Leroy's eyes before he looked away were filled with hurt, and Victoria Ann felt a quick stab of pain and hope in her guts. Mr. Dupree came up and commenced to talk to the St. Clairs. After a spell he said to the folks around, "We're goin' to borrow your company. We want the senator to toss the baseball in." The St. Clairs shook hands all around and they and Mr. Dupree went over to where a baseball diamond was scratched out in the dirt.

The ball teams came out of the brush, where they'd been changing into their uniforms. The Alto Springs team had on black shirts with a kind of white patch sewed onto the shoulders. The Junction City team wore blue and red. Some wore baseball caps and some cowboy hats, and they all had on boots. A few had baseball mitts. The only one who looked right was Frank Twelves, and that was on account of his mama had spent two weeks working on his outfit.

Everybody went over to the baseball field. Papa took Velma's and Victoria Ann's arms, and Victoria Ann toted her heavy heart along with. The St. Clairs were over on the other side of the field. Mr. St. Clair tossed in the ball and a cheer went up from the crowd.

Victoria Ann was suffocating in her white dress, though it wasn't as hot as it had been earlier in the day. It was like she was in a dream. The shouts of the baseball players as they practiced pitching and catching, the conversations going on around her sounded like they were coming from a long ways off. In the slant evening light folks moved their lips, nodded their heads, gestured with their hands, out on the baseball diamond the boys pitched the ball back and forth, like in a dream. She felt a headache coming on.

There were too many bodies crowded around her. Something tugged at Victoria Ann's skirt. It was Elgia Slate. She said, "Hi, Victoria Ann."

Victoria Ann said, "Papa, I feel light-headed. I've got to get out of the crowd. I'll be back in a minute." She pushed her way through the crowd to get to the back of it, Elgia holding onto her skirt. Victoria Ann said, "Please let go of my skirt."

"Ain't you gonna watch the game, Victoria Ann?"

"I will when I feel better."

"Hollis Mitchell's on our team."

"What do I care?"

"I want to watch the ball game."

"Well then for goodness sakes go watch it."

"I want to be with you." Elgia had hold of Victoria Ann's skirt again.

Victoria Ann slapped Elgia's hand. "Why do you keep pesterin' me all the time?"

Elgia looked up at her, shocked. Then she burst into tears. She spun away and ran back over to the crowd.

Oh, what do I care? I don't care about anything anymore. I don't even want to live. Victoria Ann brushed out the wrinkles from her skirt where Elgia's hand had crushed it. *I think I love now with a clear mind, and it's too late. I'll never see him again.*

I'll never get to Austin or ride in an automobile or do any blessed thing that counts.

She went over to the picnic tables. She took a piece of paper out of her chatelaine purse, and the gold-mounted fountain pen Papa had given her, and wrote a note.

> *Please do not give me up.*
> *Please let me talk to you.*
> *I will meet you in the cem-*
> *etery tomorrow morning be-*
> *fore breakfast.*

She wrote the note in Latin in case somebody else than Earl Leroy should get hold of it.

How can I get it to him? She wished now she hadn't chased Elgia away.

Junior Luckett was sitting under a live oak a ways off, poking at the ground with a stick. Victoria Ann called: "Mr. Luckett." He looked up as if he'd just noticed her. He scrambled to his feet and tipped his hat.

Victoria Ann motioned him to her with two jerks of her hand. He stared at her a minute like he didn't know what she meant. Then he came limping over to her. He broke into a grin. He had a double row of teeth like in the mouth of a king snake. Beauty's skin deep, ugliness goes clean to the bone. Victoria Ann didn't know whether to stand up to him or turn and run away. Who *is* this man? Where-all does he come from?

Like he was sent here.

Over on the baseball diamond somebody hit a ball—*thwock*—and a cheer went up from the crowd. Victoria Ann's whole body of a sudden broke out in a sweat. She wanted to wipe her hand across her upper lip.

She shifted on her feet. She said, "Don't baseball interest you, Mr. Luckett? You look like you're bored."

"Folks have their games." His eyebrows were dark and thick. There was a little wisp of a beard on his chin. He stood on his left leg, his right leg slightly crooked. Victoria Ann could hardly stand his tiny, pebbly teeth.

She turned away from him and commenced to walk away. He followed her. He said, "Folks got to do somethin' with their lives. They got to have picnics and horse races and go to church. They got to build it all up or there ain't nothin' there."

For a minute Victoria Ann stood under a sky so filled with endless space there weren't any edges to it at all. As quick as she thought it she forgot.

She touched the birthmark on her neck. She said, "Papa says you're his right-hand man at the store. He often talks about you. The customers like you."

"Well, sixteen ounces makes a pound, and when I'm behind the counter two of 'em ain't wrappin' paper." He laughed. It was a harsh laugh, raw and joyless.

She said, "You're honest."

"We're all honest."

"Maybe you'll do somethin' for me." She fingered the note she had tucked into her waist.

"Anything. I wasn't put on this earth just to eat and sleep."

She hesitated a moment. Then she said, "Would you fetch this note to Mr. St. Clair? Not the senator. His son. It's nothin' important, but he'll want to get it and I may not be able to see him before he leaves." She held the note out to him and he took it before she had a chance to change her mind. Thank goodness fools can't read Latin.

He said, "Miss Castleberry, it's my delight."

All her hope hung on a piece of paper that might be crumpled, lost, might never be gotten to him or, if given, never read. She saw how worrisome every chance in life was, a paper boat set on water to get soggy and sink. You could die on account of you stepped in a certain place or on account of you didn't.

Victoria Ann worked her way back through the crowd to Auntie and Papa. Everything got in her way, her clothes, the crowd, other folks' elbows and children, even, it seemed like, the light and the air. Papa made room for her beside him. He said, "Are you all right, sweetheart? Frank Twelves just made a hit."

Frank was running around the bases like he had a rattler stuffed in his britches, and the crowd went wild. A stupid game.

Over on the other side of the baseball field Junior Luckett was standing beside Earl Leroy. He handed something to him. Earl Leroy looked down at it, his hat blocking his face. He must of read it, on account of when he looked back up he stared right across at Victoria Ann. She looked down at the ground, her heart so high in her throat she was like to choke. Tears came to her eyes. *Oh, dear God, give him to me. I'll be good. I'll pray and memorize verses and listen to the sermon clear through, ever' Sunday. I'll put a quarter in the collection ever' time.*

Hollis Mitchell hit a low ground ball and the hunk of stuffed cowhide went whizzing into the brush, knocking down cedar needles.

That night, in her room, all her thoughts were of Earl Leroy. She saw his face looking at her in the orchard, or at the dinner table. She didn't blow out her lamp till past midnight, and in the dark the grief and longing were even closer. She thought she'd never sleep. Only the night breeze soothed her, and the distant silence in the sky of Regulus blinking in Leo.

15

All night long out of the darkness on the Plateau locusts and night crickets and other bugs rasped and shrilled, over and over, waves of noise swelling from the brush, lifting, breaking, or up in the trees around the house hissing in crescendo and collapse. Then of a sudden, just before daybreak, the noise quit. The whole Divide was still. To the east there was a thin crack of light. Victoria Ann had not slept.

She got up from bed and lit a lamp, rinsed her hands and face in the washbasin. Working them up under her gown she slid her stockings onto her legs, stepped into her drawers and a short petticoat, then, slipping her arms out of the sleeves of the gown, put on a lace-trimmed camisole. Her breasts were small, she hadn't a wasp waist, her hips were too wide, like those of a Spanish woman. Of a sudden the heart went flat out of her. *I ain't at all pretty. I haven't a good shape. I'm just common, not even as pretty as Alva Pryor,* and it felt like her body was so heavy of flesh, so close to death in its female weakness and grossness, hardly able to push through the world, not liable to attract anything to it at all, that she could wellnigh weep. She was in complete physical despair. She sat on the edge of the bed, the nightgown hanging like a tent from her neck, and tears sprang to her eyes. *I think I hate the world.* She was in a fury at her helplessness. Only the press of growing light, the sharp, scissors-like, wakening noises of birds, brought her back to her senses. *I've got to go before they're all up.* She slipped the nightgown off over her head and rinsed her face again in the basin. *I'll put on a pretty dress. Oh, I wish I'd never been bornt.* She put her shoes on and fastened them. She put on a black skirt with overdrape, a castor-colored shirtwaist of silk and lace and a short Eton jacket. She did up her hair, her hands awkward with grief, and pinned on a small, black sailor hat. *There.* In the mirror, with all her clothes on to hide her lacks, she looked some better. She pulled open one of the drawers of the chiffonier, found the tonic bottle and took a spoonful of Wine of Cardui. That helped. It's better just to face the world. She selected her black riding skirt to go over the overdrape. She blew out the lamp and went into the hall. It was lighter out than she'd thought.

Auntie was in the hall, headed towards the kitchen. She looked as brisk as a sparrow. She said, "What on earth?"

"I'm just goin' for an early-mornin' ride, Auntie," Victoria Ann said. "I feel so well this mornin'."

"Well, be back for breakfast. I don't want to worry about you."

"I will."

The bright morning star was just fading out of sight. The air was cool but dry, the fig leaves were pale with dust. *This is no place for angels. You'd think God wouldn't even know this place was here.*

Jésu was in the barn, already cleaning out the horse stalls. He always got there before anyone in the house was up. He was an old, hunched-over Mexican with iron-and-white, close-cropped hair and a face the color and texture of a dried, leathery prune. Victoria Ann had always thought he was a hundred years old, and she still half believed it. But he did all the yard and stable work. He tended Velma's vegetable garden and (with Auntie at his elbow) fed and watered her flowers. He hardly ever said anything, but just tended to his chores like a dark offshoot of the dirt, hovering above it.

"*Buenos días,*" Victoria Ann said.

"*Buenos días, mi hija*," Jésu said. His voice had a note of impatience, a kind of growl to it. It wasn't that he disliked her, he had his work to do. He liked doing it alone. In the summer he ate his dinner away from the other servants, at the end of the garden. He ate figs and hard-boiled eggs and troweled the egg shells into the dirt. In the winter he ate in the stable. He moved above the ground in a kind of solitude. But he was good with plants and horses.

Victoria Ann said in Spanish, "Saddle Badger for me. I mean to take some exercise."

"We all do what is necessary."

Victoria Ann waited impatiently while Jésu saddled the horse. Then he led Badger out into the street and around to the front of the house while Victoria Ann walked back through the yard to the stile. Jésu held the horse and Victoria Ann climbed up the stile steps. She put her right leg over the double horn, eased into the seat, and put her foot in the stirrup and adjusted her dress. Jésu handed the reins and riding whip up to her.

"*Gracias*," she said. The whole sky was already light.

"*De nada.*"

The morning air, though it was cool, had that flat stillness to it that means a hot day. All the dust was waiting for the heat to lift it into life. Victoria Ann rode over to the square and turned left at the corner. Smell of hay and manure from the wagon yard. She rode past the store.

A. T. CASTLEBERRY

• WHOLESALE & RETAIL •

GENERAL MERCHANDISE

The doors were open and Junior Luckett was walking a barrel out onto the stirrup-high boardwalk in front of the store. He sleeps in the shedroom at the back of the store

pallet laid down

at night amongst barrels of coal oil, molasses, sugar, coffee and lard.

A big black horsefly with isinglass wings lit onto Victoria Ann's wrist like it meant to bite her. She slapped it and it fell to the ground. "No longer an active member of the community." Junior Lucket lifted his hat to Victoria Ann, but she didn't even look at him. She sat ramrod straight in the saddle, staring directly ahead, gave Badger a lick with the riding whip and trotted past. She felt Junior Luckett's gaze on the back of her neck. She had all she could do to keep from putting her hand to the back of her neck. *I know he did me a favor yesterday. He wanted to do it. I don't owe him anything.*

What is it about him that scares me so much? He could kill a body and never show it in his face. Who is he? Where-all does he come from? Papa says Houston. Victoria Ann saw Junior Luckett in a street in Houston stabbing a man for his money. Oh, I hate ugly things! I wish he'd never of come here.

I wish he'd have a gate to fall on his toe.

Badger was still trotting and it felt good. Victoria Ann gave him his head. He broke into a gallop. Up at the high road she reined him in. The brief run had brought the blood to her cheeks. *I want to be free! I want to live my own life! God can't of give me the power to know and be so much just to torture me by denyin' me ever'thing!*

She turned left on the high road, towards the picnic grounds. The long, two-story schoolhouse threw a dark shadow. Behind it the sky was orange. As Victoria Ann rode out of the shade of the schoolhouse the sun came up like a red-hot stone.

It's Papa who's dead set on my marryin' Carson Gilstrap. Sometimes I think Papa tricked me into choosin' him. He wants me to marry a rancher and be stuck here all my life. But Carson's just a narrow-minded ninny who don't pay attention to anything but his mama and his goats. When I fell in love with him I was just a girl. I'm a woman now. I know better. I wish he'd get on a boat and hit out to China.

The red-hot stone had turned white, lifted up by its own light

and heat. The air was already getting warm. She rode past the
picnic grounds, where blue smoke was curling up from camp
fires: folks cooking breakfast before spooling their bedrolls and
taking down their tents and heading back out to their ranches.
Victoria Ann hoped nobody had noticed her.

She rode east on the high road, into the blinding sun. She
kept her eyes on the white, caliche road. There were flowers
along the edge of the road—niggerheads and prickly poppies—
and a lark sparrow sang somewhere. A string of bobbed-wire
fence ran alongside the road. A red bird, either a cardinal or a
summer tanager, followed Victoria Ann, darting from cedar bush
to cedar bush.

She turned in at the stone-arched gate. The caliche track
went up a slight rise. Earl Leroy wasn't here. It was just the
gravestones and the pale, empty sky. Oh, but he'll come. He *has*
to come. Oh, dear God, dear Jesus, if I had Earl Leroy everything would change for me!

Victoria Ann slid down from the saddle and tied Badger to a
live oak. She took off her riding skirt and flung it across the
saddle. All around her were fenced-in grave plots, the marble
shafts topped by lamps or crosses or urns—dozens of markers
above dozens of stopped suns. Here was little Cebia Slate's grave,
who had died last year, white caliche mound with toys—a sheet-
brass doll head, a dish, a tiny spoon, some loose, different-
colored marbles—scattered upon it. Here was old Bofill Grather's
grave, clam shells and mussel shells fetched up from the Nueces
and Agua Fria rivers making a border.

Where *is* he? Why don't he *get* here? The dead don't have
anything to fret them, they don't cry, they don't hurt, they don't
know the awful feeling of love.

Already it hurt to stand in the heat of the sun. It hurt to look
out at the rolling, brush-covered Plateau going on and on all
around her.

She listened hard: no sound of a nearing horse or buggy, just
cedar needles dropping to the ground. Tears prickled in the
corners of her eyes. No, I won't cry. It's no use to cry. I won't

ever cry again. She brushed a sleeve across her face. She walked, dragging her heavy skirt, a little knot of anger in her breast, towards the middle of the cemetery.

Here was her mother's grave, single shaft in the center of a large, bleached plot, a hand offering roses and lilies carved on the face of it.

CATHERINE S. CASTLEBERRY

1866—1887

Love Is Love Forevermore

Ants were making a nest beside the marble base. The dirt was yellow, like it'd been heaved from out of deep in the ground. Where my mama is. All bones. They say she was pretty, the most beautiful thing on the face of the earth. I've seen her picture. Was that my mama? Can her face be gone? What's she got to do with me? She died before I was even a year old. I've got her eyebrows and nose and chin. Oh, Mama, am I you? Is that why I'm walking above the ground, to keep some notion of you? Oh, Mama that I never knew, make me beautiful! Let me be like you. The main thing is to be pretty. Everything depends on that. Let me wear your face, let these be your hands and arms. Bring me love. If I play the piano, let it be you. I hate the dirt that's pressing onto you. If it was me, I'd heft it up, I wouldn't stand for it, and for a minute Victoria Ann saw her mama's face, deep in the darkness of the ground. Like in her picture, but smiling.

She heard a horse's hoofs. She turned and saw a horse and buggy coming up the caliche track. It was Earl Leroy. Her heart took a hitch. She turned away from her mother, wherever she was, in the shadow of the ground or in a whisking air of angels' wings, and walked a few steps towards Earl Leroy. It felt like she was stepping into a new world—the world of the blessed or the damned, she didn't know which.

He drove up to her. "Good mornin', dear girl," he said, and she was walking on air.

His grip was in the boot of the buggy and his coat on the seat beside him. Already he was on his way away from her. And yet he was *here*, as if he and the buggy had been carved by the sunlight out of thin air.

He said, "Do you mean to marry him?"

"I don't even love him."

The whole air was splinters of light.

He stepped down from the buggy and was to her in two steps. Her arms were out to him and she might'near stumbled as they met. He caught her in his arms. "Victoria Ann!" He kissed her cheeks and eyes and brow, all the time his warm breath onto her face: "My dear, dear, dear one!" They kissed, the first kiss she'd ever had in her life, or the first kiss that mattered.

He said, "How I love you! How beautiful you are!"

She said, "I prayed and prayed to the angels and they've fetched you here."

They kissed again, hard. Her legs shook so, she wellnigh couldn't keep on her feet. Oh, my love. She longed to melt into him, to disappear from the face of the earth and just be part of him, like water into water.

To have the pure wedding of him!

He said, "I thought I'd lost you yesterday, that you were just stringin' me along. And when your folks talked about invitin' Papa and me to the weddin' they could as well of give me poison."

"You wouldn't say a word to me."

"I was in Hell."

"I thought you despised me and weren't ever goin' to talk to me again."

"How could I despise a one like you? I love you too much. All my joy is in your hands."

She looked into his eyes. "My precious love." His eyes were of the warmest brown, intent but gentle, with a hazel cast to them. She wanted to kiss the lashes, to kiss the sweet gentleness of his eyes. There was a scar on his chin. She touched it. She said, "What happened to you here?"

"I fell and cut myself when I was little."

Victoria Ann stretched herself up to him and kissed it. They kissed again, a kiss that felt like it was going all through her.

He said, "But you're engaged to be married."

"My papa's dead set on it. But I'm fed up with always doin' what Papa wants. I wish I'd never heard of Carson Gilstrap, that there wasn't any such name anywheres. I was blind-haltered when I got engaged, just a schoolgirl, it was all pretend, not real like this."

"Well, there's no need to sit on the blessed thing till it hatches. The thing to do is get quit of it."

Victoria Ann laughed bitterly. "Buy him a ticket to Tokyo, I suppose."

"When you got a dead cat in the well you fish it out."

"Oh, I hate it that we have to steal our kisses. We'd be so happy if it wasn't for that."

"I'll go to your friend and tell him it's off, that you and me are in love."

Of a sudden Victoria Ann was scared. "No, you don't want to do that." She saw Hollis and Weldon Gilstrap walking her down the hall the night of that dinner three weeks back

angels

with flaming swords, Weldon with the coldness in his eyes they'll do anything to save the family honor. "You don't know what it's like here. People get killed just on account of a stretch of fence." She remembered the time she'd been on her way home from school, four years back, and she heard the shot. There was a crowd in front of Fred Maple's barbershop. When she got there Mr. Beecroft, who ran the wagon yard, was lying on the board walk. Mrs. Beecroft was trying to hold his head up and his blood was on her hands and dress. Austin Shafer had shot him on account of some little thing.

Earl Leroy said, "It don't do any good to be afraid."

"Oh, darlin', promise me you won't do that. I'm glad you said it. I don't want you to do it. We'll find a way. I'll get Papa to put off the weddin'. I don't ever mean to marry Carson Gilstrap."

"I don't mean you to neither. Well, the gentleman in question ain't here anyways. Listen, give me your hand." She held her hand up to him and he kissed it. "I got to go with Papa to Vinegarone and Del Rio. We've got the opposition on the run but we can't let up. There's a Republican faction in Del Rio. Papa will put a match to their shirt tails. I'll be back in a week. Then we'll settle this whole business."

But even if Carson lets me go free, what will the folks in town say?

Earl Leroy took both her hands and brought them together and kissed them again. He said, "Do you think we'll be happy when we're married?"

Victoria Ann looked up at him with all her passion in her eyes. A body doesn't fall in love, they soar. She squeezed his hands and said, "I swear to you there'll be no happier man than you in the world."

Earl Leroy laughed. He held her to him and she could hear his heart beat in his chest. Sunlight was all around them. The smell of warm cedar needles filled the air. He kissed her on top of her head. He said, "Our love's as true as if we'd sworn it on a stack of Bibles." He kissed her head again and held her at arms' length. He said, "Papa's waitin' for me. I got to go to Vinegarone."

She said, "With you gone I might as well be dead."

"Shhh. Don't talk like that. It won't always be this way."

"There ain't nothin' here but the hot sun and the dragged-out days."

"I'll be back. Shall we go into town together?"

She broke away from him and said, "No. No. We can't do that. I'll wait."

They looked at each other a moment. She said, "Oh my dear, sweet love!" and they were in each other's arms again. They kissed, a long, long kiss. When they came back into the world it was like she was another person. She felt so strong she could of stood waiting for him on the one spot forever. She looked at him. She kissed the scar on his chin and said, "I'm all right now. Go. I'll follow along later."

She watched the buggy go down the track, and from down by the gate he blew her a kiss.

As she rode up to the store she saw Junior Luckett out front again, sprinkling water on the road in front of the steps. She had a queer impulse to talk to him. She reined in Badger and said, "Is my father in the store?"

"He just come in. Shall I fetch him to you?" His eyes were as bright as a weasel's or a rat's.

"No, I just wondered if he'd had breakfast and got here yet." Victoria Ann of a sudden wished she hadn't stopped. Junior Luckett took a step towards her. He said, "That young 'gentleman' come by a few minutes ago. He had his gear in the buggy." He stared at her with a grin like he'd told her a fine piece of gossip, in fact like he was used to doing it every day across a breakfast table. Victoria Ann wanted to slap his lopsided face. She said, "I *don't care* who *came by*." She gave Badger a lick on the rump with the riding whip. He jerked forward and broke into a fast trot.

16

There wasn't any color to the rocks or water, which is how she knew it was a dream. Her soul must of flown the thirty miles from Alto Springs, through the dead air, here to the headwaters of the Lipano River, the Seven Hundred Springs. She recognized it: the low-water crossing on the road to Junction City, the water clear as glass above shelved rock. She was trying to get away from something, and yet she'd fetched it with her. Now, without looking, she knew: it was something terrible growing on her arm. She hiked up her dress and stepped into the water. She was barefoot. The water hadn't any feel to it at all, just its clearness above the rocks, like magic. All along the bluff, great noses and tongues of water sprouted through ferns, broke and rushed down through the maidenhair. A dab of red darted in the sycamores. But she didn't hear anything, not even the sound of water.

She bent down and washed her arm and the sore disappeared. Carson's face was in the water—lips stuttering just under the surface, sandy hair, the Gilstrap family eyes

"declivity!"

filled her with disgust. As easy as a sponge on a blackboard she reached down, brushed her hand across the surface of the water and the face was washed away.

17

 Auntie and Papa and Victoria Ann were sitting on the side gallery after supper when Louie Thallman came up the walk. Louie had been one year behind Victoria Ann in school. Victoria Ann had to say it, Louie was more and more good-looking every day—and he had gotten so tall lately! She liked his light, curly hair and his might'near green eyes, which were set wide apart so that his face had a kind of shining, open look to it. He was the son of Mrs. Thallman, who ran the hotel in town. He said, "Mr. Gilstrap asked me to come by. He just got back into town, but it's so late he figured he'd better get on out to the ranch. He says he'll come in to see you-all sometime tomorrow. He says to tell you his ma is all right."

Papa said, "Thank you kindly, sir. It was mighty good of you to come by. Would you like a glass of ice tea?"

"No, sir. I was on my way back from the store with this bucket of lard when he stopped me, and I had better get it on over to the hotel."

After Louie had gone Papa said, "Well, that was good news."

"What was, Papa?"

"That Mrs. Gilstrap is some better."

"Landsakes, yes," Auntie said. "I've been worried for her all week."

"We've never even met her," Victoria Ann said.

Auntie said, "We're goin' to be kinfolks soon."

Victoria Ann started rocking in her chair. What do I care about that old fool? Let her sit in Johnson City and catch the chicken pox. I don't even know what she looks like. She never came out to see me once. And Carson never fetched me to see her.

The sun going down made the outlines of the buildings over on the square as black as Victoria Ann's thoughts. What made Victoria Ann furious was the idea that Mrs. Gilstrap might look down on her. Victoria Ann saw a woman coming towards her on a board walk. It was Mrs. Gilstrap. Victoria Ann didn't know what she looked like, but she had a face like a horse. When Victoria Ann got near her, the woman tried to avoid her by stepping way over to the edge of the board walk. Victoria Ann wanted to rip up a board and lay it across the back of her head. And I will *not* see Carson Gilstrap tomorrow.

Already she felt a tickle at the back of her throat, and during the night she started coughing. She hardly slept all night, trying to work up a cough and fever. She worked up the cough by imagining it, tickling the back of her throat with a turkey feather, thinking of all the other times she'd been sick. Towards morning she slept and dreamt of walking on air three feet above a patch of cockleburs. When she woke she was sure she had a fever: the pillow sham seemed damp. And her cough had got worse. For a long time she lay in the growing light, hearing footsteps in the hall and kitchen, smelling the smell of fresh hot biscuits, teasing the cough, trying to get it to come out of deep in her chest, wondering whenever is Auntie goin' to come in and find out I'm sick?

For a minute she was afraid she was well, and then Auntie knocked on the door and Victoria Ann broke out into a feverish sweat on her chest and forehead. When Auntie came into the room Victoria Ann couldn't quit coughing.

Auntie said, "What on earth?"

"Oh, I'm all right."

Auntie touched her forehead. "You don't seem to have a fever."

"It likely just broke. I can get up. I feel fine." Victoria Ann coughed.

"Maybe you'd better stay in bed a spell. I'll fetch you in some breakfast."

"Oh, Auntie, I don't think I could eat a thing."

"Are you that sick?"

Victoria Ann coughed again. "I feel just fine. I'm just not hungry, that's all."

"That cough don't sound good. Are you sure you don't want somethin' to eat?"

"I'd likely just throw it up."

"Goodness sakes, now you frighten me."

Sweat prickled Victoria Ann's forehead again. She sat up in the bed. Her flimsy gown stuck to her chest. She said, "I'm goin' to get up."

"No you ain't." Auntie made her lie back down onto the bolster. "We ain't goin' to have you turn out sick two weeks runnin', like the last time."

"It's just that I have this cough."

Velma smoothed the hair back from Victoria Ann's forehead. She bent over and kissed her on the forehead. "You stay in bed. I'll fetch you in some magazines to read."

Victoria Ann spent the morning watching the sunlight move across the floor. She poked through some magazines: *McCall's*, *The Woman's Home Companion*: patterns for sleeves, bonnets, basques, knitting, crochet and tatting designs: *it is such a bore*.

I have got to change the arrangement of this room. It would be prettier with the chiffonier near the window.

The fierce sunlight poured into the room. Smell of dusty fig trees, and of half-ripe figs.

She got hungrier and hungrier. Now she wished she'd let Auntie fetch her in some breakfast. She thought of tea cakes, layer cakes, jelly rolls, a clear-seed peach. She thought of fried ham slices, a bowl of brown ham gravy, lemon snaps, the fizz in a bottle of soda pop. Her stomach growled like a bear turning over in its cave. She hiccuped and laughed. But the thing is to stay in bed and be sick.

Late in the morning Carson Gilstrap came to the house. Victoria Ann knew he was here by the way Velma's skirts swished down the hallway to the front door. She heard him talking in the front hallway. ". . . ever' single one of the w-w-water crossin's . . ." Let him sit in the parlor and look at stereoptic views. Victoria Ann turned to the wall. When Auntie knocked on the door she pretended to be asleep.

18

Sunlight came in through the cracks and knotholes, bright slices and finger-pokes of light. Dust motes hung motionless or of a sudden shifted in the light. The slices of light striped Victoria Ann's skirt bunched up around her hips. She used a sheet from the National Bella Hess catalog, then stood up and dried herself again with her petticoat, heisted her lace-flounced step-ins and let fall the skirt and petticoat. She adjusted her skirt, shaking out the pleats and smoothing them, leaning through walls and knothole rods of light. Something outside, over near the barn, made a thin, brisk, squeaking noise, once, and then a *pop*. She looked out through a knothole.

What's he doin' there? I didn't know he was there. If I'd knowed he was there I'd of stopped at the woodpile, got some sticks of kindlin' and gone right on back to the house.

Junior Luckett was over by the barn. He was fitting a pane of glass into the mullions of a wooden frame.

That's what that noise was. Glass cutter squealing along a straightedge, scoring glass, then with the side of your hand you can hit the glass and break it with a *pop*. Victoria Ann had seen Mr. Dunlop, the carpenter, do it, that time after a pecan branch had come down in a high wind and broke a window in the parlor.

Papa's sent him over to finish Auntie's cold frame.

The box of the cold frame, white, fresh-painted, like a bottom-less coffin, leaned against the barn.

Junior Luckett worked in the narrowing morning shade in front of the dark opening to the barn. He bent over the lid of the cold frame, fitting the pane of glass into place. I don't think he saw me. He must of been inside the barn.

Now he went into the barn. Victoria Ann slipped out of the privy and walked as quick as she could to the woodpile, halfway to the house. But she stopped and hid behind the fig tree next the woodpile, on account of Junior Luckett was back out with an-other piece of glass.

The sun, high up but still towards the east, held over every-thing. It was like a blinding mirror that if you were to look direct into it might-would kill you, but if you looked away still followed you everywhere, wellnigh stopping your breath, smoth-ering you with its heat and light. The heat made Victoria Ann's hair tighten and feel heavy. She brushed a hand against her forehead as if to push away the weight.

She reached into the fig tree, holding a branch aside so as to see. A leaf snapped off and milk came out of the break like white blood. Junior Luckett leaned above the sheet of glass, pressing a steel square onto it: the cutting diamond squealed across the glass. Then he shifted the glass to the edge of the board it was laid on, readjusted the straightedge and came down with the side of his hand on the piece of projecting glass. The waste popped off.

Why does Papa keep sendin' him over here to do things? Why don't he keep him to the store?

As he bent over, in his shirtsleeves and without his vest, the small lump on his back hunched up.

Who *is* he? What's that thing on his back?

So ugly he'd have to slip up on a dipper to get a drink out of it.

The dark shade amongst the fig leaves shifted.

As if he was sent.

Where was my art? Why didn't I think on it? Even the ugliest thing in the world has a use to it.

The sunlight held close around her as if it was her whole thought. She didn't know until now she was breathing so fast. She put her hand to her chest and her heart pounded.

Once when she was little she'd fallen and got a bump on her head. Auntie had put the flat coldness of a knife against it. It hurt, but it stopped the hurt. That's how close she felt of a sudden now to being free.

If I ain't ruint it. I've bit off his head enough times he might cut and run.

She took a deep breath. The fig tree was all light and shadow and purpling, ripening fruit.

She turned and went down the path to the house. When she got to the gravel walk she stopped. She looked down at the ground a minute. Then she looked up and over towards the barn.

Like she wanted, he was watching her. But he turned away and bent down again to his work. She walked towards him on the gravel path, past a bag of clabber cheese hanging in the chinaberry tree, past Auntie's melons ripening in the garden. The whole pitch of morning light seemed to make the ground alter in front of her feet.

She came right up to him but still he didn't look up. He kept shifting from one foot to the other, one foot to the other, over and over like some kind of dance, his back to her. The small, winglike thing under his shirt moved, bunched feathers that might any minute split out of their sheath and grow. His head with its thinning, reddish-brown hair was too big for his body. His shoulders were strong and broad, but one was lower than the other. He didn't have any waist either, or if he did it had climbed on up his back into the general area of his armpits. Victoria Ann wasn't even certain sure he had a backside, it was so flat. He stayed bent over his work, his feet doing their queer little shifting dance.

He probably won't even talk to me. Maybe I hate ugly things, but I ought to of knowed to of kept my mouth shut.

"Mr. Luckett?"

He straightened up and slowly turned to her. He wasn't much taller than she was. She hadn't noticed before the color of his eyes. They were as chocolate brown as a nigger's. With its high, shiny forehead and big chin his face was long and heavy, like it was some kind of animal to itself.

She said, "You didn't even notice I was here."

He glanced off to one side. Then he looked directly at her. He said, "Well, I'll tell you. Sometimes when you feel an earthquake comin' it's best just to pull in your head."

"Do I bother you that much?"

"The ground gets to be a little bit like jelly."

She said, "What's that on your neck?" There was some kind of rash on his neck, like Spanish-American War itch.

"I don't know where I picked it up. It won't quit."

"It looks like Spanish-American War itch. Come over here a minute."

He paused, then came to her. The look in his eyes was so flat she couldn't tell what he was thinking. She said, "Turn your head, let me see." The red splotch came out of his collar and up behind his ear. She touched his neck. "I think that's what it is."

She drew her hand away and brushed it on her skirt. He stood there like he was rooted to the one spot. She said, "You can get quit of it."

His face had a dumb, angled look to it, or maybe it was the queer flatness of his left cheek. He seemed to be trembling. He said, "Get quit of what?"

"All you got to do is rub it with a root of rain lily. Serafina taught me that."

"I can't tell weeds from grass."

"They come out all over the place after a rain. I'll show you."

A sly look came into his eyes. He said, "What's rain?"

"Well, maybe somethin' else'll work. I'll ask Serafina."

She looked at him a minute. She said, "I think I've just learnt somethin'. When you get used to a body's face, when you see it enough times, it gets more and more interestin'. I like a strong face. It shows what's inside."

Of a sudden she remembered where she was. She looked over to the house. No one was there. She said, "I've got to get out of the sun." She went past him into the barn. The barn was open at both ends. With the sunlight stretched across the other, street-side opening, it was hard for her eyes to get used to the inside dark. She heard her heels on the board floor. She smelt the straw and dust and hay and dried horse dung. Up overhead in the loft, streaks of dusty light stabbed across. She looked into the horse stalls. Like she figured, Badger and Blue had been led out earlier in the morning and staked out in the vacant lot across the street. Nobody was in the barn, or out in the street either.

A fly hovered in the air, stalling and standing still just in front of her at the opening to the barn. There wasn't any sound to it at all.

From somewhere a long ways off, like it was from another world, somebody called. The call hung in the air with no weight to it. Likely it was some boys playing. Victoria Ann turned back to Junior Luckett. He was watching her. She walked back to him, dust lifting in little drifts where her skirt hems touched the floor. When she got to the opening where Junior Luckett was waiting, there was more light than she could handle. She said, "Can you come in here?"

In two shakes he was to her.

She said, "You've been awful faithful to my papa. You might even be faithful to me."

"I take that to be a religious word."

His nose was funny the way it slanted to one side.

Victoria Ann started walking back and forth. She said, "Oh, Mr. Luckett, sometimes I wish I was a man."

"Oh, you don't want that!" Of a sudden he laughed. It was a queer kind of laugh, not what she expected from him at all.

She stopped in front of him. She hardly even saw him, she was so worked up. She said, "It's nothin' to laugh at. If I was a man, I could do what I wanted. Women aren't free. They just do what they're told. If I was a man, my papa couldn't make me marry somebody I hate—I'd get quit of whatever bothered me, even if I had to take a whip or a gun to it." She started to walk back and forth again. Tears burnt in her eyes. "I was just a schoolgirl. Girls don't know what they want. I'm not a girl anymore."

"No, I don't reckon."

Victoria Ann stopped in front of him again. "Or if there was a man I could trust, to help me. Somebody I believed in."

For a minute it was so quiet you could might'near hear the dust ticking in the barn. Then Junior Luckett said, "I think you've just hit on him."

"What would you want to help me for? I've been mean as all get-out to you."

Of a sudden Junior Luckett did something that scared her. He dropped down onto his knees and grabbed hold of her skirt. He pressed the hem against his face. She stepped back, but he wouldn't let go of her skirt. Victoria Ann said, "Get up!"

"Use me. Don't miss your chance. What do I care what's happened b'fore? You think horses won't eat an apple even after they've been rid?" There was a bald spot the size of a quarter dollar on top of his head.

"There's more scariness in what I want than what you read about in books."

"If only you knew how sweet it'd be to do with any act of yours."

She said, "Get up." She looked around. Thank goodness there was nobody in sight.

He stood up. He said, "Just tell me what the job is." He was older than she'd thought, older than Carson Gilstrap even, she saw that now. Is it safe to fool with a man like this?

Oh, to get quit of the whole business! But I'll have Earl Leroy, I don't care what. She felt it pushing in her like some kind of blind, white wall. She said, "Here, take this. It's worth somethin'." It was Carson's engagement ring. She pulled it off her finger.

"What do I want that for?"

"I mean to pay you somethin'."

"Oh, I know that!"

"I wish even the thought of him was wiped from the face of the earth."

"Who?"

"Carson Gilstrap."

A queer look came into his eyes. He said, "Don't bother your pretty head about it no more."

"I don't know! It's awful risky."

"Risky is as risky does."

"It scares me. You might get caught."

"Both our lives depends on bein' smart."

"If you got to you can go to Mexico. I'll get you money."

"We'll talk about that later."

"You're—different from what I thought."

He laughed. "I'm scared too, for one thing."

"I don't want to think about that."

Somebody drove by the other barn opening in a two-seated hack. Victoria Ann didn't catch who it was. She said, "I've got to get to the house." Of a sudden she was like to choke in the closeness of her clothes. Her hair felt heavy with heat and sweat. She was soaked right up the backbone with sweat. Behind her the dusk ticked onto the floor. Or something ticked. She went out of the barn and up the gravel path. Her skirts hissed. The gravel crunched under her feet. The sunlight was brighter than before and it hurt even to look at the shade, it made her dizzy. It seemed hard to walk in the weight of her skirts. I don't think I'm even here. The fig leaf snapped off from its branch again and bled. Anyways, it's all just some kind of dream I'll likely wake up from.

19

When they came into church Earl Leroy was back, standing just inside the door, talking to Mrs. Thallman. Papa invited him to sit with them in their pew. He sat on the other side of Papa, and Victoria Ann could see his hands—so clean and slender-fingered and nail-trimmed—resting on the creases of his gray-and-white summer-weight britches. She could see the light, brownish hairs on the backs of his wrists. It made something flip over in her belly. But now it was the call to worship and then a hymn, "Come, Thou Fount of Every Blessing," and she heard him singing on the other side of Papa, a fine tenor voice. Two people were missing from church this morning. Victoria Ann felt their absences, but just for a minute: she was already moving into another, bigger world. She put her mind to the sermon and heard every word of it. The Green Tree and the Dry. "Look at this green tree. How beautiful it is. It has no twisted branches. There are no worm-eaten or withered leaves, no weather-beaten blossoms, no bitter or rotten fruit. Behold here the symbol of Jesus. His birth was as pure as the making of an angel, his childhood as spotless as sunshine," and Victoria Ann's soul spread through her breast, pressed against her ribs and breastbone, filling her with a painful joy. She could of wellnigh risen on a shaft of light, she was that joyful. It hurt worse than the time she'd cut her finger and the pain had been so bad she'd taken pleasure in it. Ever'thing in the world, the good and the bad, is blessed! "It casts a cool shadow at noontide. So Christ is a refuge, a medicine." Even Preacher Mayhew with his pale eyes and pale skin and bald head was beautiful. The heat outside the windows, the sunlight pouring in, the flies dodging the *swish* of cardboard fans were blessed.

When it was time for the collection basket to be passed around, Victoria Ann put two quarters in it.

After church Papa invited Earl Leroy to stay to the house. "I've taken a room in the hotel," Earl Leroy said. "I got in late last night and I mean to cut out early tomorrow mornin'. Papa sent me back here to attend to some last-minute things. He was headed up into Sutton County and I'm to meet him there."

"Well, sir, have dinner again with us."

Earl Leroy glanced at Victoria Ann and then at the ground.

Auntie said, "You're always welcome, Mr. St. Clair. We took such pleasure in your and your papa's visit b'fore."

"Thank you, ma'm. It's an honor I'd be foolish to decline." He smiled and said, "B'sides, I remember your cookin'." Auntie reddened and laughed and adjusted the watch pinned at her belt.

Papa said, "I wonder where Mr. Gilstrap is this mornin'. I would of liked to of introduced you."

Earl Leroy bowed and said, "It would of been an honor, I'm sure."

Victoria Ann said, "If we don't get out of the sun, we're goin' to get the heatstroke."

All that ain't real anyways.

They walked together to the square and then turned left towards the house, Auntie talking to Victoria Ann about the visit she'd made before church to fetch a cake to Anice Nettleship, who was old and bedridden "and don't look like she's ever goin' to shed her winter coat and get up." Papa and Earl Leroy walked in front of them, chatting. Up overhead it was another cloudless sky.

* * *

At home Victoria Ann changed into her rose-and-white organdy dress with the belt of soft-crush rose silk. Earl Leroy
hadn't seen her in this before. She looked pretty in this dress,
she knew it, like in a painting. In this dress she ought to be out
under a tree, holding a book in her hand. Her face was flushed
with happiness. She was perfect in this dress.

At the dinner table Papa said, "What's this I hear about
somebody named Percaris?"

Earl Leroy said, "Perdicaris, I believe his name is."

"Some bandits or other kidnapped him?"

"A Moroccan hard case named Raisuli took him from his home
in Tangier and demanded seventy thousand dollars in ransom."

"And we paid it, no matter that we sent a passel of warships
there."

"Well, he's an American citizen."

"Mr. Roosevelt has made hay out of it. The Democrats don't
stand the chance of a snowball in Hell in the national election."

Victoria Ann said, "Mr. Satterwhite says Judge Parker got
the nomination at the convention."

Papa said, "We could as well of nominated a brass monkey."

Out on the side gallery after dinner they talked of the burning of the ship *General Slocum*. Victoria Ann said, "In Mrs.
Haines's *Harper's Weekly* it says more than nine hundred people died in it. It was mostly children."

Auntie said, "Oh, do we have to talk about these awful
things?"

Auntie and Victoria Ann and Earl Leroy went down into the
yard to look at Auntie's flowers. Auntie said, "Well, it's too early
yet for my four o'clocks." There was a long bed of rich green
leaves up on stalks, sprinkled with red and yellow specks of
unopened blossoms, alongside the walk. Earl Leroy said, "*Mira-
bilis jalapa.*" He said, "Do you keep them as an annual or a
perennial?"

"An annual, usually. I start 'em from seed."

"Mama treats some like a perennial. She digs up the tubers

after the plant's died back and stores 'em. She dusts the roots with sulphur."

"I'll have to try that."

"Your roses have cabbaged up real good."

Auntie showed Earl Leroy her zinnias and pinks and yellow cannas. Red and yellow and pink and rose and coppery-orange and cream and coral flowers floated in the air, knee-high and waist-high. She said, "I'd like to put in ranunculus bulbs but it doesn't stay cold long enough to set 'em back in winter." She said, "Oh, my nasturtiums've gone past."

Earl Leroy said, "You've done wonders. You'd be the envy of my mother's Oread Club."

While Auntie was pinching wilted, dead-monkey-looking twists of faded flowers from a hollyhock, Victoria Ann said softly to Earl Leroy, "Go back and chat with Papa. He gets impatient sometimes." Later, after Auntie had done some poking around in the roots of her bouncing bets, she and Victoria Ann went back onto the gallery and rejoined them.

In the late afternoon, while Papa washed up and Auntie put a cold, early supper on the table, Earl Leroy and Victoria Ann sat in the parlor. They sat on the horsehair settee, amongst the needlework and embroidered cushions, smell of dried bouquets, a copy of the *Pictorial Review* open on their laps. Earl Leroy said, "I'm goin' to tell them about us."

Victoria Ann touched his hand where it lay on a picture of "John Drew and His Daughter Riding in Central Park." It was such a live hand. The photograph under it was like something washed up on a shore, dead long ago. She said, "It's not the right time." She leaned her head towards him so that it was touching his shoulder and whispered, "Ever'thing will turn out right for us."

He looked at her and said, "You have more faith than I do." His brown eyes made her heart turn to melted wax in her breast. She gave his hand a little squeeze and said, "Wait." Then she straightened up.

She read out loud, her finger moving like a teacher's rule

across the page, "Whenever Mr. Drew is playing an engagement in New York, some part of each day is sacred to a brisk
ride around Central Park, accompanied by his daughter Louise.
This young girl, the only child of the actor, has but recently
entered her father's profession. She is now appearing with Miss
Virginia Harned in *Iris*."

Earl Leroy kissed Victoria Ann on the neck.

After supper Papa walked Earl Leroy back over to the hotel.
Victoria Ann stood at a front-room window and watched them
walk towards the square. The sun, which was still high but to
the west, gave a harsh edge of light to everything. Papa and Earl
Leroy walked through the sunlight. Its harshness made them
seem so real it hurt. *There go the two most precious men in my
life.*

Velma was in the front room with Victoria Ann. She stood
for a moment at the window with her. She said, "That's quite
a fine young man."

Victoria Ann chatted with Auntie and Papa the rest of the
evening until she couldn't stand it any longer. She went out onto
the side gallery and sat on the steps. Auntie came to the screen
door behind her. She said, "Do you miss your beau, sweetheart?"

Victoria Ann said, "Yes, I do." She said, "I'm goin' to take a
turn in the orchard."

But it was joy she felt. In the orchard she walked amongst the
peach trees and the plum trees. *Here's where we found the
fossil.*

The first of a night breeze stirred the leaves. The orchard
trees stood up into the air like miracles, miracle after miracle of
pale smooth or dark scaly trunks, explosive branchings, forkings,
red-tipped twigs, pointed leaves, hanging sailing peach suns and
dark, purple moons. In the fierce sunset they were like swords of
fire of a sudden hammered into the shape and softness of trees.
She felt the fire in her, joy to be alive and in the world.

20

To the west, in the blood-red sky, the evening star showed, brittle as a diamond. And when Victoria Ann turned back towards the barn she saw the orangish moon above it, as if it had just popped out of the roof peak. It was so close and big you'd of thought it'd come up at the edge of town. She could make out the oceans on it, it was that close. But it got smaller the higher it rose, until it was finally its own size.

She walked back and forth between the trees. The third time she stopped. She hadn't noticed it before: there was somebody standing over by the barn, motionless, hard to make out against the dark siding. It was Junior Luckett.

Nobody was in the kitchen at the back of the house, there wasn't any lamp lit there, and of course nobody would be in her bedroom. Papa and Auntie were likely in the front room, reading. Victoria Ann walked over to the barn.

She said, "Did you have to come here?"

He said, "Shhhh."

The barn door was partway open. He slipped into the barn. She followed him, but stopped near the opening. She said, "What-all happened?"

"I shot him off a windmill, out by the stocktank. I went out to visit him yesterday evenin'. He was up there workin' on the windmill. He had a rifle in the wagon. I shot him with his own rifle."

She said breathlessly, "Did anybody see you?"

"There's a Mexican out there, but he wasn't anywheres around. I passed Mr. Crooms on my way into town. But I was might'near into town when he saw me. Today I just stayed in my room."

She said, "I'm goin' to the house."

"You ain't goin' to talk to me?"

"What about?"

"I didn't do all that for nothin'."

"Auntie'll be wonderin' where I am."

He said, "*Wait!* I've got somethin' for you."

"What?"

He held something out to her, soft and white. It was a handkerchief and he unfolded it. There was some grass in it, and what looked to be a little, dead, bloodied, baby mouse. She said, "What is it?"

"Look again."

It was an ear.

"Oh, my God! What've you done?" She felt like she'd been hit across the front of her face with a board.

He said, "Is that worse than shootin' the back of a man's head off?"

She stepped back from him. The ear fell onto the floor. She said, "Pick it up!"

"Let the ants have it."

She said, "We can't leave it here!" She got down onto her hands and knees and began feeling frantically around on the floor. She said, "Please! Pick it up!" He bent down and picked it up and put it in the kerchief. Victoria Ann got up onto her feet and backed against the barn door. She said, "*Take* it. *Bury* it."

Somebody rode by outside on the road, the horse's hoofs muffled in dust. The two of them stood stock still. Victoria Ann managed to get hold of herself again. The hoofbeats got farther and farther off, then quit.

She said, half under her breath, "You can go to Mexico. I'll get you money."

"Do you think I'd kill a man for money? I could of hired a Mexican to do it and stayed on home."

It was getting so dark they could barely see each other. Outside, the moonlight shone onto the tops of the orchard trees. Victoria Ann said, "You've got to get away from here. Go back to Houston."

"I ain't goin' nowhere without you."

"Oh, I think you must be crazy."

"If I'm crazy, it's for love of you. I don't sleep nights for thinkin' on you—that mouth, them eyes. Even the way you walk makes me hurt all through." He took a step towards her.

She backed away from him. She said, "I don't want to hear that? How *dare* you talk to me like that?"

"You think just because a man's ugly he ain't a man?"

"You don't leave me be. You keep doggin' my tracks."

"I'd crawl on my knees from here to Junction City if that's what it'd take to get to be near you. It's like it's night if you ain't somewheres near at hand. If you smile, it's the sun, if you turn on me it's like I'm naked in a fit of hail. But you know all that. You know how sick in love with you I am."

"*No, I don't.*"

He touched her on the sleeve. She could hear his raspy breaths in the dark. He said, "There ain't another like you. All the self of you, all the thoughts behind them eyes! You *know* what I went and done. I did it for you. I'd give my life for the havin' of you. All the rest don't mean nothin'."

She turned abruptly from him. She said, "I'm goin' up to the house."

He grabbed her wrist. He said angrily, "No, you *ain't*. You're in it as deep as I am. You talked me into doin' it."

Victoria Ann was so shocked she couldn't speak.

He wouldn't let go of her wrist. He said, "Do you think I'm some toad you can step on and then kick into the brush?"

"Let loose of me! Oh, God, I'd as soon of married Carson Gilstrap as have to hear this."

"You're what you've gone and done, woman. You're the same as me."

"What?"

"Yes, you murderess. Pretty is as pretty does. We ought to both of us take out a subscription to *The Texas Christian Advocate*."

Victoria Ann thought she was going to be sick. She said, "I can't believe you're so cruel as to carry on like this."

"If I can't have you I'll go down onto the square and yell out the whole business."

"Mr. Luckett."

"I kiss the ground you walk on. I pray to your little shoes."

"Mr. *Luckett*."

"Folks laugh at me. They wonder what rock I was born under. They wonder should I be allowed to walk above the ground. But I'll have *this*."

"I'm just a girl. I ain't hardly had a chance to have a life. If you'll let me go I'll be good to you, I won't never say a mean thing to you again."

"As easy knock a star out of the sky with a stick as change this. You better make up your mind to it: I'll have you or the whole town'll know." He pulled her to him and kissed her on the face.

Victoria Ann backed away from him and bent over, sick. "Oh, to think it should come to this!"

"Shhhh. I ain't about to hurt you. I done what you wanted me to. I'd do it again. There ain't nothin' that matters in my life but you." He kissed her on the neck. He slid his hand down her spine and let it rest on the small of her back. A little knot of terror tightened in her gut.

21

She thought now he'd leave her alone. She thought once a horse has had its fodder it'll be satisfied. Two nights later pebbles ticked at her window. She elected not to hear. The window rattled. Papa and Auntie'll hear! She slipped her felt nullifiers onto her feet and went to the door. It was pitch dark out but she could feel him there, she smelled his close, raspy breaths. It was like he thought he was going to come into her room! He said under his breath, *"I got to talk to you."* She said, "What're you *doin'* here?" *"I got to have you."* Her heart sank to the soles of her feet. Of a sudden he had hold of her wrist. He led her off the gallery and into the yard. He led her through the gate and into the vacant lot across the street. If there were stars overhead, they were blind stars. She was blind her ownself, walking the edge of an abyss. Something caught at the hem of her nightdress. On the lot Junior Luckett pulled her to him. He kissed her face and neck and the front of her dress. They were frantic kisses. He said, "Christ, I love you! Christ, I want you!" She wished she could kill herself right here. He fell down onto his knees and held to her. He kissed her belly through her nightdress. Her skin prickled up her back. Oh, I hate it! I wish I was dead! Then the queer thing was, it was like her mind got switched off and all that was in her was the stone dark. He lifted her dress and kissed

her knees. Her legs shook. She was going to be sick. He pulled
her down and crawled with her under a scrub oak. He kissed her
breasts again, and her belly. Then he was onto her and in. *That
hurts!* She would of cried out, but somebody'd hear. All she felt
was the pain, the terrible weight of the hell of it. He made a
noise that hurt in her ear and he was done. She just lay there.
Something hot and wet spilled onto her neck. Junior Luckett
was crying and his body shook. "Oh," he said, "the—sweetness
—of you, the—ever'lastin' prettiness of you." He quieted. He
touched her face and hair. "There ain't no other woman like
you. There ain't no other hair so soft as this." She turned her face
away. The thing got small and came out of her. She stared up
into the dark. She was filled with disgust.

Junior Luckett blew out the candle in the shedroom at the
back of the store. Smell of coal oil, green harness, glaze on new
calico. He put his arms around her and tried to kiss her. She said
angrily, *"Don't tear my nightdress!"* She took off the dress. He
was like a bee gone crazy on a windowsill dish of honey. He
kissed her breasts and ribs and belly and neck. He said, "Victoria Ann, you're so pretty it'd make a stone get up and walk!"
He never seemed to get enough of her. *Am I that pretty? Could
I do another man that way?* Her heart sank and she was filled
with bitterness. *No, no other man'd have me, not after what
I've done.* Earl Leroy stepped into the edge of her mind and she
pushed him away. *Only if he don't know it.* Junior Luckett got
her down onto the pallet, into the desert of bitterness. Then he
was into her. It hurt, but not so awful as before. She closed her
eyes and began to see another face behind the lids. It was a
man's face. He had dropping lids, a girl-like length of lashes.
His eyes were helpless with passion and tenderness. She held to
him with all her longing and grief. "Victoria Ann!" he said. He
kissed her, he put his tongue into her ear. She lifted her breasts
towards him. Of a sudden threads of fire shot through her guts.
But Junior Luckett was done. He kissed her again and again.
"Victoria Ann! Victoria Ann! Victoria Ann!" Victoria Ann was

discombobulated, the warmth went all through her. Junior Luckett was kissing her on the neck. She put her hands on his body.

Junior Luckett gave her gifts, a bracelet of twisted silver, a waist pin that used to belong to his grandma, a cake of buttermilk soap, a tiny French gold watch that he said had been his mama's. The watch had a high, thin stem and a case that looked like a seashell, with little stars between the ribs. The case was might'-near as thin as a silver dollar. When you opened it there was an enameled photograph inside the lid, that he said was of his mama. She had thin eyebrows, a delicate, china-boned face and what looked to be light brown hair. A second hand was on the face of the watch, and the numbers around the edge were raised gold. The chatelaine clasp was solid gold. Victoria Ann didn't make any show of these things. She hid them in a chiffonier drawer, beneath her underthings. Once Junior Luckett gave her a kerchief full of ripe plums, from some that somebody'd turned in in trade at the store.

She felt his body with her hands. His left side had a caved-in feeling to it, like he was missing a couple of ribs. His backbone snaked from side to side. A little roll of bunched-up muscle was next his right shoulder blade. He was moving in her. He was like some queer, wild critter that'd crawled out of a river somewhere and got hold of her. There were the quickening breaths and the deep, feeding thing in her. She opened herself to it. He kept thrusting into her, and of a sudden she wanted to open her legs wider. She was going past herself and now she saw she might get across. She felt the nearness of it. But Junior Luckett was done and she was left in a tangle of irritability. Her heart thudded like it was half sick. A headache commenced in the front of her head. Junior Luckett said, "I can't get quit of the thought of you. Your hands, your voice. I hear your voice even in my sleep. I know all the changes in it." She was might'near in a fever. There was that fence she hadn't gotten over. She'd felt how close she'd been, the frenzy, the wildness. She wanted to hurt herself. She wanted to go out and hurt her feet on stones, prick her skin with cedar needles, press her breasts against the roughness of a live oak. She wanted to be dirt under somebody's feet if that's what it'd take to get her across. Junior Luckett tried to kiss her and she got up from the pallet and put on her dress.

A ringtail screamed in the lot outside the shed. A star twitched outside the window. "Christ, Victoria Ann," Junior Luckett said, "I'd go through hell and high water for you." He didn't try to pull her down to the pallet. He stroked her hair and kissed her on the forehead. Victoria Ann got more and more irritable. Her nerves twitched like the star outside the window. She said, "Touch me!" She put his hand on her breast. She said, "Touch me hard!" He squeezed her breast till it hurt and she said, "I *want* it to hurt." But she was getting in a rage. She wanted to kill him if she could. She began to hit him with her fists. He forced her hands aside. She bit him on the arm. "Oh, Jesus Christ!" he said. Of a sudden he slapped her so hard her ear rang. "Yes yes yes yes!" she said, and she smothered his hands and face with kisses. She pulled him down to the pallet. "Victoria Ann! Victoria Ann!" he said. "*No, not that way,*" she said. She got down on her hands and knees and pulled up her nightdress. He threw himself onto her. He held her breasts, he felt her belly and the hairs at her crotch. She opened herself to him and he came in from behind. Cedar needles shook from the bush. At last she might be free.

She liked the cinnamon smell that came off his body. She loved the way his hands touched her in certain places, places not mentioned in *The Woman's Home Companion*.

22

"I'm beginnin' to believe the stars're arranged in a slipshod way." Ira Hance, the sheriff, was sitting on the side gallery talking to Papa. Victoria Ann, who had hurried to her room, stood at her window—the window was open but the outside shutters closed—and listened. She was careful not to make a sound. The whole world was so still, even the air was solid and still, only the creak off and on of one or the other of the wicker chairs the two were sitting in, and Sheriff Hance carrying on in his soft, lazy, slightly irritable drawl. "For ever' way I tried to get a handle on it it none of it turnt out right." A chair creaked. "You was smart to stay shut of it, A. T., even after four weeks it still fair makes me sick. I sent Leon and Charlie to pull down the cedar stake. *A short spell after what had happened to Carson Gilstrap, Earl Leroy had come to town again. He came to the Castleberry house. Papa and Auntie were in black, Victoria Ann in dark blue or gray, whatever-all it was she had on that day. That was several weeks ago. She was wearing a black armband. She'd begun to get some notion of what it might be like to be a new widow: you don't get any choice of colors or anything. At first she didn't even recognize Earl Leroy. Ever'thing she'd been doing lately was like in a dream. She'd stand a long ways off watching herself sit down to eat or walk out onto the gallery or strip to the last stitch and*

*hadn't any more feeling connecting her to that one than a fish
has for turnips.* Ever'time I go by there it's still a big black circle.
But you wanted to get all the facts straight, A. T., and I come
here to tell you. Jay Altonsall was out to the Gilstrap place that
Sunday evenin' and found him in the south lot, out by the
windmill. You couldn't tell front nor back: his face and the back
of his head was half shot off. Jay hit right into town, but he
didn't get here till way after dark. I got up a posse quick as I
could and we hightailed it out of there. You know I sent Walt
Haines to tell you. I'm sorry it was him had to do it, but I
couldn't think of nobody else might-could carry off a bad piece
of business like that. *Earl Leroy had come to offer the sympathy
of the St. Clair family. Then he stayed on in town. He didn't
stay with the Castleberrys but at the hotel, but he visited with the
Castleberrys every day. He seemed half a stranger to Victoria
Ann. It was like she was so lost to the world of what she knew
now was simpleminded purity that it took something simple-
minded to fetch her back to it. But once she grabbed Earl Leroy's
hand and said, 'Oh, I need you!' They were in the parlor and
Earl Leroy had been talking to Auntie and Victoria Ann, and
Auntie had gone for a minute from the room and Earl Leroy
said in a half whisper, 'Ever'thing's goin' to be all right, dear
girl' and she grabbed his hand and said, 'I need you!' He kissed
her on the neck. She put her hand to the birthmark on the back
of her neck.* We got out to the ranch way late. That Meskin had
took off for somewheres. There weren't a thing we could do
b'twixt suns: it was a good moon up but we couldn't make out
anything on the ground. The next mornin' we struck his trail.
He was ridin' shanks' mare, and I figured with him on foot thataway we'd come up on him quick enough. I sent Jay and Leon
and Proc Mayer over to the Henry Secor ranch to watch the
sheepherders' camp, but he never showed up there. *Later, when
Auntie said, 'Poor darling, I think we should pack some things
and you and me go visit to San Marcos—or maybe go visit your
cousin Cebia in Corpus Christi, we both of us need a chance to
pull ourselves together,' Victoria Ann said, 'I'm going to stay*

here. I'm goin' to be gay despite ever'thing.' When Earl Leroy
and Victoria Ann took a walk in the front yard to look at Velma's
rose bushes, Victoria Ann said, 'I want to be engaged to you. I
want ever'body to know we're engaged.' He said, 'Aint' it a mite
previous?' 'Previous to what?' 'Previous to when ever'body else
in town might think it was proper.' 'I won't wait.' Of a sudden
Earl Leroy laughed. He said, 'I figured you had spunk. If you've
got grit enough, dear girl, I'm right along with.'

"Me and Charlie and Tom Crozier and Lum followed the trail
through a brush pasture and over to the section line. We had to
cut the wire to get the horses through. It was rocky, sheeped-off
ground, and we had a hard time construin' a trail, let me tell
you. It looked like it was headed in sixteen dozen directions. I
sent for more men from town. Some hit over to the Winedecker
ranch, the rest of us cut through the Jordan pasture, down along
the Nueces breaks. The ground was so rough we had to follow
the trail on foot, and I never pushed through so much brush in
my life. Victoria Ann and Earl Leroy waited a few days and then
—when they could get him alone with them in the parlor—Earl
Leroy said to Papa, 'Sir, I know things are in a state of discom-
bobulation. The time may not seem at all propitious, but I'm
goin' to presume and ask you most respectfully, sir, for the hand
of your daughter.' Papa said, 'Excuse me, sir?' 'Mr. Castleberry,
sir, I have ever' regard for you and your family, who've lately
become so dear to me—.' 'It's true, Papa. He's asked me and I've
accepted.' 'But my dear, dear child—.' 'Papa, I'm not goin' to
spend all my days livin' ever' inch of my life by the town's yard-
stick. I've had my grief and—and—I've learnt to live with it and
I love this man—.' Earl Leroy said, 'Victoria Ann—.' Papa turned
to Earl Leroy and started to say something. Victoria Ann flung
herself at his feet and clasped his knees. Tears flooded her eyes.
She pressed her face against his leg. She said, 'Dearest, dearest
Papa, I've suffered so much! Yes, I've lost him, but does that
mean I have to crawl on my knees the rest of my days till there's
nothin' left of me and nobody'd have me anyways?' 'Child, it's
only been four weeks.' 'It's been four hundred weeks to me!' and

she burst into tears. She heard Earl Leroy take a step towards her but Papa must of stopped him. She pressed her face against the rough weave of Papa's britches. She felt his hard knee bones, the hot strength of his legs. 'Child, you break my heart when you carry on like this.' 'I love you, Papa!' 'Get up, Victoria Ann.' He helped her to her feet. She saw there were tears in his eyes, too. He said, 'You love this young man all that much? As quick as this?' 'It's been growin' and growin', Papa—the last three weeks.' Papa said to Earl Leroy, 'And you love this one—my daughter?' 'With all my heart.' Papa didn't say anything for a minute, and then he said, 'It ain't wise for me to do this. There're so many things at stake. But I guess—I give my consent!' 'Oh, Papa!' Victoria Ann flung herself into his arms and begun weeping with joy. I don't know how that Meskin done it. Far as I can make out, all he had to eat was agarita berries and the seeds of bull-nettle. When it come night on us we wasn't any closer to smokin' him out than when we started. The next mornin' I got a dog out there, but he wasn't but half-trained. Still, he helped some. He struck the trail of a lone man on foot and we followed it about three miles through the pasture east of the Ugalde road, headed in the general direction of town. We decided we'd follow it to the fence and if it crossed the fence we'd know it wasn't made by a herder on the ranch. The ground got worse and the brush heavy and we had to lead the horses again. *And the sun came up and the moon went down and sometimes Earl Leroy would kiss Victoria Ann or sometimes touch her or put his arm across her shoulder and she would go all tingly, goosebumps would prickle up her back and her knees tremble, she'd get an ache in her guts, couldn't hardly wait till night, and the dark would come down onto her and she'd go to Junior Luckett.* Tom took the horses, and Charlie and Lum and me tried to smoke out a trail but lost it at a line of brush drift-fence. We figured he must of turnt up the draw. Lum wanted to study the ground some more there, so Charlie and me went up the draw with the dog. We hadn't gone but halfways up the draw when we heard a shot back behind. That Meskin had been stretched on the ground flat as a crazy quail in the mountains of New Mexico, and he fired on Lum. The bullet left a yellow streak on the crown of Lum's hat. *Victoria Ann made her way back across the lot towards the house. The moon had gone down, what thin sliver of it there had been, all she had to see by was a passel of stars. The night breeze hissed through the mesquite trees and shinneries around about, all over town windmills creaked. Of a sudden a light, wooden-spindle wagon came around the corner next the house. It had a wagon lamp. Victoria Ann stepped back from the edge of the road. She couldn't tell who it was driving the team.* Charlie was up on a rise above the draw and he saw the Meskin hunkered down, slippin' through the brush. He got off a shot, but said it was like tryin' to hit a dragonfly on a quick dart. I was afeared somebody'd get kilt and decided to hold off till Tom had fetched the rest of the posse. Meanwhile me and Charlie and Lum poked around. We couldn't find sign enough to scare up a turkey tick. *The team and wagon came towards her. She pressed against the mesquite she was next to and pulled close the hem of her dress. The horses went by. She could might-near of reached out and touched the haw horse, it was that close. The circle of lamplight brushed the hem of her dress. She held her breath. Whoever it was didn't see her. The team and wagon went on over to the square.* When Tom got back with the others we scouted in all directions but couldn't rouse doodly. That Meskin must of been runnin' two feet above the ground, like some sort of Jesus. Even the dog give up on it. It looked like the boy was goin' to give us the slip. I didn't know what the douse to do next. But late Wednesday evenin' Dick Sanders and Perry Kincheloe seen him at a distance, near the northeast corner of the Sutton pasture about five miles out of town. They also found a pocketknife dropped there that was identified as his. We fetched the dog, but a herder had been there a few hours b'fore and the dog trailed him direct to his sheep camp. We had to put up in the sheep camp for the night. *Papa and Victoria Ann stood at the front door. Weldon and Hollis Gilstrap were coming up the steps. Weldon said, 'We've got a bone to pick with you, sir.'*

*Papa said to Victoria Ann, 'Go into the house.' Victoria Ann
went in and hurried quick as she could to the front room,
where she stood behind the curtains at the window and listened.
Weldon said, 'What kind of woman is that, anyways?' 'Who,
sir?' 'Your daughter, Mr. Castleberry. My brother ain't hardly in
the ground and we hear tell she's took another man to her. It's
all over town she's wearin' his ring. She changes men like Texas
does the weather.' 'I gave my consent. The responsibility's mine,
sir.' Hollis said, 'Oh, ever'body knows when Victoria Ann says
frog you jump.'* Thursday we got onto the trail again and followed it through the Benskin and Quarternight pastures to the
Fisk pasture east of town, then northeast to the cemetery. But a
passel of folks was to the cemetery Tuesday at the-uh-burial,
and we lost the trail. Lum picked it up down by the gate. It went
through the Stackbine pasture to the north edge of town and
then south to about forty yards from the Tomás Cantú house,
where he'd likely scared off and hit out into the brush again. It
was hot as blazes and we'd run the horses into a big limber and
I'd begun to think we wasn't never goin' to come up onto that
Meskin. It'd been ring-around-the-rosie the whole way. Then
Frank Tober and Jimmy Wittenburg found him asleep in a
clipping shed out to J. C.'s place and got the drop on him. Jimmy
held him at gunpoint till Frank could get me and my posse out
there. *'The responsibility's mine,' Papa said. Hollis said to Weldon, 'Like I told you, Weldon, these folks're as common as pig
tracks.' Weldon said, 'We want to know what happened to our
brother.' 'A Mexican killed him.' 'What'd he go to do that for?
He didn't take no horses. He didn't take no money.' 'He took
your brother's rifle.' 'That's somethin' to kill a man for? That
Mexican weren't stupid. He'd figure white folks hereabouts'd
suspicion him. He'd need somethin' to protect hisself.' 'What's
that got to do with my daughter?' 'Nothin', as far as we know.
But it don't sound right.' Hollis said, ''Course that Mexican'd
been out to the ranch two years runnin', workin' for our brother,
and he never done Gip no harm b'fore.' Papa said, 'Fine. Now
I want you two to turn around and hightail it right on back out*

that gate. Don't ever come onto my property again.' I had eight men with me. We headed to town to put the Meskin in the jailhouse, but just outside town met up with that mob, close on one hundred men from all over the county. They came right for us, and they were armed. We hadn't the chance of a snowball in Hell, they meant business. I had to turn the Meskin over to 'em. Found out later they'd already built a brushpile over on the other side of town. I tried to reason with 'em, but I might as well of been talkin' to a pack of hydrophobic dogs. Some of my own men wanted to go over to 'em! I kept my foot on *their* necks. We waited till the crowd was out of sight, pushin' the Meskin ahead of 'em, then the boys went with me to the courthouse where we all set down, with our mouths shut, and made like we was workin' on court reports and tax records. I never spent an hour that had more Hell in it. *Weldon said to Papa, 'We'll keep our eyes peeled.' Papa said, 'What's that supposed to mean?' 'Just, we'll keep 'em peeled.' Hollis said, 'There's a nigger in the woodpile somewheres and we mean to smoke him out.' Papa came into the house and slammed shut the door. Hollis yelled after him, 'Put that in your pipe and smoke it!' Papa stomped down the hall to the back of the house. Hollis said, 'The sonofa-bitch.' Weldon said, 'Let's get the hell out of here.' They went down the steps and out into the street, leaving the gate wide open behind them.* Later, when the mob had scattered, we went out to the spot and held an inquest. They'd poured coal oil on the brush. Likely the Meskin was dead in three or four minutes. But it was a christawful mess: eyes popped out, body half-burnt, bones stickin' out—the asshole end of an episode. I ain't been sick to my stomach in a good many years, but I was then."

23

 It was a mite cooler this evening. The lamps were lit. The soft linen tablecloth glowed in the lamplight, the weave of the cloth seemed might'near alive. Serafina took away the leavings of chicken and white gravy, fried okra, beets and butter beans. She put the bottle of pepper sauce on the sideboard and fetched in the marbled cake, peach cobbler and fresh coffee. They were all—Victoria Ann, Auntie and Papa—at one end of the table: Auntie thought it made a family that way. But they were all ghosts. There wasn't a thing in the world that was real to Victoria Ann. Even the food hadn't had any taste in Victoria Ann's mouth. Papa and Auntie sat there like pieces of cardboard propped up on chairs. If they'd spilled coffee on their fronts they'd of sopped on down out of sight. Papa and Auntie chatted. Victoria Ann didn't even want to hear. All it was was the noise folks make on their way to the grave: words hadn't any meaning at all.

Auntie said, "What's the matter, darling?" Victoria Ann said, "Nothin'. I think I'm about to fade into thin air." Papa and Auntie laughed, and the two pieces of cardboard started chatting again.

24

Her mouth was open, head back, eyes up into her head, couldn't get—couldn't get a breath, trying. To. Get. There with all her might, hips about to break at the joints, her belly to split.

"*I told you there was tracks in the yard!*"

A flash of light filled her skull, as if something had broken in her brain. She lay stunned, her legs apart, her petticoats up around her hips.

"A pair of beauties!"

That was Weldon Gilstrap's voice, and Victoria Ann sat up quick as she could. But Papa was standing in the room. He had fetched a lantern and the room was naked bright from the light of it. Victoria Ann scrambled to her feet and pulled her dress off the nail where she'd hung it. She held it in front of her. Junior Luckett had got his pants up and managed to hitch his belt.

Papa said, "*Victoria Ann.*"

Victoria Ann backed into a corner. She didn't know what she'd of done if somebody'd tried to touch her: scream or go crazy and make to bite them, one.

Papa stared at Victoria Ann, but it wasn't as if he saw her. It was like he was staring through her into a nook or cranny of Hell. Hollis took the lantern from him and held it towards her.

She shrank against the wall. He said, "Here's your good name, the one who figured when God made her He was done and the rest of us just happened."

Papa took a step towards Victoria Ann. He was shaking all over. He raised his hand as if to hit her. He said in a thick, choked voice, "Jezebel!" How horrible those words were! They twisted everything to ugliness. They made even her face ugly!

"A melon spoiled early don't get no better with age."

Victoria Ann fell to her knees. She leaned towards Papa and said, "Yes, Papa! Kill me! Put a bullet through my head!"

Junior Luckett started towards Victoria Ann. Hollis said, "Hold that sonofabitch." Hollis thrust the lantern into Victoria Ann's face. "Look at this. So well brought up you'd take her for a saint."

Victoria Ann bent down to the floor. She wept into her dress.

"Let me go to her!" Junior Luckett broke away from Weldon and rushed to Victoria Ann. She felt him touch her shoulder. "Victoria Ann."

She screamed. "He's the one who brought me to it, Papa. He forced me." She said to Junior Luckett, "I hate you. *Don't touch me, you murderer!*"

Weldon said, "Jesus Christ."

Victoria Ann screamed again. "It's true. He killed your brother. It's in that snuffbox there!"

Junior Luckett said to Victoria Ann, "You poor fool, are you gonna blame me for ever'thing? I see that's how the world is: if a body loves he's got to take the blood and dirt with it."

Weldon said, "You sonofabitch. Henry Secor was fixin' fence that day. He saw you comin' off the place, and Mr. Crooms passed you ridin' into town."

Hollis said, *"Did you kill Gip?"*

"Fools talk. The rest of us keep our mouths shut."

"I'll cut your heart out and stuff it in your mouth."

Weldon said, "Put that lantern up, Hollis. You'll kill us all."

Hollis said, "Snuffbox. She said somethin' about a snuffbox."

He started hunting around on the shelves. On a shelf, next a cracked mirror, comb and other truck, was a tin snuffbox. Hollis put the lantern on the shelf. He opened the snuffbox and a black, shriveled ear dropped out.

"Holy Jesus!"

Weldon turned around and hit Junior Luckett in the face. Junior Luckett fell to the floor. Blood came out of the side of his mouth.

Hollis just stood there. His shoulders were shaking, he was weeping. Weldon shoved him. He said, "Get a rope. We'll trim this bastard's comb quick enough."

Weldon turned back to Junior Luckett and kicked him in the ribs. He said, "We're gonna settle your hash so's you won't know ass from eyehole."

"*Ah*," Junior Luckett said. "*Ah!*" He doubled over and held his side. "We'll . . . all . . . slide down to . . . Hell . . . on splinters."

Papa said, "Victoria Ann, you'd of done better to of cut my throat in my sleep."

"Don't come near me, Papa. I'm slops to be dumped in the privy. Pitch me aside like you would a stick or a poison weed."

Weldon said, "I always knew there was somethin' rotten behind them looks."

Hollis said to Junior Luckett, "Why'd you go to kill Carson?"

"I had a mind to do it and I did it."

"*Why*, you goddamn bastard?"

"I took the notion."

"Goddamn you to Hell."

Papa hadn't moved from the one spot. He said to Victoria Ann, "Were you ever my daughter? Did I ever know anything that went on in your head?"

Weldon said, "We're in a fair way to study Hell."

Papa said, "We're in Hell. It's right here."

Victoria Ann said, "You think you know what Hell is. This town is Hell. The whole town's watchin' you, you can't never be free. All a woman's life is, is what ever'one else ever done, and you might as well never of been bornt."

Papa said to Victoria Ann, "Go to the house. I never mean to speak to you again."

Victoria Ann said, "What's it matter? Are you going to lay out another dress for me to be a fool again tomorrow in? I'd rather go naked in Hell."

IV

September 11,
1904

25

To the west there were still hundreds of stars, brightest close to the earth. Eastward the sky was pale, the morning star commenced to dissolve in the brightening air. Here and there on the Plateau a windmill poking above the scrub and brush got hit by the orange light. Below were the breaks of the Nueces and West Nueces rivers, and to the south the rivercourses themselves between bluffs. The sun stoked itself white as it rose.

Near the river, on a narrow track, a caliche cut that passed for a road, two men rode horseback. A third limped along behind them on foot, his hands tied together with a rope dallied to the horn of one of the riders' saddles. Caliche dust was in the prisoner's hair (he was hatless and coatless) and on his shoulders and shirtsleeves.

Up overhead a hawk circled, a speck in the cloudless sky.

The two horsemen had on hats and coats. Each had the same long, narrow face, thin-nosed but with strong mouth and chin, the same close-knit eyebrows and close-together, bright blue eyes.

They had got to the river.

The one on foot said, "It was sweet, sweet, sweet, sweet! She didn't hold nothin' from me. She needed me and she gave me ever'thing. There ain't nothin' on earth I give a damn about but that."

"Shut up, you bastard."

A grasshopper's wings grated as it flew in the brush at the edge of the river.

"She was shameless and I loved her for it. What do I care about a shikepoke stutterer?"

Hollis slid down from the saddle and was back to the prisoner in two steps. He said, "How an ugly sonofabitch like you ever got into the world I'll never know. Your ma must of took up with a horse turd."

The prisoner grinned. He said, "And now, O Lord, wash away their sins and make them white as crimson snow."

"Why'd you kill my brother?"

"Sometimes a body gets fed up with certain faces."

"Christ a'mighty and little bitty fishes."

Weldon grabbed up a broken elm branch and hit the prisoner smack across the back. The man fell into the water but managed to crawl back up onto his hands and knees, choking and coughing.

"Pair of spit bugs."

Weldon hit him up the side of his face. It laid the cheek open to the white bone, blood ran down his shirt front. The man tried to grab hold of Weldon's leg. Weldon kicked him in the face. He spat at Weldon. Then he slid slowly into the water.

Weldon said, *"Don't let him get up!"*

Hollis shoved his face in the water. He kicked and thrashed like a sonofabitch. A bone broke and stuck out of his leg. It took all Weldon and Hollis could do to hold him in the water. Hollis picked up a rock and hit him several times on the back of the head. Finally the body quit. Blood was all over everything.

The blood in the water was bright red but then it thinned away. The two men got up, stumbling and shaking. But Hollis said, "I'd kill the bastard again if I could."

Weldon said, "Leave it be." He stood over to one side and threw up.

A dove called, down along the river.

Weldon said, "Let's get the bejesus out of here."

They lit up onto their horses.

Hollis said, "He sure showed spunk."

Weldon said, "I don't want to think on it."

They spurred their horses and went on across the river. A red-bird showed in the bushes, *pi-ti-tuck, pi-ti-tuck.* The two men rode up onto the caliche track.

A dragonfly lit onto the hump on the hunchback's shoulder. It had a tail like a blue darning needle, blue head and eyes and lace-looking, see-through wings. It held there, motionless. Already the man's shirt and britches were turning dry, the rocks all around were dry. The skin of dust on the water began to grow together again.

A cliff swallow flew across. The stones of the riverbed shimmered in the heat and light, the well of light shone. Even the leaves of the hackberry bushes along the riverbank seemed made up of light.

Up overhead the white of the sky ruled.

The dove called again.